UNNATURAL SELECTION

by

DENNIS WHEATLEY

authorHOUSE®

AuthorHouse™ UK Ltd.
500 Avebury Boulevard
Central Milton Keynes, MK9 2BE
www.authorhouse.co.uk
Phone: 08001974150

First published by AuthorHouse 8/2/2007

ISBN: 978-1-4343-1642-4 (sc)

Printed in the United States of America
Bloomington, Indiana

This book is printed on acid-free paper.

This work is dedicated to my wife Beverly, to my daughter Chantal (who was the creative influence behind the front cover) and my son Brett, they have been a source of strength, pride and inspiration. I also want to mention my mom and dad, and my brother Raymond, they were the foundation upon which I built the rest of my life.

CHAPTER 1

'The Blight' crept in quietly like at thief in the night, so quiet no one was even aware of its arrival, didn't even know of its existence, I mean why should they, people die all the time don't they? Even healthy people die and sometimes for no obvious reason; fine one minute, gone the next. That's life, it happens. It's part of the natural order of things, an everyday event. The dead make way for the living.

But when it did announce itself the consequences were so shocking that there was nothing in human history to compare with it (but then again that might not be true, at least I personally am not too sure that it is but to be honest it's impossible to be certain about anything anymore).

Sure, the religious nuts talked of God's wrath being exacted on humankind. 'A curse on all our houses!' they trumpeted. They said it was divine retribution for the decadent society we had created. I'm not sure about the retribution bit but the decadent society part was definitely true. At least it was a change from the never ending newscasts and sensational journalism of global warming; I had gotten really fed up with all the doom-laden stories of melting ice caps, holes in the ozone layer, carbon emissions and energy efficient light bulbs.

As 'The Blight' or Sudden Death Syndrome to give it its official title (SDS for short everything gets reduced to letters), tightened its grip of death on the soul of humanity, some of these very same religious nutcases involved themselves in unspeakable acts of barbarism by organising human sacrifices to placate their vengeful God, atonement they had claimed for our evil and wicked ways. You shouldn't be surprised at the depths of depravity to which humankind will sink when the thin veneer of civilisation is stripped away.

I can still remember how it was; a reporter from one of the popular British tabloid newspapers claimed to have infiltrated one of these lunatic fringe movements; I think they called themselves 'The New Dawn'. His report spoke of them kidnapping their victims, usually some poor wino whose senses were sated in cheap plonk, or a down-and-out bum who just wanted to be left alone, then bundling them into a car and taking them to some secret location. In this particular report it was one of the dozens of disused shipping warehouses somewhere on the River Clyde in Scotland.

He reported seeing a church alter, probably taken from one of the many abandoned places of worship, in the centre of a large storeroom, it was draped in a gold-coloured cloth with a white cross roughly stitched in the middle, he estimated that about a hundred and fifty followers were crowded into the warehouse.

They had drugged their victim and dressed him in a white shroud before laying him out on the alter, then the self-styled lunatic leader who was wearing priest-like vestments harangued the gathering, reminding them of the depths to which society had sunk which had caused the 'God of Life' to turn His back on the world and become the 'God of Death' and that the only route to redemption and a return to their God's good grace was to offer Him a sacrifice, in the same way as the Israelites had done in the Old Testament, except in this instance because of how far humankind had distanced themselves from the Almighty, the sacrifice would have to be something more than a mere lamb or goat.

Playing to the gallery, in somber tones he reminded the congregation that God Himself had sacrificed His only begotten Son on Calvary's Cross, to atone for the sins of humankind and that anything less than blood from a human sacrifice, could not possibly appease His wrath.

The gathered devotees had appeared hypnotized by the priest's words and were soon 'in the spirit', throwing themselves on the floor in self-induced ecstasy, crying out in tongues, tearing at their clothes and bodies, calling on the Holy Spirit to reveal Himself.

Then with perfect timing as the faithful bayed for the blood of redemption, the 'High Priest of Death' took up an ornate dagger that was lying on the alter next to the motionless body and raised it high above his head, holding it aloft in an act of pure theatre for all to see. By this time he'd worked his audience well and they were at fever pitch and then amidst the cacophony of noise he plunged the blade into the chest of the victim, tearing through skin and muscle and bone, laying open the wound and revealing the innards in all their red pulsating glory; he then slowly and deliberately put his right hand into the gaping wound and ripped out the poor drunkard's heart in a bizarre parody of the ancient Inca sacrifices, and then like the Shaman of old, he held up the dripping heart as if it were the ultimate prize, showing it to the frenzied faithful who cheered and cheered in rapturous ecstasy.

Sacrifice or no sacrifice, it seemed that God's wrath had not been appeased after all because people still carried on dropping like flies, it wasn't long before the 'Sacrificers' became the 'Sacrificed' as anarchy swept the world and they became victims of 'The Blight' or the terror they themselves had helped to unleash, either way they didn't last long. At that time there were too many people looking for a quick and easy fix to the problem and if dispatching a few dozen of their fellow citizens in ritual sacrifice would take care of business, then what was the issue?

I remember telling some of my colleagues that there was nothing strange or unique about human beings sacrificing themselves or each other, whether for religion, or some other 'just cause.' I hate 'causes' don't you? When emotion rules, logic goes out the window and what is right or wrong ceases to have any meaning; the only thing that matters is 'the cause'.

The world had seen lots of 'causes' in its time, take the Middle East, especially in places like Iraq and Israel and Palestine, people blew themselves up with monotonous regularity and anyone else who happened to be around at the time for the sake of the 'cause'. They even extended their reign of terror to the US, Madrid and London.

If it wasn't the 'Jewish Cause' it was the 'Palestinian Cause' or the 'Muslim Cause' or the Christians, Hindus and Sikhs. It sure was a time of 'causes'. That was before sense had finally prevailed and peace had largely settled across the land but not before rivers of blood had drenched the streets of cities from Tel-Aviv to New York, Washington to Madrid to London and soaked the desert sands.

But this time there was nothing that could stop what had been set in motion, absolutely nothing at all, the die had been cast and perhaps in a way the religious nuts had been right after all, it might well have been part of 'God's Master Plan.'

It doesn't matter now; it's academic, I mean, who's left to debate the issues anyway?

Even so, as humankind faced up to the onslaught, questions that had baffled scientists for centuries were at last being answered or were on the verge of being answered, cures for a multiplicity of diseases were well within our grasp; Cancer, MS, Alzheimer's, Parkinson's the cures were all close at hand but there was no excitement or euphoria, no rejoicing, no anticipation of a new dawn. And then again, some of the answers had only raised new questions that would never require answering anyway.

Theories concerning humankind that would have been considered crackpot only a short time ago were now being postulated by respected academics; some of the theories were fanciful, others were downright frightening.

All this was because of 'The Blight.' That was the name given by the media for what in truth was the defining moment in the history of the world, the ultimate cataclysmic event that ever could or ever would befall the human race.

We had built our Tower of Babel, stood on its very pinnacle, turned our faces to the sky and shaken our collective fist in defiance of the Creator, or Allah, The Manitou or whatever name you give to your ultimate deity.

The fate of the builders of the original Tower of Babel was little or nothing compared to what the Almighty had in store for the builders of the new one.

CHAPTER 2

You ask where, how and when it had all begun? When the world had first realized how serious the situation was and what the frightening implications were? And when we finally did face up to what we were up against, it was too late anyway. All humankind's knowledge, accumulated over thousands of years was powerless to help. The world's greatest minds were assembled to define and solve the crisis but they might as well have been a collection of minds from any local pre-school group because that was about as effective as they were.

But let me not get too far in front of myself, I need to go back to the time after the beginning. Can it really be only a year or so ago that the first warning bells started to ring? It seems unbelievable; so many things have happened, so much water (and blood too) has flowed under the bridge and at this stage looking back, it's hard to put everything into context and at the same time remember what the sequence of events were as they unfolded with mounting devastation, imposing themselves onto every human being in every country on earth.

Let me concentrate, I need to remember and get it down because whoever eventually reads this (and I fervently hope and pray that someone will), has a right to know what happened and why it happened, I don't want 'The Blight' to become another of history's great mysteries like the Pyramids, Stonehenge, Crop Circles and UFO sightings.

Sure, it was a mystery at first but once the awful truth had been unlocked it held no mystery anymore, the truth had been exposed and what it revealed couldn't be unrevealed, Pandora's box had been opened with no possibility of putting anything back in.

Thinking back to the beginning (or was it really the end or better still the beginning of the end?), I'm pretty sure it was when one of those smaller European countries had noticed something strange happening to their population; death rates were gradually increasing and it wasn't a seasonal thing either, no severe winter nor a hotter than usual summer, people just died and kept on dying in higher than usual numbers, nothing to panic over at first but enough to create a spike on a graph.

Autopsies were carried out as a normal routine but their findings revealed no particular cause of death; no infections, no signs of cardiac arrest, no toxins, no medical history pointing in any particular direction; nothing, nada, people just stopped living; many literally dying on the spot.

I remember reading somewhere that someone who'd actually witnessed one of these 'strange' deaths, had described it '…as if their light had simply been switched off.'

Even stranger, prior to them dying there had been no complaints of pain or discomforts of any kind, in fact no signs of illness at all. They had just inexplicably died.

The medical authorities had been baffled but weren't overly concerned because the numbers at that time were still relatively small. They asked the European Union's Health Commissioner in Brussels, if any other EU country had reported anything similar. They hadn't, so as a routine precaution, the EU sent out requests to all member states asking for reports concerning any unusual and sudden rises in mortality rates.

A week or so later, they heard back from Luxemburg and the three small Baltic states of Latvia, Lithuania and Estonia of unusual rises in their death rates (all had smallish populations, which made the monitoring of these things that much easier), it was the same story; children, the elderly, youth, middle aged and across all social backgrounds, death was no respecter of age or position. It seemed that all sections of the population were simply dying at a higher than usual rate with autopsies revealing nothing. They reported that they had no idea what was causing it.

In those EU countries with larger populations, like Germany, Britain and France, the mortality rate anomaly had gone largely unnoticed, lost in the morass of figures and statistics.

In the USA, with its even larger population, if any anomalies had existed at all, they had gone completely unnoticed and no reports had been received by federal agencies from state health officials. Whatever was going on in Europe seemed not to be occurring in the US. But it was. It just hadn't gotten itself noticed yet.

The Office of the EU Health Commissioner after reading the reports, realised something was not quite right and sent alerts to all member states. It also sent an advisory to the World Health Organization (WHO) in Geneva, Switzerland.

What had started out as a fairly routine matter was turning into something quite a bit different when the bigger EU states finally realized they too were experiencing the same rising mortality rates in their countries?

CHAPTER 3

I guess I should pause here and tell you a little bit about me, if only for posterity's sake and just in case this account is ever found and read in the future by who knows who, or what.

My name is Eve James; I'm 32 years old, a widow and grieving mother for the past what, I'm not sure anymore, it seems like years but it can't be that long. God how long has it been now?

I work, sorry worked, as a micro- biologist at the Center for Disease Control in Atlanta, Georgia, in the United States of America but for you to fully understand how I became part of all this and the role I played, I need to go back to the time when I was asked by Professor Frank Burke, Director of the Human Genome Project at Duke University, to accompany him to a meeting at the World Health Organisation's headquarters in Geneva, Switzerland.

I'd known Professor Burke from my time at Stamford where he was Head of the Department of Biology and I was one of his students. We just seemed to hit it off from day one; I was totally immersed in the subject and was always an enthusiastic participant in his lectures. He noticed my enthusiasm and sort of started to keep an eye on me almost like a father, coaching and helping me wherever he could; it was one of the happiest times of my entire life. It was in some large measure thanks to Professor Burke, that I graduated class Valedictorian.

After graduation, I got a job with the CDC and some time later, Frank (we had become friends by then and were on first name terms) was appointed Director of the Human Genome Project at Duke. We kept in touch after I graduated and a firm friendship developed; we often visited each other's homes. I really admired Frank and yes more than that even loved him in a daughter/father way. He'd always taken a genuine interest in both my career and me encouraging and guiding me. Later on he would often tell me I was the daughter he'd always wanted but never had, Frank had never married, unless that is, you can be married to your work.

Not surprisingly, when Bill and I decided to get married, Frank's name was pretty near the top of the Guest List. Bill had already fallen under his fatherly spell as easily as I had and they soon became firm friends. They had so many things in common; football, basketball, Budweiser and me. Boy those were happy times.

After about two years into the Genome Project, Frank asked me if I would be interested in joining his team, he said they were involved in cutting-edge research that was just up my street and that the opportunity would be great from a career point of view, he said it was too good to miss. He told me it would be no problem for him to arrange a secondment from the CDC to his project.

Although going to Duke would mean moving home, after talking it over with Bill I/we decide to accept and no sooner said than done, in no time at all, Bill, our three year old twin daughters Wendy and Suzanne and myself, had loaded all our worldly goods into one of those Pensky rental trucks and we were on our way to Raleigh, the state capitol of North Carolina.

Bill was an architect and a damned good one, he had his own one-man business and since he worked mainly from home, the idea of relocating to Raleigh was very appealing to him, in fact to both of us. We figured the twins would soon settle into their new home. You know how it is with kids, they always do.

I had been part of Frank's team for about two years and had formed a particularly close working relationship with him, so being in tune with his moods, I noticed something was troubling him and when I enquired what it was, he just fobbed me off with something about him being tired and needing a rest. I didn't believe him for one minute.

A few days later he told me the World Health Organisation had invited him to a meeting at their headquarters in Geneva and that persons from the Pasteur Institute in Paris and Oxford University in England would also be present. He said the meeting would be dealing with a number of topics that were related to the research work we had been undertaking. He asked me to accompany him.

He said the meeting would specifically look at higher than normal mortality rates in several European countries and that it was important for the US to be aware of what was going on and to be ready to deal with any type of pandemic or something of the like that might be lurking just over the horizon. I thought he knew more than he was saying. I hoped I would soon find out what it was.

CHAPTER 4

American Airlines flight 6207 to Geneva lifted off from JFK right on time at 9.30pm. I have hated flying ever since I was a little girl and I was with mom and dad on a flight from Chicago to Nashville, we ran into a violent thunderstorm. It was one of those small twenty seater planes and it had been tossed around the sky like a cork on a raging sea, I became violently ill and had vomited over myself, the passenger in the seat in front of mom and me and the poor guy who was sat on the seat next to mine. I still shudder at the memory. This time thank God, the flight was uneventful and I slept fitfully for most of the way, Frank on the other hand seemed to be lost in thought, definitely not his usual ebullient and talkative self. It was like he was trapped inside a multi-dimensional puzzle that only he knew existed and only he knew what the answer might be.

Every time I opened my eyes and glanced in his direction, I could see him staring into a deep nothingness and for reasons I couldn't quite fathom, fear trod softly but unmistakably up my spine.

Some WHO functionary met us at Geneva Airport but not before we had been whisked at almost breakneck speed through Immigration and Customs. I remember thinking that I could easily get used to that kind of treatment; it sure beat the hell out of the Thanksgiving holiday weekend crowds that choke up every one of the country's airports at that time of year.

'Good morning Professor Burke, good morning Doctor James, welcome to Geneva.' The voice belonged to a squat blond-haired man of indeterminate age, 'I trust you had an uneventful flight. My name is Doctor Wolfgang Maier and I am here to take you to Professor Ricardo Valdez, Director General of the World Health Organization, he is waiting for you at headquarters. If you don't mind, your luggage will be taken directly to your hotel. Kindly follow me.'

He didn't leave any room for argument and I assumed from his accent that he was either German, or from Switzerland's German Canton.

My prior involvement with Germans had suggested a people who were dead serious about everything they did and away from the annual Oktober Fest celebrations, when they could show a Rio Carnival dancer how to have a good time, they are not famous for their free-spirited approach to life, but if Frank was surprised by the 'warmth and congeniality' of the welcome, he didn't show it, he just nodded and strode after Maier out of the airport and into a waiting BMW. I almost had to run along side them, like a child trying to keep up with parents who are striding off too quickly.

We traveled in silence, Maier was up front with the driver and no one spoke. Frank was still wrapped in his deep silence, lost in a space only he could imagine; his face was wreathed in an inscrutable expression the like of which I had never seen him wearing before.

Again fear started to assert itself, pacing up and down my spine. I could tell something was wrong, I could almost touch it. I was afraid to ask Frank what it was all about; what with flights to Geneva, meetings at the World Health Organization, the involvement of the famed Pasteur Institute and Oxford University and us, Frank and me. What did it mean what were we really here in Geneva to talk about? I was no longer sure I wanted to know the answer and I thought of the adage, 'ignorance is bliss when it is folly to be wise'.

The limo came to a stop at a solid looking security barrier that blocked the entrance to the parking area; we had arrived at the WHO headquarters on Avenue Appia. Dr Maier lowered his window and said something in German to the guard; he passed him some papers and what looked like an ID wallet.

The guard examined them closely and then peered into the back of the car and examined Frank and me more closely still. I guess we must have checked out ok because he raised the barrier allowing the vehicle access to the parking area.

We drove down one of several roads that crisscrossed the enormous parking lot but we didn't pull into any parking spaces. We drove past the Staff and Visitors' Car Parks, past those slots reserved for Directors, VIP's and Dignitaries, swept on past the front of the building and then turned sharp left at the corner of the office block and disappeared down a steep slope that led to a heavy metal door at the bottom.

The Bimmer glided to a halt. Maier spoke into what looked like a microphone in the center of the car's dashboard and immediately, a panel slid open in the wall next to Maier's window, he lowered the window and a small screen revealed itself. Maier placed his left palm against the screen. When he removed his hand the screen retracted, allowing the panel to slide shut. When I looked, I couldn't see where the screen had come from; it just blended into the wall.

Seconds later the large metal door slid noiselessly open to admit us into the cavernous room it had been concealing; clinically clean and totally bare, it looked anti-septic. Concealed overhead fluorescent lights dimly lighted it, the illumination didn't reach the outer walls.

The driver took the car forward and stopped in front of a bank of elevators, as we got out I happened to look in the front and was surprised that the car had dual foot pedal controls, one set for the driver, the other at the feet of the passenger. I had seen cars like this before; driving schools used them. This was to enable the instructor, who usually sat in the front passenger seat, to take control of the vehicle if there was an emergency that an inexperienced driver couldn't cope with. I was sure the Bimmer driver could never be described as inexperienced, so why the dual controls?

The thoughts fairly sped through my mind without stopping to take up residence, in one side and out the other so to speak. It was only later that the answer to this little conundrum was supplied and then it made perfect sense.

At last we had arrived at or more precisely in, the headquarters of the World Health Organization.

I said before that I'd been disturbed by Frank's self-imposed silence and introspection which had set in almost as we took our seats on the flight and had showed no sign of lifting on the journey from the airport to the WHO HQ. Now as we stood outside the stainless steel elevator door, with Maier punching in a multiple digit code, I stole a glance at him again and noticed he was still mentally jousting with something he preferred not to share. More cause for concern, or was I just being unduly sensitive, my thoughts playing mind games? In any event, that feeling of unease and disquiet cranked up another notch.

We left the BMW driver stood outside the elevator, Maier inserted a card into a reader and to my surprise the elevator went down instead of up. He saw the look of surprise on my face and said the DG had asked for us to be brought to one of the small meeting rooms as soon as we arrived. The rooms, he explained, were below ground level.

The elevator button- board read LL2 in bright luminous green letters and numerals; I took it to mean Lower Level 2. The car stopped, we had traveled two floors down.

The elevator doors slid open to reveal a wide corridor of bare bone-white walls with air conditioning vents interspersed at regular intervals and a bank of fluorescents that marched down the ceiling for about fifty feet before coming to a halt where the corridor abruptly ended.

'This way please,' said Maier, as he turned to the right, we dutifully obeyed. We walked for about twenty feet down a tiled corridor and stopped outside an imposing oak-looking door that bore no handle or other obvious means of entry. Even so, the door seemed to sense our presence and with a mind of its own, opened with an audible click to let us in. Maier stepped to one side to allow Frank and me to enter the room first.

Frank led the way into a rectangular shaped room, measuring about thirty foot by twenty. In the middle was a long, wide handsome mahogany table, with comfortable looking leather chairs running down both sides. At the end of the table to our left, was one of those newly integrated laptop computer/cameras and a six by six video screen.

A handsome man about six foot tall, slim with jet black hair and in his mid fifties, rose from one of the chairs and strode confidently across the room, hand extended, to greet us.

'Professor Burke and Doctor James, how good of you to come and at such short notice.' He took Frank's hand first shaking it vigorously and then mine but instead of shaking it, he lowered his head and gently brushed the back of my hand with his lips in a gesture of old-time gallantry. When he stood up he smiled pleasantly revealing even, white teeth. His face wore a tan and his smile was deep and genuine. I decided straight away that I liked him.

'Welcome to Geneva, I am Professor Ricardo Valdez, Director General of the WHO but please, if you don't mind, let us dispense with the formalities, I would much prefer it if you called me Ricardo; I have a feeling we will be having quite a lot to do with each other over the coming months, we might as well break the ice now at the outset. I never saw him or heard from him again after this first meeting.

Before we could reply 'Ricardo' had quickly moved on.

'I am so sorry you had to fly half way around the world but in the circumstances and given the nature of your research, I think you will see that it was very necessary.' He paused for breath; Frank wasted no time moving in.

'Professor Valdez, uh I mean Ricardo, he said in his clipped Bostonian accent, I've no problem dispensing with the formalities, so let's get right down to business. Is this meeting to do with the funny goings on in Europe?'

'Yes and no' said Ricardo, 'yes it is those funny goings on, as you put it but no, in that the funny goings on are not confined to Europe. As far as we can tell from the reports we have been receiving, they probably mean that every country on earth is being affected in the same way'.

Up to this point the conversation had made no sense to me at all, so I sought to clarify the situation. 'Excuse me,' I interjected, 'could someone please tell me what funny things are going on and why these funny goings on require Professor Burke and myself to fly at a moments notice about six thousand miles, sorry, about nine and a half thousand kilometers, to meet the Director General of the World Health Organization?'

'Oh, my good Doctor James,' said Ricardo, 'He spoke flawless and almost accent-less English, please forgive us for talking over your head; quite unforgivable, allow me to try and explain,' but before he could, Dr Maier, who had been standing to one side, indicated with a well-timed cough that he needed Professor Valdez's attention. The DG looked in his direction.

'Yes Dr Maier?' he enquired, he sounded distracted.

'Sir, I thought I should remind you of your other guests, they will soon be here.'

'Oh of course, thank you Wolf, I had forgotten the time, how silly of me. Frank, Eve, I know you are aware that we are to be joined by colleagues from the Pasteur Institute and Oxford University. They are not going to be here in Geneva in the physical sense; they will be joining the discussion via a two-way video link, from their respective laboratories in Paris and London.

They are already working on the problem and can't take the time off to come here. Thank goodness for modern technology. They are due to join us at two o'clock, in about ten minutes.'

He must have noticed that we had all been standing since Frank and I arrived because he suddenly gestured to the chairs, 'Oh dear, my manners get worse, how impolite of me to keep you standing all this time, please, won't you sit down, perhaps you would like something to drink?' We both said we would like water.

At the request of Dr Maier, who spoke into an intercom, four bottles of chilled Perrier and a matching number of crystal tumblers were brought in on a tray by a stern looking lady in her sixties, her iron grey hair pulled tightly back into a bun. She deposited the tray in front of Frank and me and left without saying a word.

CHAPTER 5

At precisely 2.00pm, Professor Valdez, I mean Ricardo, asked Dr Maier to dim the lights and switch on the monitor. Two scenes side by side greeted us on the same screen; both showed views of laboratories festooned with equipment. It could easily have been my lab back home in Duke. Thinking about it put my mind on Bill and the girls, six thousand miles away and a feeling of panic swept over me. It soon passed.

The sound came through a few seconds after the image.

'Good afternoon gentlemen, are you there?' As if it had been choreographed, two guys appeared on the screen side by side, at exactly the same time. They might have been clones. Both wore long white lab coats, both sported white shirts and dark neckties, they looked about the same age, sixtyish, both wore thick black-framed glasses and both stood with their left hand leaning on the top of a desk. Tweedle Dum and Tweedle Dee came to mind and I put a hand to my mouth to stifle a chuckle. I looked around the room at the other three but no one else appeared to be the slightest amused, so I looked back up at the screen, re-asserting a serious expression on my face.

'Good afternoon Ricardo' they said in concert. Their timing was good but their voices were very different. One sounded like one of those BBC newscasters, all plums and marbles in the mouth and the other wonderfully French, he even made a 'good afternoon' seem deliciously suggestive.

Ricardo spoke to the screen again, 'Let me introduce our American colleagues, Professor Frank Burke, Director of the Human Genome Project at Duke University and his colleague Doctor Eve James, the project's senior micro-biologist. Dr Maier is also with us, you already know him quite well of course,' turning to Frank and me he said, 'our distinguished friends on the monitor are Professor Ron Davies from Oxford University and Professor Jacques Rombert from the Pasteur Institute'. The four of us smiled and waved.

'Does anyone object to the use of first names? No? Good, 'professor this' and 'doctor that' can be so cumbersome and time-consuming and we can't afford to waste even a moment,' 'Frank, Eve, let's get right to it. A very small number of people on this side of the Pond are in possession of facts that if widely known, would cause widespread panic throughout the entire European populations. Something we all want to avoid. I know you have heard whispers and rumours concerning high European mortality rates, they are true but it goes far beyond that. The same thing is happening in your own country and we believe in every other country on Earth as well.'

I saw the grave looks and imperceptible nods that signified agreement on the two faces staring back at me from the video screen. I looked at Frank and even he appeared to have some understanding of what was being said. Maier too was obviously part of the plot, because he sat there impassively but me; I hadn't a clue what they were talking about.

'I guessed as much,' said Frank, 'Do you have a handle on how many, which categories of the populations are affected and most importantly, the cause?'

'Frank, in answering your questions, the numbers dying are growing daily but not in epidemic proportions, at least not yet, secondly, all categories of the populations are affected, it appears to be totally random in that the victims are young and old, rich and poor, fat and thin, male and female. There is no discernable pattern we have been able to identify and as to the cause, so far we have been unable to come up with a thing, that is unless Jacques or Ron has made a magic breakthrough,' he paused and looked at the screen perceptively, when no one responded he continued 'so far we have simply failed in all our attempts to isolate the cause.

We have been working on it for the past several months but we're no nearer than when we started. That's why you're here, to bring a different and new perspective to the investigations. This matter has gone as high as your president. Only he and his inner sanctum are aware of the situation. He readily agreed to you becoming part of the team.'

Up to this point I had sat there silently taking in as much as I could but now I needed to ask some questions of my own.

'What are the symptoms?' I asked, 'is there fever, pain, swellings, changes in body temperature, vomiting, bleeding, anything that could be considered neurological?'

Jacques Rombert answered, 'Eve, we have spoken to many family members and friends who were there when death occurred, not once did they say the victim complained of feeling ill, of pain, headaches or nausea. They appeared to be fine, chatting and laughing one minute, dead the next. Some were eating; others were watching TV or reading a newspaper, in fact doing the ordinary things we all do, every day of our lives. There they were, healthy and well and then someone pulled the plug on them and disconnected them from life.'

'That has been our experience as well,' said Ron Davies, 'There is nothing I can add to Jacques' account; here today and gone before tomorrow.'

'But what did the autopsies come up with?' I asked.

It was Ricardo's turn now. 'Nothing, nada. Everything inside and outside was exactly as it should have been. The medical examiners missed nothing, left no stone unturned in the pursuit of the truth.

They didn't know what to put on the death certificates. I suppose 'Death by Unnatural Causes' would have fit the bill but that smacks of foul play and there was certainly none of that. The authorities became very suspicious and started asking all kinds of questions. In some instances there were arrests but given the lack of evidence, no charges were made.'

' Her Majesty's Government has confirmed reports that in some African countries and southern parts of India, there were many reprisal killings when people in one village suspected another village of somehow poisoning their food and water, or of putting a hex on them. They attacked each other with machetes and anything else they could lay their hands on, burning huts and killing as many as they could as the poor sods fled the flames. The victims were women, children, old and young alike, it made no difference.

Some reports described the carnage as the work of depraved maniacs in the grip of a blood lust. The local police weren't equipped to handle it, so the army was called in to bring the situation under control but not before hundreds and probably thousands, paid with their lives.'

Jacques told us of the terrible violence that broke out in parts of Israel and Palestine when residents in a Jewish settlement took matters into their own hands. They suspected their old foe of poisoning the deep-water wells that served the settlement. Seeking revenge they infiltrated the outskirts of Ramalah and shot dead at least twenty Palestinians before returning to their settlement. Palestinian retribution was swift and deadly; suicide bombers entered Jerusalem, Tel Aviv and Haifa, targeting cafes, shopping malls and public areas.

Jacques said it was like the Intifada of the early years of the century being played out all over again. Fortunately times have changed and the Israeli and Palestinian Governments enjoy excellent relations and both clamped down on the trouble before matters got completely out of hand.

An analysis of the well water was carried out and showed there was no contamination. Several hundred innocent people lost their lives in that catastrophe but at least the region was saved from being plunged into another fifty-year war.

Frank said he recalled the incident clearly but the news reports never portrayed the situation as being anywhere near that serious.

'I know,' said the DG, 'The Permanent Members of the United Nations Security Council were already aware of the 'funny goings on' as Frank put it, through 'Top Confidential' WHO reports and through them we were able to 'persuade' appropriately placed people in government and news media personnel, to play down the seriousness of the matter. It really is difficult to refuse the big boys' requests, especially once they said it was for the sake of continued peace and stability in what used to be a hotbed of violence and hatred.'

'So that's how our government became aware of the problems, through the United Nations?' I said.

'Well not exactly,' Ricardo replied,' they already knew something was going on from their own intelligence sources but they didn't know to what extent, it was only after the Permanent Members of the Security Council were appraised of the situation that any government became fully aware. It was decided by them that the fewer governments who knew about this, the better. There was already too much instability in the world as it was and they felt that until the WHO had a better handle on it, information would be made available strictly on a need to know basis.'

'Remind me,' asked Frank, 'who are the Permanent Members?'

'The US of course,' said the DG, 'And France, China, Great Britain, Russia, Japan, South Africa and Germany.

Remember, Japan, South Africa and Germany were added to the Council in 2020.'

'My God' said Frank, 'what an incredible, unbelievable story, the scale, the magnitude, it staggers the imagination. The entire world, except for a few privileged presidents, prime ministers, UN staff and government high ups, is caught up in a web of deception that stretches from pole to pole, east to west, and tell me please, how long has the deception been going on for and who gave these people the right to play God?' Frank was mad, he was a doctor not a bureaucrat and understanding the politics of situations was not something he was particularly sensitive to. 'The people have a right to know.'

'People have a right to know what Frank?' this was Dr. Maier speaking, 'the right to know that literally at any second they, or one of their loved ones might drop down dead, the right to know we don't know why or when, the right to know there's not a damned thing we can do about it. What exactly do they have a right to know?'

Frank and I stared at Maier; he had hardly said a word and now here he was making a speech and making no attempt to hide his anger.

'Wolf, ' said Professor Valdez soothingly, 'I understand how you must feel but Professor Burke's reaction was how you too would have reacted in normal circumstances, in fact how you did react initially but there is nothing normal about these circumstances, nothing normal at all.'

Maier turned to Frank, 'Please forgive me Professor Burke, I'm so terribly sorry for my unforgivable outburst but you see, my wife and son died within two days of each other from this.... this, whatever it is. He was three years old my son, his birthday was two weeks away...' He never finished the sentence; it was just left hanging in mid-air.

I looked at Frank; the colour had drained from his face, his mouth moved without making a sound. Finally, he got control of himself, 'Doctor, I don't know what to say. I guess we deal with figures and statistics a little too much and we sometimes miss the nub of the matter and can't see the wood for the trees. It's the real life human tragedies that are what really count and yours is too tragic for words. I'm real sorry.'

Maier simply gave a nod of resignation and settled back into his chair.

An awkward silence followed before Professor Davies said, 'We have looked at this problem from every conceivable angle except the right one and that is the one that continues to elude us and since we don't know what we're looking for we are just running blindfold. Believe me Frank we have applied every standard test, our best teams are on the job. Ricardo is co-ordinating the investigation from the WHO HQ, which means that Pasteur and Oxford are holding hands and working very closely. We seem to be barking up the wrong tree but where are the other trees to bark up? We need help.'

'Frank, Eve, said Ricardo, 'your government has promised to throw its weight and resources behind this project, we have to come up with answers and we don't have that much time. They will formally advise you and answer your questions as best as they can, details like funding, confidentiality and the like will be between you and them but the matter is so serious that work will be suspended on the Advanced Human Genome Project to enable you to direct the energies and talents of your team into helping solve the puzzle.

I don't want to sound melodramatic but the situation probably presents the greatest threat humankind has ever had to face, even its very existence.'

For a moment we were all frozen in a tableau of silence, Professors Rombert and Davies on their video screen, Professor Valdez, Dr Maier, Frank and me in Geneva, whilst the words of Valdez insinuated themselves into our minds. I involuntarily shuddered.

Addressing the video screen Valdez said, 'Do you have anything new to report?'

Rombert was the first to speak, 'No, nothing at all. The tissue samples from Zaire appear perfectly normal. Almost all the victims were in good health, many in the prime of life; at the time of their deaths they were doing nothing remarkable, mainly routine mundane stuff. They just died,' he snapped his fingers for effect, 'just like that'.

'Ron?'

'The same I'm afraid. We received tissue samples from Russia and China, there was nothing. No clues, no leads to work on, to all intents and purposes the people should never have died. The dreaded question all of us working on the problem ask is who will be next? It's like a lottery, a game of chance and the spin of a roulette wheel. Whose number will be up next? It's really frightening.'

'Do you know even in ballpark figures how many we are talking about?' I asked.

'It's difficult,' said Ricardo, 'most countries, especially the poor and underdeveloped ones don't have the means of recording and reporting these things. Their populations live day to day without the central government ever really getting involved with them; many of them don't even have the slightest idea what the size of their population is. Look at India, a vast country of over a billion people, so much poverty and overcrowded slums, there's nothing particularly new or alarming about people dying, it's an every day occurrence, a few hundred or a thousand more, especially in the big cities, would simply go unnoticed, part of the fabric of life itself you might say. And China with one and a half billion people, how can any government keep tabs on a population of that size? At least, as a Permanent Member of the Security Council, they are in the information loop and are co-operating as much as they're able.

Then there's Mexico City with over thirty million people and San Paulo with thirty five million more. Would a couple of thousand additional deaths make any difference to anyone except loved ones? I don't think so, just another drop in the bucket. I'm sorry if I sound callous, I don't mean to, it's just the way it is.'

'So you have no way of knowing the extent of the problem?' said Frank.

'Well we do have good and accurate reporting from most of Europe, Great Britain, the USA, Canada Australia and New Zealand. The Caribbean islands of Jamaica, Barbados and Trinidad are also providing good data, although they have no idea what the information is for; their UN Ambassadors were asked to provide information on several health topics, HIV/Aids for example and communicable disease stats and of course mortality rates, which was what we really wanted.

You will understand that at this stage it is important not to create suspicion amongst the other countries. We know that we are living with this on a day-to-day basis. Some countries, like Australia and Canada are already asking questions, they know something's going on. It's only a matter of time before this thing can't be contained anymore, the lid will blow off and then God help us all. In the meantime we are working against the clock to find some answers but the time bomb is ticking away. We desperately need something, anything we can announce with confidence to the General Assembly.'

'What does the available data show?' asked Frank.

'Actually it's remarkably consistent,' said Oxford University, 'about a 2% rise in mortality rates, not enough to cause a tidal wave of concern but enough to make some countries health authorities sit up and take notice.'

'Eve, gentlemen, enough I think for now. I will be meeting again tomorrow with Frank and Eve. They must be exhausted from their flight and then coming straight here, As important as this is, they need some rest and a little time to digest what they have heard. We all need to be feeling fresh for tomorrow.' Then addressing the screen he bade farewell to Rombert and Davies, promising to keep them advised of our up-coming meeting and anything else of importance. We all said our goodbyes and the screen went blank. That was the last time they had anything to do with Professor Valdez this side of eternity.

'Wolf, why don't you escort our friends to the hotel; it's the Noga Hilton isn't it, almost round the corner from here?' 'I think enough is enough for one day, you need time to relax and no doubt reflect on all you have heard today. It has been a lot for you to take in and I'm sure you have more questions forming in your minds already. Time enough for that tomorrow.'

Ricardo walked us to the door and we shook hands for the last time.

We retraced our steps back to the elevator and Dr. Maier followed the same procedure as before to take us up to ground level. When we stepped out of the elevator a different driver was waiting for us. I think Maier must have read my mind because he said that the previous driver had finished his duty and this was his replacement. I wondered if I was starting to get paranoid.

CHAPTER 6

We got back into the Bimmer and drove up to the same large metal door, Maier spoke into the magic microphone and his abracadabra brought out the palm reader, in no time at all we were gliding up the ramp and into the car park. We soon cleared the security barrier and turned onto the approach road that would eventually deposit us at the hotel.

Every thing looked so damned normal, cars everywhere, people going unsuspectingly about their business and for a brief moment I thought of George Romero's classic horror movie 'The Night of the Living Dead' when healthy humans became flesh-eating zombies.

Was this one of those examples when life mimics art and everyone out there on the streets of Geneva is auditioning for a part in a new version of the movie, entitled 'The Time of the Living Dead?' 'What is happening,' I thought,' where is this crazy ride taking us.' I wasn't looking for an answer.

By now it was late afternoon and the sun was already beginning to set, a true sign of winter. I became convinced of my paranoia when I started to look for a set of car pedals at my feet. 'Just in case,' I told myself, 'just in case I need to stop the car because someone else can't. Because he's….' I couldn't finish the thought, I tried to banish it from my mind but it wouldn't go. 'Dead! That's the word. There it's said. 'Dead', in case the driver and Dr. Maier suddenly die.'

Fear was stomping all over me in concrete-laden boots. I imagined some blind malevolent god, a Colossus atop Mt Olympus, amusing himself by randomly pointing a finger at one of us lowly humans as we scurried around like ants and wheresoever the finger rests, the prize is instant death, just because He wills it.

All fall down, like in the kids' game of 'Ring-a Ring-a Roses', except in this new version, people don't suffer, they simply fall down dead but this is not a game; just death stalking the land.

Frank was oblivious to my silent ranting and stared out of his window, though I doubt he actually saw anything, you could almost hear the cogs spinning in his head. He had a brilliant brain and I was sure it was cranked to the top and already working in overdrive. Like a computer, he would be tabulating and analyzing what he had learnt at the WHO, perhaps he had most of it worked out by now. Frank was like that, a brilliant man, there was no one better qualified to be on the project, and his knowledge of the human genome was probably unparalleled. With due respect to the Pasteur Institute and Oxford University and taking nothing away from Professors Davies or Rombert, this conundrum seemed made to measure for Frank, it seemed so closely related to our research programme. Personally, I couldn't wait to get started, I felt already that the answers were tantalizingly close, I would have voted to head straight out to the airport and get back to the lab at Duke as soon as possible. Give us one week, two at the most and we will have this thing licked.

What I really meant was that I wanted to get home to Bill and the girls, find them well and then solve the problem before it became too personal. Wishful thinking I know but I was a wife and mother first and a microbiologist next.

The hotel was only a couple of miles from the WHO and we were there within minutes. I was still gathering my thoughts when the driver opened the car door and I was walking into the lobby area.

Dr Maier escorted us to the reception desk and waited while our reservations were confirmed; everything was in order, Frank had a message in a hotel envelope and we were given our keys, 520 for me and 522 for Frank. The clerk told us our luggage was already in the rooms.

We shook hands with Maier and thanked him for looking after us. He said Professor Valdez had suggested he could pick us up at the hotel at about 10.00am tomorrow, if that was convenient. It was. We then made our way through the busy lobby area to the bank of elevators. I pressed the call button and one of the doors opened straightaway.

Frank had hardly spoken since we had left WHO.

'What do you think Frank?' I asked 'Any first ideas?'

'I'm at a loss;' he said 'I've never heard of anything like it. It's too weird; nothing fits into anything I've ever come across. Maybe it's because I'm tired and my brain's not fully in sync. I think I'll take a nap and then shower that should brighten me up. Then we could get a bite to eat if you feel like it, say about 8.00. What do you think?'

'I think yes,' I said, 'I'll ring you at 8.00.'

The elevator faithfully deposited us on the fifth floor and we followed the signs to our rooms.

'Later,' I said, letting myself into the room. I heard Frank's door open next door, as mine closed.

The air conditioning must have been set at the lowest possible temperature because arctic blasts of air were coming through the vents in a subdued roar; it was freezing cold. A quick search quickly located the temperature setting dial and I set it to 'off'. The room fell silent.

The desk clerk was right; my two pieces of luggage had already made themselves at home and were there waiting to greet me. I was about to risk death by freezing by taking off my coat when I noticed the red message light flashing on the phone. I figured it had to be Bill trying to reach me, because I had promised to phone him as soon as I arrived at the hotel, I didn't think we would be whisked off to a meeting quite so quickly.

I punched in the numbers that activated the message facility. A small voice said, 'Hi Mommy it's me.'

Another identical sounding voice said, 'Hi Mommy it's me as well.' The twins, my God I had never been so relieved to hear their voices.

And then a third voice said, 'Hi darling, can you guess which three people are on the phone to you?'

One of the first two voices said, 'Of course she can Daddy, it's us, who else would it be?'

'What happened honey, forget about us already?' 'You can give your poor forgotten family a ring if you want.'

'Yes Mommy, give your foor regotten family a wing if we want,' chorused the twins.

'Oh Bill, Wendy, Suzanne,' I realised I was crying and I was annoyed with myself for doing it, it were as if crying sort of confirmed how serious the situation was and the fear, the near panic I felt for the safety of my little family.

That damned blind Colossus on Mt Olympus wasn't going to point his finger at any of mine. I'll stop him in his tracks. I'll find out how he works his evil spells and put an end to them.

I finally removed my coat and surprisingly, I didn't freeze to death; just almost.

Geneva was seven hours in front of Raleigh; it was six here, that made it twelve noon back home. I decide to call home there and then.

I followed the dialing instructions and was rewarded with a burr, burring sound. The phone was picked up on the fourth ring.

'Mommy, Mommy, is it you?' Yelled one of the twins, I didn't know which; hell it was difficult enough to tell them apart when they were stood in front of you, on the telephone it was impossible.

'Hi darling,' I said 'yes it's Mommy, how are my two cherubs?"

'We're fine, how are you?'

'I'm fine too; I wish I was there with you guys.'

'We do too Mommy, we miss you. Have you bought us a present yet?' Kids are great aren't they? Always get their priorities right. Get the pleasantries over with quickly and then get down to the important stuff.

'No honey not yet, I've only just got here but I will.'

'Ok Mommy, here's Daddy.'

'Hi honey,' Bill's dark brown voice resonated in my ear and I was weeping again, 'how are you doin'?' He asked.

I was going to tell him everything that had happened, from when we got off the plane, to this telephone call; the whole crazy story, then I remembered Professor Valdez stressing the need for confidentiality and I clamped up. I told him instead, there was a new strain of the flu virus that had surfaced in South East Asia and that it had proved resistant to normal treatments, the WHO had asked Frank and I to pool our resources and knowledge with other research institutions, primarily Pasteur and Oxford University, to see if between us, we could come up with a vaccine.

I hated to lie to Bill but there wasn't an acceptable alternative. Time enough for him to find out for himself, I really saw no need to lay that kind of worry on him right now and anyway, this thing might not be anything as bad as it sounded, then again, it might be much worse.

Bill said he had to go because of a meeting he had arranged with some business clients, the call seemed to be over almost before it had begun. All four of us shouted our goodbyes into our phones at the same time, I couldn't bear the thought of them hanging up all I could think of was whether I would ever see them again. I told myself I was over-reacting.

CHAPTER 7

I wasn't tired, I was exhausted but my brain was going at a thousand miles an hour, there was no way I could nap. I just lay on the bed and tried to imagine what in heaven's name could be behind these deaths. Nothing came to mind.

Obviously my brain knew better than I that I had used up my stock of endurance and I unceremoniously slipped into sleep. In my dream I was riding in a fire engine and we were rushing to the scene of a fire, the bells on the fire engine seemed to be right next to my head and they were ringing so loudly that the sound obliterated every other sense of awareness. The ringing seemed to go on and on. Then I experienced a blurring of two realities and the fire engine started to loose its substance, to be replaced instead by a bedroom scene. My dream state was evaporating rapidly. The fire engine was gone now and the ringing was no longer coming from a fire bell but from the telephone on the bedside table next to my head. Reality finally kicked in and I realised where I was. The dream state gone, I reached out and picked up the phone, it was Frank, since I hadn't rung him as promised, at 8.15 he had decided he'd better check on me.

I must have sounded real dopey because Frank was apologizing for having disturbed me. I told him not to be silly and twenty minutes later I was stood outside his door, showered, dressed and ready for something to eat. Frank suggested we visit the café and eat gourmet American style; cheeseburgers and fries, I thought it was a great idea. You can't beat a touch of home when you're far away and I figured everything would be complete if they had apple pie on the menu.

When we stepped out of the elevator, scenes more appropriate to one of those disaster movies than a busy hotel reception area, greeted us. The flashing red light of an ambulance was visible through the hotel's glass entry doors, people were running in every direction around the lobby in a state of utter confusion, voices were raised everywhere in a cacophony of pure sound, it was difficult to understand what they were saying as it seemed that everyone was trying to talk at he same time, it didn't help of course that most of the languages were not English. Opposite us was a team of para-medics in white coats bent over what appeared to be a body lying on the floor in front of the reception desk.

Frank and I threaded our way through the confusion to get a better look at what was going on; we arrived just in time to see a man in a white coat, down on one knee beside the body shaking his head; whoever was on the floor wouldn't be getting up, he was dead. Then the impossible happened, the very desk clerk we had dealt with only a couple of hours earlier suddenly collapsed behind the reception desk, at first it looked as if he'd fainted then someone screamed, I think it was the telephone operator, one of the para- medics vaulted the counter but it was too late, the guy was dead already.

The hotel's duty manager appealed for calm by shouting to make himself heard above the growing babble of voices and general cacophony. By now some of the guests were clearly frightened, which was hardly surprising what with dead bodies in the hotel, ambulances with flashing red lights, men running around in white coats and general mayhem ensuing all around them.

Frank identified himself to one of the medics and asked him what was going on. The medic said they had got a call from the hotel that a guest had been checking in when they had simply collapsed. The hotel telephone operator said they thought it must have been a massive heart attack because it was so sudden. The medic confirmed that the guest was dead by the time they had arrived fifteen minutes later (apparently the ambulance was on it's way back from a similar situation and was quite close to the hotel when the call came through).

The medic's take on the desk clerk was that he had probably suffered a heart attack, which could have been brought on by the shock of the incident with the guest.

I asked him who was the leader of the para-medic team and a short stockily built man involved in an animated discussion with the hotel manager was pointed out to me. I waited until he had finished his conversation before approaching him.

'Excuse me sir, I can see how busy you are but may I introduce myself and my companion?' He looked up at me uncertainly but didn't raise an objection, 'this is Professor Frank Burke, head of a major research institution in the USA and I'm Dr. Eve James his assistant, we're in Geneva for a medical conference.' He nodded to us but still looked unsure, I showed him my Duke ID, it seemed to do the trick.

'Your colleague was telling us it looked like both fatalities were due to cardiac arrest; unusual but not unheard of. He also said you were on your way back from having dealt with a similar case.' I left the statement hanging.

He no longer viewed me with suspicion. 'Yes, we were called out to an incident in a shopping mall not too far from here, same thing really, a young woman, I would say in her early thirties was out shopping with her husband and two children when she collapsed to the floor. She was already dead when we got there. The husband was distraught and the children were in tears, he said they had just come out of a toy store and she was looking at a teddy bear they had bought for one of the kids, she was tickling the tummy of the bear and the kids were laughing when she suddenly keeled over. No warning, she had not been ill and hadn't been complaining about anything at all.' For a moment he stood there in silent contemplation and then added, 'It was unreal, she looked the picture of good health lay there where she had fallen, she looked as if she were asleep. But she was dead. She didn't look to me to have been a heart attack victim and now these two. We're living, or maybe dying, in strange times. This is the seventh call like this one, we've answered in the past four days; it's been the same story, a healthy person going about their everyday business, eating or talking, or shopping with the family, just everyday things, then poof, gone, like their life was snatched right out of them. I suppose the autopsies will show something.'

He asked us to excuse him and he turned back to the business of finishing up with hotel. I said a silent prayer that there would be no further incidents, if there were, I wouldn't want to predict what the peoples' reactions would be, many of the guests were already showing signs of anxiety.

'Frank?' I said inquisitively.

'I don't know Eve, I just don't know. I would have to think that the calls these guys are answering are related to what Professor Valdez was telling us. None of it makes any sense. If 'Pasteur' and 'Oxford' had been able to form an opinion from their investigations, I might have been able to offer an observation, a thought or something but if they can't find any leads…' His sentence just tapered off to nothing.

I thought again of my blind god, he had somehow become 'my god' and I didn't like that a bit, playing his own version of Russian Roulette and knowing that me and mine occupied slots on his spinning wheel, filled me with a deep, dark, dread.

Fear changed its form of attack and instead of stomping up my spine; it swapped its boots for a long pointed icicle and plunged it into my heart.

The hotel settled down very quickly into something approximating normal, the bodies were removed and with the excitement over, the onlookers drifted away. Guests started to arrive who had not been witness to any of the recent events and they were dealt with in the usual friendly and efficient manner and dispatched to their rooms with a minimum of fuss, blissfully unaware of the excitement of only moments ago.

'Are you still hungry?' I asked Frank.

'Not really,' he replied, 'but we ought to eat something, do you realise we have had nothing to eat since the stuff on the plane, let me see, that's more than twelve hours ago.'

We made our way to one of the cafés, it was about half full and we chose a table for two next to a window that looked out onto the gardens. Of course being winter, it was dark outside except for the sodium vapour lights that illuminated the pathways.

We both ordered cheese burger and fries, I asked for a soda water and Frank chose a Bud, like I said, nothing beats a taste of home.

We sat in silence until the food arrived, then Frank said, 'Are you worried about Bill and the girls?'

'Only out of my mind,' I replied, 'This isn't like a real bad flu outbreak, or even getting sick from gastric bug that's currently doing the rounds, there is no vaccination against it, no tablets, no medicine; nothing. I feel so damned helpless. And with Bill and the girls five thousand miles away, it makes matters that much worse, I know that if I were there it would make no difference, I mean what could do, but just being there would be a comfort. I spoke to them earlier and they're fine but they would be wouldn't they, I mean everybody's fine until the thing hits them and then zap! You're it and you're gone.'

'Did you tell Bill anything at all about this?'

'No, not a thing, what's the point? He would be less likely to understand it than we do and we don't have any ideas at all right now. I think he would just worry himself sick about the girls and me. It's better that he knows nothing, then he can't worry.'

We finished the food; I guess it must have been ok because I couldn't remember what it tasted like. We didn't look to see if apple pie was on the menu, we just ordered coffee.

Our reverie was broken by the hotel's public address system paging, Frank and me, asking for us to go to the front desk. We quickly signed the room bill and hurried to Reception.

CHAPTER 8

A semblance of normality had returned to the foyer and reception area, Doctor Maier stood to one side looking as if the troubles of the world were resting on his shoulders, in truth I guess they were.

'What is it doctor?' I said.

'I'm afraid I have some rather bad news for you, Professor Valdez is dead.' Before we could respond he continued, 'I received a call from the Head of Security, he said the Professor's wife came to pick him up; they were going to a function. He rang the Professor but he didn't answer his office phone, they tried his pager still nothing and his mobile went unanswered too. They went to check his office and that's when they found him, sat behind his desk, dead, like all the others, dead.' This whole situation had become unreal, we hadn't known Ricardo Valdez very long but Maier's words still fell like hammer blows.

'My God, what is this thing?' said Frank, 'what in heaven's name are we up against? We need answers and we need them quick.' Still talking to Maier, 'There was a message waiting for me when we got to the hotel, Dr James and I are to report to Washington as soon as possible, apparently there are pressing matters that need to be addressed, they want a briefing on what we have learnt here and there's now some urgency in getting our side of the business set up. They said there were also other things they wished to discuss; I can well imagine what they might be. They also instructed that we must not discuss the matter with anyone, outside of your people at the WHO and our own personnel.

'Dr Maier, would it be possible to have a quick video meeting with Rombert and Davies tomorrow morning, say at eight? There are a couple of things I would like to raise with them before we return to Washington; we're booked on AA 6206, it departs Geneva at 12.15 for JFK.'

Maier agreed to set it up and then left. Neither he nor we thought to shake hands or bid each other a goodnight. I guess the three of us were already lost in our own personal kaleidoscope of thoughts.

I was elated at the thought of going home but what would we find when we got there. I was certain of one thing, whatever it was, it would be that much worse than when we left. I had a horrible feeling that this, whatever it was, was gathering momentum.

How long would it be before governments were forced by deteriorating circumstances to tell their people something, if only to try and halt the speculation and reassure them that they were in control of the situation, and what would happen when it was obvious that they were anything but in control but were simply being carried along in the tidal flow? How do you tell people not to panic, that the government has everything under control, when increasing numbers of the population are dropping down dead all around you? If it reached those proportions, Civilisation's very existence would surely teeter on the edge of the abyss. The world would go up in flames; rioting, death and destruction like a giant tsunami would engulf every continent on earth and the streets would run red with blood.

My God, what a nightmare scenario, it staggers the imagination; it's like something out of 'Revelations' in the New Testament. Armageddon would surely be upon us.

There has to be an answer and we have to find it, no matter what it takes. There is a responsibility to the whole human race to turn back the tide. The answer might come from a test tube in Duke, Oxford or Paris, or anywhere else but it has to come, the alternative is too frightening to contemplate.

I once remembered reading an article about 'Black Holes' they were likened to enormous cosmic vacuum cleaners meandering round the universe and that over many billions of years all the galaxies would eventually be sucked into them, like water gurgling down a plughole. I recalled thinking at the time, what an ignominious end to everything, more like glug, glug than kerpow. I didn't pay too much attention to the article, because billions of years is a long time to wait for any event to happen and it wasn't really of pressing importance to me, but this new version of 'Ring-a Ring of Roses' was here now, galaxies might not be dying but people were and now not in billions of years and worse still, I was convinced the process was speeding up.

CHAPTER 9

By now I was feeling exhausted, the flight, the meeting at the WHO, deaths in the hotel and finally, I hoped, the terrible news about Ricardo Valdez. Such a nice man, I liked him, I hardly knew him of course but my woman's intuition told me he was a nice man.

Frank and I rode the elevator to the fifth floor and I held his hand all the way. We stopped at my door and I looked up at him and said, 'I'm frightened Frank, not just for Bill and the kids; I'm frightened for all of us. I'm frightened for all humankind.' It didn't sound the least bit melodramatic.

Frank's expression needed no words; his own fear was etched deep in his face.

'Good night Eve, pray, pray for us all.'

I opened my door and went in; it closed behind me with a faint whoosh and a click. I stood there for a long minute staring into the darkened room. It was inky black, my eyes hadn't had time to adjust and it struck me that I could have been peering into the emptiness and blackness of space. I prayed there would be no encounter with black holes tonight.

I'd booked a wake up call for six but I didn't need it, I'd tossed and turned for most of the night and finally come fully awake at four. I lay for a while with my head on my pillow staring at the ceiling; the faint green glow of the numbers on the bedside clock my only company. I felt so alone, so vulnerable and so afraid. I put my hands together, like when I was a little girl, closed my eyes and prayed. I prayed for strength, for my family and loved ones, for Frank and for deliverance from this 'plague' thing, or whatever it was. I topped it all off with the Lord's Prayer, just like when I was a kid. I felt a bit better.

I was now fully awake and knew sleep would remain out of reach for the rest of the night so I reached for the TV remote and found CNN, it was the European version, some woman with a British accent telling us that temperatures across the middle east were below the seasonal norm, something I could have gotten through the day without knowing.

I seem to be unlucky with CNN, whenever I switch on back home; I either get the weather or the ads, never the news. I scrolled up the channels and came to BBC World, there was a news clip showing some civil disturbance or other and I was about to move on when I caught the voice-over, '.... the people are convinced the government is holding back from telling them the truth and they're demanding a statement from the prime minister.

A spokesman for the villagers said they're convinced that the high number of deaths in many rural villages across the land is a direct result of what they describe as their government's hideous policy to reduce the rural population and concentrate resources in the major towns and cities.

A spokesman for the prime minister's office described the accusations as outrageous and preposterous. He said it was the government's policy to improve the living standards of the rural population and enumerated the many initiatives they had taken since becoming the government, just over two years ago.

The villager's spokesman posited what other explanation there could be when people dying in numbers the like of which had never been seen before were decimating so many villages throughout Bangladesh. He said the deaths were not confined to any particular age group, everyone was dying; old, young even babies and that most of the people were not even ill.

This looks likely to become a developing story, we'll keep an eye on it for you and update you in future bulletins. 'This is Nick Carter, live in Dhaka, Bangladesh for the BBC.'

I didn't hear the next item, even though I hadn't turned the TV off nor turned down the volume, I just sat there stunned, staring at the screen and seeing nothing. My thoughts raced in all directions, 'Is this where the end begins, the disintegration of civilisation, in some remote villages in rural Bangladesh?'

There was no doubt in my mind what the root cause of the protests were; the Bangladeshi government couldn't have respond in any other way, it had no idea what it was up against; in truth, none of us knew what we were up against but I had a horrible feeling it wouldn't be long before we found out.

CHAPTER 10

I left the BBC on and took a shower, by the time I was dressed and my luggage packed for the return flight home and I was ready to face the world, it was 8.00am. There had been no further news from Bangladesh. I rang Frank's room and was gripped by a sudden dread that there wouldn't be an answer, that Frank would be lying cold in his bed but sweet relief; he picked up on the fourth ring.

'Did you see the news this morning?' I asked

'Good morning Eve,' Frank responded very deliberately,' Thanks, now you ask, 'did you sleep well last night? Oh you did, great, why don't we go have some coffee and donuts or something and catch up with what's happening?'

'Ok,' I said, 'Sorry about the morning's greeting or should I say lack of it, no need to be sarcastic. Sure, I would love a coffee; I'm never quite human in the morning until I've had my first injection of caffeine. See you outside in ten minutes.'

A last look in the mirror told me what I suspected, puffy eyes and telltale dark circles, compelling evidence of a poor and restless night's sleep. 'Oh well,' I thought, 'Let's go see what the world looks like this morning.'

Frank was just exiting his room as I stepped into the corridor; I walked up to him and hugged him tight.

'Hey what's this about?' He said, 'I needed that.'

'Yea, me too, come on let's go down, I can smell the coffee from here.'

On the way down to the café I told Frank about the BBC news item, he hadn't seen it but he too felt it was the 'thing' that was responsible, (what the hell else do you call it? I had no better word than 'thing' right now).

We talked about going home and getting started on the lab work but never said exactly where we thought we would make the start, it didn't really matter either at this stage, and in truth the comforting thing was the getting home. Bill was there and Wendy and Suzanne. I hoped the answer would be there as well.

By the time Dr Maier arrived I felt sustained by the hot coffee and donuts, I asked him if he had seen the news out of Bangladesh, he said he had and that it was extremely disturbing. He said there must be many potential flashpoints all over the world. 'There has to be,' he said, 'this, whatever it is, is happening everywhere. Where will the next demonstration be and then where after that? I fear the snowball is already rolling down the hill, it can only get bigger and bigger and go faster and faster, as if it's rolling all of humanity up into one big ball, taking us on a journey that can have only one end, obliteration when the snowball smashes into whatever waits for it at the bottom of the mountain We have to find a solution and quick.'

As we got into the BMW, I again noticed the dual pedal controls, this time I felt brave enough to ask Dr Maier if they were a precaution against the driver dying at the wheel and the car careening out of control. A nod of his head was confirmation enough. I thought of my blind god with the pointing finger, sowing seeds of discord in the hearts of humanity all across the world and wallowing in the wretched misery of what he was responsible for. Again I mentally warned him to back off from my family.

'We're real sorry for what happened to Professor Valdez,' Frank said,' it must have been a terrible shock.'

Maier looked down at his hands they were resting like sleeping birds in his lap, 'Thank you Professor, Ricardo was not just the boss; he was also a good friend. He was loved by many and respected by everyone who knew him. He will be sorely missed.'

I wondered who and how many would be around to do the missing. I wish I could describe the feeling of helplessness, cornered like a rat, with no way out. My blind god was calling out to me, 'One Two Three YOUR DEAD!' I shuddered.

The drive took no time at all and we were soon in the elevator dropping down the same two levels. Dr Maier led us to the same room, which was equipped with the same equipment. We took our seats and Maier switched on the equipment. At exactly 10.00am the screen came to life, Rombert and Davies were there in their same white lab coats but this time looking very somber indeed.

We greeted each other.

'Wolf,' said Professor Rombert, 'what can I say? Ricardo was a fine man, an excellent administrator, knew his way through the various political mazes, a highly trained physician but most of all I will remember him for his humility. My heart bleeds for all of us.'

'I agree with Jacques, he was all those things and then some more,' it was Professor Davies.

'Thank you my friends, we already know that this particular hand of death strikes with impunity, when and where it wishes, it is as if it knew Ricardo was leading the charge against it and struck him down as in battle. We must continue the fight and be true to his memory by finding the answers to these stubborn and so far unyielding questions before time runs out.' He paused reflectively, his eyes and mind temporarily focused somewhere else and then he was back with us.

'Have you heard the news from Bangladesh?' He asked, 'I felt sorry for the government spokesman, they haven't a clue what they're facing. The villagers are frightened and news travels fast, village to village, especially bad news. Most are uneducated and they see things in simple terms; the government doesn't enjoy the trust of the people and the politicians are perceived as corrupt and self-serving. It is not surprising that they should see the government as being behind the events. To them there is no other rational explanation. Of course the accusations are horrendous and without foundation but someone has to be held responsible, who better than the government?'

Professor Davies said 'This will give the Security Council something to think about, because I can't see this remaining an isolated incident. They are going to have to come clean on the issue. You know what they say, 'you can fool some of the people some of the time but you can't fool all the people all of the time.'

'Gentlemen,' said Frank, making a timely interjection in the conversation, 'I'm sure Dr Maier told you Eve and I would be flying back to the States later today, I wanted a chance to raise a couple of things with you before leaving, so thank you for agreeing to this meeting, I really appreciate it, I know you don't want to be dragged away from your work but a couple of things occurred to me last night and I would like to highlight them with you before we leave.

' Not a problem,' said Professor Davies, 'we have to pool our resources and ideas if we are to break this thing. The answer will probably come through close collaboration between our collective research institutes and us as individuals.

'Ok, great, thanks, tell me, have you had any reports of a rise in the death rates of animals, especially primates; perhaps from zoos or safari parks, maybe the big game reserves like the Kruger National Park in South Africa, or the one in Kenya, it might be something that is affecting humans and simians?

What about some new virus jumping the species like mad cow disease did at the turn of the century. Remember, initially there was a great deal of disagreement amongst scientists as to whether mad cow disease had jumped from one species to another; the British Government went on record denying the possibility and then there was the stupidly embarrassing spectacle of a government minister appearing on TV, beaming broadly with his family at his side, eating burgers made from British beef and telling the world how safe the beef was.

They even ridiculed their own government scientists when they first alerted them to their suspicions. The view of many people at the time was that the Government's strident denial of any link between cows and humans was cynical and based purely on economics, because the domestic consumption and export of beef was worth billions of pounds sterling a year and that if the scientists were correct it would devastate a significant section of the British economy.

If you recall, there were many claims that other foreign governments, the US included, conspired with the Brits to suppress the truth because of fears of a world-wide anti-beef movement that could have destroyed the beef industry from Greenland to New Zealand and caused incalculable damage to the profits of large corporations, many of whom supported the political parties in power.

The fallout affecting the world's farming community, the fast food industry, world unemployment, poverty, bankruptcies and God knows what else staggers the imagination. The economies of some nations like Brazil and Argentina that had a heavy dependency and an enormous political investment on beef exports, would have been at risk not just from an uncontrollable economic decline but also from political instability as well. I haven't even mentioned the supermarkets and even the small corner shops. No country and no individual would have escaped the fall out.

As it was, sanity prevailed and the British Government and its friends did a superb job of damage control. Another nasty example of a lack of corporate conscience is the suppression by the cigarette companies of the incontrovertible results of medical research linking tobacco smoking with cancer. They would rather have had people dying from cancer than see a dent in their profits and they have known for some considerable time of the dangers of cigarette smoking and chose to ignore the evidence and continued to vociferously deny its existence. In crude terms, a dollar was more important than a life.

Even after the evidence, which as I said was irrefutable, was widely publicised and subsequently sales started to fall in the developed world, they still pushed and promoted their death-in-a-packet, to the developing world. Why didn't the governments protect their citizens and stop the tobacco companies peddling death? They knew what tobacco consumption was doing to their populations but they chose to ignore it too, tax revenues being more important than a healthy population.

Do you see the parallels between the British government's mad cow disease crises and the tobacco companies and how the spin doctors dodged and weaved on the facts and why the Bangladeshi villagers are so suspicious of their government? Their accusations, while we know them to be ludicrous, seem not quite so ludicrous to them and perhaps now we can understand why.

Sorry for that lengthy digression, at first glance it might seem a million miles away from what we've got here but then again maybe not. I just want to be sure in my own mind, that we are covering all the bases and examining the evidence from every perspective, no matter how fanciful that perspective might seem.'

I realised I'd been holding my breath during Frank's little speech, it had been riveting and so typical of Frank's ability to see the side issues as well as the main focus. I admired him so much.

No one spoke for several long seconds, I guess everyone was digesting what Frank had said, and it was certainly food for thought and demanded to be taken note of.

Professor Davies was the first to break the silence, 'My goodness Frank, I had been looking at this from almost a purely academic point of view, I can see clearly now that we will have to be mindful of other related issues, especially when we are sifting through the evidence. The order of the day is to take nothing for granted and accept nothing on face value.

On the question of the other primates, I confess I never thought of it and when you do think of it, what would a few additional monkey deaths in zoos mean, they are hardly likely to get much coverage outside of Reader's Digest or the National Geographic Magazine? The game reserves are even less likely to take note of dead gorillas and chimpanzees, I mean, their natural predators would probably quickly eat the carcasses and the bones would be picked clean by scavengers. In a short time there would be little or no evidence that there was anything unusual going on. Still, it's certainly worth making enquiries.

Now that I'm thinking about it, there may be more reliable information from the safari parks we have dotted up and down the country, there are not so many predators lurking amongst the trees as in the large African game reserves and higher mortality rates would quickly be noticed. If this could be added to whatever we find going on in the zoos, it might give us a pointer and a new line of investigation.'

'On the question of some as yet undiscovered virus or organism being at work, I would have to say that it is very possible but the problem so far is that we have not been able to establish a pattern, no common thread, nothing that points us in any particular direction. We had expected to discover evidence that somehow linked each patient, perhaps some organ deterioration, a toxic substance, evidence of a sudden falling off in the body's functions, or a weakening of the immune system but after examining hundreds of specimens and having applied all the standard procedures, we have found nothing unusual. Most of the victims were robustly healthy, enjoying life to the fullest and then puff, gone. Then there are the hundreds of thousands of autopsies that have been routinely carried out by pathologists all over the world, they also have come up with nothing. There is only one common factor, death and so far death is giving up none of its secrets.'

'Are you collaborating in your work,' I asked, 'or are you following your own paths?'

'So far the WHO has been co-ordinating the effort and is keeping the Council advised almost daily, the research institutes also advise their own people on a need to know basis. Up to now we have only been able to report negatives.' This was Dr Maier responding. 'We hope that your input will add a new dimension and impetus to the investigation. There is a suspicion that we are not dealing with a disease as such but something far more fundamental.'

I glanced at Frank, he was staring off into space, he seemed to articulate his thoughts and my own as well, when he said 'Do you realise what this means; if we can't find what is causing these opportunistic deaths and if they don't stop as spontaneously as they seem to have begun and if the mortality rate continues to increase as it appears to be doing, we will reach a situation, and I have no wish to appear melodramatic, when the human race comes face to face with its own extinction.'

More silence, this time no one seemed the least bit eager to add to Frank's observations.

After what seemed like an eternity Dr Maier was the one to break the uneasy silence. 'Jacques, Ron, I want to thank you for joining us today at such short notice; I hope you both agree it was worthwhile, it was correct for Frank to share his thoughts with us, he has added another dimension to our thought processes and anything that stimulates our investigations must be positive. I'm now going to arrange for Eve and Frank to be taken to the airport, then I have a meeting with the 'Overview Committee' in about an hour, some decisions have to be taken as a result of Ricardo's death, all most unpleasant, but very necessary nonetheless. Whatever the Committee decides, there will still have to be continuity and co-ordination of the various inputs from the three of you. The WHO, in conjunction with the Council and your own governments will ensure that everyone is aware of what the other is doing. Good luck and God speed.'

We again said our goodbyes but this time there were four of us instead of five, next time we spoke we would be down to three.

CHAPTER 11

I looked at Dr Maier; I had been trying to pluck up the courage to raise the deaths of his wife and son without appearing insensitive. I decided there was no easy way so I plunged in headfirst. 'Dr Maier, I mean Wolf, I'd like to ask you a few questions concerning your own tragic loss, if you don't mind.' Frank shot me a speculative glance,

'No Eve,' he said, 'I really don't mind at all. I still find it painful to talk about but I do appreciate the importance of your wish to raise the matter, especially in view of my unique position in the investigations, so please, go ahead.'

'Thank you, I'm sure you must have talked about it a hundred times and re-run the events through your mind on countless occasions but can I ask you to do it one more time, it's just possible that you may remember something you hadn't recalled before and Frank and I, coming to you with fresh eyes, just might pick something up that had been previously missed? So please take your time and tell us exactly what happened.'

'Hm, the first to die was my wife,' he paused and took a deep breath before continuing, it was obviously going to be very painful for him; we waited for him to continue, ' it will be four months on the thirteenth, a Sunday, since…since it happened.

We were at home, I was in the study reading reports on the latest SARS outbreaks in Canada and the US, there was to be a meeting at HQ the following morning. My wife Steffie, was in the kitchen preparing lunch and Dieter, our son, was with her, I could hear them talking. Dieter could never say anything quietly, what three year old can and his side of the conversation was very clear, he was giving Steffie a list of all the things he wanted for his birthday, it was a couple of weeks away. Steffie's answers were not quite so clear but I'm sure she was agreeing to his every request, she couldn't refuse him anything. You see we called him our little miracle; we had been married for twelve years and for much of the time we'd wanted children but nothing had happened, eventually we sought help and both of us underwent the usual tests, they found I was the problem; a low sperm count they said, Steffie was fine. They told us it was unlikely I could ever impregnate her, so impersonal don't you think? I thought it sounded awful. I remember we both held each other and cried together that night but forgive me I digress. More than three years went by and then the impossible did happen, Steffie became pregnant; the gynaecologist said it was a million to one shot. Seven months later our little miracle was born. Their conversation in the kitchen reminded me I was hungry and I glanced up at the clock, it was two minutes past one. Dieter suddenly shouted,' 'mommy, mommy what's wrong?'

I wasn't really paying attention so when I realised he was shouting I didn't panic or anything but I was concerned enough to get up and go to investigate. Steffie was collapsed in a heap on the floor; I rushed over to her and felt for a pulse, there was nothing there; I tried the various resuscitation techniques but still nothing, no signs of life. She was quite dead. Lying there on the floor, my lovely Steffie, she looked as if she was sleeping but it was a sleep she would never wake up from.

I stayed knelt at her side for what seemed like an eternity but it couldn't have been all that long, I guess time had lost its meaning. Then I realised Dieter was talking to me and I turned to look at him, the expression on his little face will live with me forever, it was one of total bewilderment mixed with fear and confusion.

I picked him up and hugged him while I climbed the stairs to his room. I told him it was ok, mommy was just resting and he must be quiet like a little lamb and play with his toys, I said I would come back and play with him. I tried to marshal my thoughts, I kept repeating like a mantra, 'don't panic, don't panic, she's ok, she's ok.' I knew she wasn't but I said it anyway. I had to keep a hold onto reality for Dieter's sake and for my own sanity.

I went back into the kitchen, I suppose I was in some kind of fugue and half expected to see Steffie picking herself up, smiling and explaining what she had been doing on the kitchen floor. But no, nothing like that, she was still exactly as I had left her. I went back to where she lay, said a small prayer and felt again for a pulse, still nothing. I lay down next to her, cradled her head in my arms and wept. The tears ran hot down my face, I wept for Steffie, I wept for Dieter but more than anything I wept for myself.

I suppose I must have lay there for about ten minutes when I was aware of movement to my left, it was Dieter, perhaps he'd heard the sound of my weeping and had come downstairs to investigate, he slowly, almost gracefully, walked up to me, I was frozen like a statue, I wanted to move, to get up but the sheer weight of grief kept me pinned to the floor, I didn't want Dieter to see me like this but I seemed to be powerless and had no control over my limbs. He stopped in front of me, a brave little three-year-old boy with big blue eyes and a shock of blonde hair, what he said next were not the words of a little boy but rather those of an angel they were so incredibly comforting and will stay with me for as long as I live. 'Daddy,' he said in barely a whisper, 'mommy's dead, I know, before she fell down she looked at me and smiled and while she was still smiling, she fell down dead.' Then he walked the rest of the way to me and tried to lift me up from the floor. I struggled to my feet and together we went into the sitting room and rang the hospital. I told them my wife had just died.' Two days later Dieter was dead as well.

'My God,' Frank said, 'how can anything be so cruel and heart breaking?'

'You can imagine, I was still deep in mourning for Steffie so much so that when Dieter died, it was like piling grief into a container that was already full. You couldn't get anymore inside so it just spilled over and poured out everywhere.

Dieter's death was even less spectacular than Steffie's. I had left him playing in the yard, in his sandbox; I shouted him to come in and wash his hands and face, I was taking him over to Steffie's parent's house, we were trying hard to comfort each other. He didn't answer so I went out to see if he was ok, he wasn't. He was lying face down in the sand. At first I thought he'd fallen over but as I got nearer to the sandbox I could see he hadn't, fear put a large hand over my heart and squeezed hard, I ran the final few paces and even before I touched him I could see he wasn't breathing and I knew without any shadow of doubt that he was dead. Of course I checked anyway to see if he had somehow suffocated on the sand but his mouth was empty. The same thing that had claimed my wife had now reached out across space and time and had claimed my son as well.

I called Steffie's parents and they came across, we had twice as much comforting to do now.

The final pieces in the puzzle and it were a puzzle where nothing fit, were the results of the two autopsies; nothing, they found absolutely nothing. The medical view was that they should have still been alive. I agreed with their conclusions but for different reasons.

There has to be an answer and I have to be part of what finds it, sometimes I think it's the only reason I'm able to keep going and my greatest fear now, is that I will become another of it's victims before we have it. Without the answer, Steffie's and Dieter's lives lose some of their meaning, as if something really important has been stolen from them and I want it given back and I won't rest until it is.'

I thought of Bill and the twins back home in Raleigh, normally I would imagine them having fun together, maybe playing ball in the yard and Bill rolling around on the grass with the girls jumping all over him but this time my mind's eye saw a different scene, I saw three coffins laid side by side, I didn't dare look inside them.

My eyes felt moist and I got up from the chair and walked over to Dr Maier, I reflexively put an arm around his shoulders and pulled him to me, slowly I felt the tension beginning to leave his body.

Frank sat there looking down at his hands; for once he seemed lost for words. I knew how he was feeling. What could you say to someone who had suffered the losses Wolfgang Maier had suffered; there were no adequate words. He slowly, almost painfully raised himself out of his chair, walked to where Wolf and I were and rested his hand gently on his shoulder. For a few seconds the three of us we were frozen in a tableau of grief, Wolf sat with his head slumped, Frank and me stood at his side like silent sentinels watching over him.

'What's going to happen now that Ricardo's no longer in charge?' I asked.

' Nothing much,' said Wolf, 'as the DG, he was the head of the organisation but as you can well imagine, he was such a busy man, he could hardly handle everything personally so he had several Directors reporting to him, I was one. Because of the nature of this particular project, which we refer to as Sudden Death Syndrome, SDS for short, he had become much more closely involved than would normally have been the case. In fact, the Secretary-General charged him to take personal responsibility for directing the work of the project and he appeared before the Permanent Members, with the Secretary-General, to provide regular updates.

I was his right hand and I expect that to remain the case when the new Director General is named, no one knows the project as intimately as I do.

This afternoon's meeting will be to announce the appointment of a new DG and she will address the senior teams of clinicians and administrators.'

'She?' I exclaimed.

'Yes, Professor Yasmine Patel, Professor Patel is one of the world's most respected biologists.'

'I know,' I interrupted, 'I heard her speak when she delivered the keynote address at last year's launch of the UN's 'Good Health For All' programme at the Kodak Center in LA. She's brilliant.

Who was it that said beauty and brains don't go together? She was Miss India in the 2040 Miss World competition, she was eventually placed first runner up to Miss Jamaica. When they asked her at those asinine interviews they conduct as part of the competition, what her ambitions were, I remember she said she wanted to play a part in creating a healthier environment for the world's impoverished children. At the time it seemed like one of those stock answers the contestants always trot out on those occasions but this time it was true, she meant every word of it. She even donated her winnings to the UN's 'Save the Children Fund.'

'Wow,' said Frank, 'she obviously made a big impression on you.'

'She certainly did and she is one of the reasons I went into that particular field. I admired her so much; I wanted to be just like her. She was sort of a hero to me, a role model; pretty, like I wanted to be but with brains and a focus. I continued to follow her progress as best as

I could and when I learned of her planned appearance at the launch, I wasted no time in obtaining an invitation.'

I wasn't aware of all of that,' said Wolf, 'I will look at her through different eyes now. Well my friends I must go and prepare for the meeting, I have been asked to give a little welcoming speech. I will arrange for you to be taken to the airport. It has been a pleasure and an honour meeting with you, I'm so glad you came; I know it was at short notice. I think it is important to meet in the flesh so to speak, those persons you will be working closely with and on this particular project, a close working relationship is as desirable as it is inevitable.'

He pressed the intercom button and summoned the driver, we all three rose from our seats and walked to the door, we stopped and turned to face each other, I couldn't resist the urge to reach out to him and hold him to me, so I did, I felt he had shared some of his inner and most private thoughts with us and that a bond now existed between us. Frank took his hand and looked straight at him. 'We'll get to the bottom of this Wolf then you can restore that that has been stolen from your family.'

'Thank you so much, both of you, you are very kind. I wish you a safe journey home, please let me know that you have arrived safely; my email address is on the card I gave you yesterday. The driver will be here in a couple of minutes. Now you must excuse me, I really have to go.' He opened the door and was gone.

CHAPTER 12

'This is just going from bad to worse. Every time we talk about it the prognosis always appears less favourable than the time before. I have to wonder exactly how many deaths are attributable to this Sudden Death Syndrome or whatever it is; my guess is more than a million and increasing by the day, or even the second.

In previous pandemics, even if they couldn't be stopped in their tracks we had an handle on the cause of it, maybe not straight away but pretty quickly thereafter, but even with the best minds singularly focused and dedicated to the investigation, not to mention the hundreds of thousands of autopsies carried out all over the world, not one ray of sunshine, not one insight into what is causing the deaths, not one single clue to pursue. It flies in the face of anything I have ever known, been associated with or read about. The human race is slowly dying out perhaps not so slowly and we don't know from what or why.' He shook his head and sat back down.

I wanted to tell him it was a blind giant who lived atop Mount Olympus who was responsible for the deaths and that all we had to do to vanquish him was identify his brand of magic and neutralize it. It was simple but regrettably only a figment of my imagination. Instead I put my hands in his and gave them a little squeeze of assurance,

I hoped it wasn't a whiff of hysteria I had detected in my thoughts.

Two drivers arrived to take us to the airport. This time the wheels was a Benz and like the BMW it had dual controls, it was a comforting thought. Our luggage had been put in the trunk, everything being in order we were soon on our way to the airport.

I contemplated the dual controls on our vehicle and wondered at the millions of other vehicles throughout the world with just the one set of pedals. I couldn't help but imagine how many people might have had their 'lights switched off' while they were at the wheel and how many crashes there had been as a result.

I sat there musing on this strange topic and as my imagination drifted away, I saw a gas tanker being driven at speed down an interstate, boy, some of those rigs really move; I imagined the driver listening to some hillbilly radio station, lost in his thoughts, when zap, 'lights out'. He slumps forward over the steering wheel and the death weight of his foot presses the gas pedal to the floor.

The rig lurches forward as it picks up momentum, faster and faster it goes, engine at maximum revs and screaming in protest. It hits the vehicle in front and sends it spinning out of control so that it collides with another vehicle and that one in turn hits another then another. The inevitable, almost pre-ordained outcome is now set in motion, there is going to be one of those terrible multiple vehicle pile ups that seem to happen when there's thick fog about and reckless drivers seem hell bent on committing suicide and manslaughter by ignoring the conditions and continue to drive like maniacs possessed.

Vehicles were now being shunted into each other as one collision followed another, some turned over and others were set on fire; death and destruction were everywhere, mayhem reigned supreme. But things were not over yet, not by a long way. The tanker, engine revving furiously is still in full flight, careening down the highway under the control of a dead man slumped over the wheel, still intent on keeping it going in a straight line. The road curves to the left but the dead man doesn't see it, he's still keeping the tanker moving in that arrow-straight line; the rig starts to enter the bend pulling its trail of death and destruction behind it, it arrows across the outside lanes scattering the vehicles on its left side like ants, then hitting the central crash barriers that separate both sides of the highway, snapping the light poles as if they were thin, brittle matchsticks. It clears the central reservation then plows into the oncoming traffic, like a bowling ball striking the pins; the air is filled with the screeching of rending metal, fiery explosions are all around with smoke belching everywhere, reducing visibility to zero and then the pitiful screams of the injured and dying, the worst sound of all.

The dead man hears none of this. His vehicle, like something possessed by a demon from Hell, seems determined to complete its mission and although it has swayed precariously on its axles as a result of its multiple collisions, has somehow managed to remain upright. God, if only it had toppled.

With its intended target now firmly in sight it veers to the left, not too much but just enough to keep it unerringly on target; its satanic guidance system keeping it locked on its destructive course. The driver of its intended target sees the mayhem unfolding in front of him from a distance of about a quarter of a mile but as yet doesn't suspect the starring role fate has selected for him; then emerging through the smoke, silently, almost dreamlike, the gas tanker, it seems to blot out everything around it, he hits the brakes and tries to steer clear of the oncoming missile but too late he's rendered powerless by speed and circumstance, it's as if what is about to happen has been pre-ordained and therefore, can't be avoided.

The gap between the two behemoths closes and time itself slows to a crawl; if the tanker driver had been alive he could have read the lettering on the side of the other tanker, 'Danger Explosive Chemicals.' Then with an ear-splitting concussion, the gas tanker hits the chemical tanker in the dead center of its load; a blinding white flash, brighter than the sun, a deafening explosion that would perforate the eardrums of many in the vicinity and would be heard several miles away, and a fireball that resembled the mushroom cloud that follows a nuclear explosion. White-hot death spews everywhere as the deadly cocktail of chemicals and gasoline erupts from the torn carcasses of the tankers, bathing dozens of victims in a deluge of fire and death. My blind god had hit the mother of all jackpots with this one.

All of this flashed through my mind in the time it took for the lights to change from green to red and back to green as we queued at a busy intersection on the way to the airport. I shook my head to try and clear away the images left by my nightmare scenario. 'Good God,' I thought, 'can this be real?' My world had turned upside down in just a couple of days; I could no longer take for granted those things that were as natural to me as breathing. And here was the point, breathing itself was something that could no longer be taken for granted.

CHAPTER 13

'A penny for your thoughts,' said Frank.

I tried to put on a smile but it didn't quite reach my eyes, 'Oh nothing really, I was just thinking about how much my world has changed over the past couple of days, I was also wondering how much it will have changed by tomorrow and the day after and the day after that. Where in heaven's name is it going to end Frank?' I said I didn't believe anyone knew the answer to that one but I had a pretty good idea what the answer would be if solutions were not found and I didn't really want to go down that particular road.

We rode in silence for the rest of the journey, Frank probably thinking about how he would start working on the problem when we got back to Duke and me thinking of Bill and the girls and trying hard to dispel the notion that they were not at home waiting for me to get back but on some mortuary slab sliced open like a fish being filleted, so some medical examiner could try and locate the cause of death. 'Stop it!' my inner self shouted, 'stop the morbid thoughts right now!' But that was easier said than done.

The rest of the journey to the airport was without incident, no careening tankers, no explosions, no death and destruction, no blind Cyclops with hangovers. The Benz glided into a space close to the concourse used by American Airlines. The chauffeur retrieved our luggage from the trunk and in no time we were making our way to the check-in counter.

There was quite a long queue and I was about to take up my place at the back when Frank asked me what I was doing. I looked at him quizzically and he held up his tickets, 'first class Eve, we're sitting up front on this one.'

I nodded, 'It's hard to break a habit of a lifetime. First class tickets are for politicians and bigshot businessmen; I don't qualify on either account.'

'Come on Eve, you don't think Uncle Sam would let you fly with the plebs in the back of the plane do you?' He retorted jokingly. 'I mean, a bigshot doctor like you? I don't think so.'

I was glad for the levity and found myself smiling for the first time that day; I joined him at the empty first class check-in counter.

We had three hours before boarding so we strolled to a café and ordered pastries and coffee, Frank ordered a beer, a Bud if you must know. You know how parochial we Americans can be.

'What's going to happen when we get back?' I asked Frank.

'Well, I guess we'll be met at the airport and taken somewhere for debriefing. Then we'll be brought up-to-date with what's going on domestically and internationally, then we'll be flown to Raleigh and then we'll start work the day after. Or something like that.'

'We're seven hours in front of home, which puts it at about 6.00am, too early to ring. I'll see if there is time before we board.'

'Don't worry Eve, if anything had happened back home, someone would have rung me on my mobile, I've got roaming on it. So for now let's work on the assumption that no news is good news.'

I nodded my agreement. The coffee and pastries were delicious; Frank drank his beer more quickly than usual and ordered a second.

'I needed that Eve, the first one hit the spot, the second I'll sip and enjoy.'

'Let's make our way to the gate.' I suggested, 'I want to get something from the duty free store. I always buy something for the house whenever I visit a new country; I try to buy something that's representative. I don't have much of a collection because I haven't been to that many countries but I bought some silver craft from Thailand, a bier stein from Germany, a lemonade bamboo set from Jamaica, remember we vacationed there last year and two or three other things from wherever we went to. I want some Swiss chocolate for the kids and a Swiss watch for Bill; he busted his Seiko two weeks ago.'

'Fine, lets go,' said Frank draining the last of his beer.

We cleared immigration and found ourselves in the bowels of the airport; I set off in search of the shops.

I was soon in my element, looking at all the fine clothing, shoes and French perfumes. I made my way to Mattie and Tissots, makers of fine jewelry. They had a lovely window display of fine English bone china, Waterford crystal, Lladro figurines and watches.

I looked very carefully trying to imagine which of the watches Bill would like best. I liked the Rolex Mariner but the sticker price was a bit high, there was also an exquisite looking Omega but that was a bit heavy too. Then I saw the one I wanted, a Tissot, black face with golden numerals and those separate dials on the face, buttons in gay profusion and a handsome titanium strap. 'Perfect,' I thought, 'just perfect.'

Bill liked those watches that seem to tell you everything but the time. He once told me he liked the ones that looked as if you could launch Space Shuttle Challenger with; all dials, buttons and rotating bezel. This one met all the required criteria, at nine hundred dollars it wasn't cheap but Bill was worth that and then some.

Frank had wandered into the large supermarket-type store and was at the checkout. He had a small trolley filled with a variety of Swiss chocolates and candies, two cuddly reindeer, one wearing a green jacket and the other one red for the twins, a large box sat atop the pile.

'Can I buy you this as your special Swiss memento, it should look real good in the family room?' It was a cuckoo clock, 'you can't get more Swiss than that and it's easier to get on the plane with than a ten foot glockenspiel.'

I picked up the toy reindeer and gave them a hug, they felt soft and inviting and brought thoughts of the girls a little closer, the feeling was good. The cuckoo clock was the perfect 'Gift from Switzerland' I was looking for. 'Thanks Frank, your right, it is perfect and the twins will love the reindeer. You're so thoughtful.'

CHAPTER 14

We set off with our duty free purchases in search of the boarding gate. We passed a bookstore on the way that also sold newspapers; I lingered at the newsstand looking for an American paper, something to read on the plane. Der Spiegel was prominently displayed, so was Le Monde and the British Daily Mail; I spotted a copy of the New York Times and removed it from the rack.

The headline shouted 'BRAD KRUGER IS DEAD' with a file photo of the Boston Red Sox star in typical pose. I read the storyline. 'Brad Kruger the 29 year old Boston Red Sox star was found dead at his home yesterday by his maid Monica Reyes. She said she arrived for work at her usual time of 9.00am and let herself in, she was making her way to the kitchen when she heard the TV playing, she figured Mr Kruger must be up so she went into the TV room to see if he wanted her to fix him breakfast. She saw him sitting in the chair in front of the TV, the drapes were closed; we asked her to describe in her own words what had happened.

'I tell him good morning but he don't say nothin', I say again to him good morning Mr Brad, he still say nothin', so I say, 'Mr Brad, you ok, you want me fix you some breakfast?' But he still sit and don't answer. I walk across the room to him and he don't even move his head or nothin'. 'Mr Brad,' I say again, but I know now somethin' wrong is with him, 'are you ok?' So I go and touch him and he just fall over on one side, in the chair, I never push him hard only gentle and then I run out of the room to kitchen and I ring the hospital and they come out quick.

When they come and look at him they tell me he's dead. I was sad and I cried. Mr Brad is a good man, I like working for him for one year. He always treat me so nice.'

The New York Times has learned that the likely cause of death is from a heart attack, although it is reported that Mr Kruger has no history of heart trouble.

Brad Kruger had an outstanding record of.......... etc, etc.

I didn't need to read anything further; it looked to me as if the blind god had struck again.

I called Frank over, he was looking for a book on the Second World War, and he was passionate about that particular period in history, that and the old Stephen King novels. He said that King's novel 'Christine', about an automobile with a mind of its own, that in a jealous rage killed people who were a threat to its owner, was his favourite. He claimed to have read it at least six times. It's probably true but Stephen King gives me the creeps so I steer well clear of him.

'Frank, look at the headline, we're only getting to know of the famous ones, there must be many more; I wonder how much longer the authorities can keep the lid on this thing. My guess is another two or three months, because if by then no answers are forthcoming, someone will have to say something either to the American people, or to the world through the UN. What do you think?'

'There's no way this can be sat on for much longer; some governments must already be asking what the blazes is going on. For example, I can't imagine the governments of Canada, Australia, Italy and Switzerland sitting back and twiddling their thumbs while their populations die all around them.

We've already seen protests erupting in Bangladesh and passions must be running high in many other places. Even the populations of those countries who are Permanent Members of the Security Council have no more idea of what is happening than that of any other country. My guess is that there will have to be an announcement by the UN's Secretary-General to the General Assembly. It will have to be very carefully crafted or the results could be incalculable. The shockwaves would be felt around the globe and not one country would be immune to the fallout.

Imagine if you can; stock markets would crash across the world, economies would collapse; civil unrest would tear many countries apart. There would be panic on the streets, looting and violence of unprecedented proportions. Marshall Law would be declared, probably in our own country but the tidal wave of violence would sweep across continents, security forces couldn't possibly hold the line. Law and order would soon become a memory and civilisation would implode into a state of pure anarchy.

And that's only for starters. What about the accusations that would fly back and forth from certain quarters, that it's an American inspired conspiracy to kill off the Arabs, Muslims, Blacks, Asians, Hispanics and any other minority group with an axe to grind. Terrorist attacks the length and breadth of the US would follow on the heels of the accusations. The European Union would also bear the full brunt of the terrorist onslaught; London, Paris, Rome, Berlin, nowhere would escape and nowhere would be safe. The maniac leaders of North Korea would probably launch a pre-emptive nuclear strike against their neighbours to the South and Japan, China would use the opportunity to invade Taiwan; India or Pakistan or perhaps both, would launch their own nuclear missiles, hoping to catch the other off guard. The world would go up in flames.'

'Please Frank, stop, my God, for goodness sake stop. When did you become an apocalyptic prophet, you should leave that kind of thing to Nostradamus? What you just described were scenes right out of Armageddon. The end of the world, the final battle between good and evil, except in your version there is no 'good', just pure unadulterated evil. I refuse to believe the fate of the human race is so delicately poised, we're not that close to savagery, are we? Surely thousands of years of civilisation must count for something.'

'Do you really think so Eve? What about the Holocaust with the death camps, the First and Second World Wars? The Nazis were supposed to be civilized human beings; take Hitler, he loved music, opera, art, in fact he was a decent artist himself, he loved fine buildings and architecture but he was a monster, some would say

Satan incarnate. He and his cohorts were responsible for the deaths of millions of people.

And then there was Stalin, the leader of the Soviet Union; he ordered the deaths of more than twenty million of his fellow countrymen. What about Pol Pot's Khmer Rouge in Cambodia and its reign of terror, the Slave Trade that started in the sixteenth century and lasted more than three hundred years, perhaps the best example of man's inhumanity to man? Apartheid in South Africa, the Spanish Inquisition, the 9.11 attacks by Al Qaeda on New York and Washington DC, the 7.7 suicide bombers on the London Underground, the burning of innocent young women who were accused of being witches, the American Civil War, the genocide in Rwanda involving the Hutus and Tutsis.

Tell me when to stop. I could go on and on with examples and even more examples of the depths of barbarism that we humans have repeatedly sunk to over the ages and are still capable of sinking to today.'

I felt as if I had been slapped in the face, Frank was right, I could see it all clearly, civilisation as a delicate flower, a beautiful bloom but flawed with something potentially rotten at the core.

I know most people scoff at the Armageddon story in the Book of Revelations in the bible, I do or rather did myself, but listening to Frank I found myself thinking that it wasn't so fanciful a story after all. History is littered with too many examples of humankind's lust for blood, conquest and power and the ends they are prepared to go to satisfy its insatiable appetite.

'I hate to admit it but you do make a convincing argument, humans have always found it too easy to slip in and out of extreme acts of barbarism and justify their actions, it isn't just nations or groups within nations either; look at the serial killers, the murderers and rapists, the paedophiles; all good examples of how close we are to the jungle.

It almost suggests that civilisation is nothing more than a thin veneer covering the true nature of man. And yet, there are good people, true, honest and dedicated, I would like to think there are more of them, than the others. I believe there's enough goodness in the world to give me faith, that in spite of all the frightening uncertainties we will have to face, we will still win through to a better day.'

'I hope you're right Eve, I really do.'

I heard sirens blaring somewhere away to the front of the airport, 'Another one for the Cyclops,' I thought. Trivialising it seemed to make it a little less frightening.

CHAPTER 15

We were at the gate by 12.00 noon, fifteen minutes before boarding, when I suddenly had a terrible thought, suppose the pilot dies at the controls with the plane somewhere over the middle of the Atlantic Ocean, what happens then? I remembered that with large aircraft, there is always a second pilot on board; I figured everything would be fine until I thought, 'What happens if the second pilot dies?'

First class passengers get to board ahead of everybody else, so when the boarding announcement was made, Frank and I were the first to show our passports and boarding papers at the gate and make our way down the skyway to the aircraft.

It was one of the new super jumbos; nine hundred people in three separate cabins, an elevator from the first floor cabin to the upper two cabins for those who can't use the stairs.

Our seats were in the third tier cabin, mine a window and Frank's an aisle. A comforting thought struck me, these super jumbo's carried three qualified pilots; the Cyclops would have to be in a particularly belligerent mood to wipe out all three of them. I crossed my fingers; I had no intention of tempting providence.

The plane lifted off right on the button and I settled back into my big comfy first class seat for the journey home. Frank was reading his World War Two book, 'The Rise and Fall of the Third Reich' by William L Shirer, Frank said it was the definitive publication on the subject, at over one thousand pages, I decided I would take his word for it.

I relaxed with my copy of The New York Times. I re-read the story on Brad Kruger, the circumstances of his death were too close to the descriptions we had been given by the WHO on the other deaths to be a coincidence. He was another victim, no question about it, one of a growing army.

I flipped through the sport, lifestyle and fashion pages, eventually finding my way to the markets and currency section. There was an article that caught my eye on the world's dwindling oil reserves; prices had hit one eighty dollars a barrel and production was down twenty five percent from the same period last year. The cost of premium gasoline was thirty dollars a gallon and hydrogen-powered automobiles were now outselling gas-powered vehicles and there was good reason for optimism that the new electrical cells developed for the space industry could be made to work in a modified form in automobiles. Companies involved in developing alternative energy sources were doing well on the world's stock exchanges with 'Advanced Energy Systems' of China leading the way.

It's hard to believe that China is now the world's second most important economic and military power.

It might not yet rival the US with its weapons arsenal but it's only a matter of time before it overtakes us in the economic stakes. It's amazing what democracy can do for a nation, of course China had been a democracy in all but name for many years and did well but since the first free multi-party elections of twenty years ago there's simply been no stopping it.

In the international section I found the story on the protests in Bangladesh. The authorities had met with a delegation from the rural areas and sought to assure them there was no government plot or policy directed at rural dwellers.

They conceded that there had been a few more deaths than usual but that this was also true for urban areas as well. A spokesman said that this was not an unusual occurrence, as sometimes it is not the actual death rate that had increased but improved reporting of deaths, especially in the rural areas, which made it look as if there was an increase in the mortality rate. He promised the government was keeping an eye on things and would continue to do so but at the same time they were committed to improving the living conditions of everyone in the rural areas.

I flipped back to the national news section, which was dominated by president Cooper's initiative on establishing a social medical programme patterned on Canada's National Health Service. 'Fat chance of that happening,' I thought, 'not with the private medical lobby so powerful and only interested in maintaining its high profit and income levels.'

Lower down the page was a story about an incident on the New York subway, apparently a train driver had suffered a heart attack whilst at the controls of his train and but for the operation of the rail track's fail-safe mechanism, there could have been a serious accident as a train was already on the platform filled with passengers. If the automatic brake sensors had not halted the oncoming train, it would have plowed into the rear of the stationery one with catastrophic results and probable high loss of life.

I was about to bring the article to Frank's attention but he seemed to be so engrossed in his one thousand-paged tome, that I decided not to disturb his concentration. There would be time enough for that after we touched down.

After a lunch of scotch salmon, blue cheese and crackers, washed down with a chilled bottle of Chardonnay, I started to feel tired, so I removed my shoes, reclined my seat all the way back and closed my eyes. The gentle hum of the aircraft's systems and the furtive movement of people about the darkened cabin lulled me to sleep in no time.

I was in a village astride a white horse and I was wearing a green tunic, there were other people in the village, I noticed a blacksmith at work shoeing a horse, a baker was pushing a handcart filled with loaves of bread and some children were sat on the grass and under trees reading books.

I guided my horse to the village store, dismounted and went inside. Strangely I was not surprised to find lots of weapons in the store, not guns and bombs but weapons that belonged to bygone times; there were bows and arrows, swords and shields. The storekeeper was a portly man with ruddy cheeks, he seemed to know what I wanted because he handed me a sword and scabbard and a silver shield with gold on the outer edges. I took them from him and paid with some money I had in a pouch. I thanked him and left the shop.

Walking back to my horse, I held the shield in front of me examining its appearance; I took in my reflection in its mirrored finish. The face looking back at me gave no pause for concern, I was wearing a green hat that matched the tunic and a thatch of corn-coloured hair crept out from beneath the hat. I attached the shield to the horse's saddle, strapped on the sword and scabbard and swung effortlessly into the saddle. I rode the horse out of the village.

I found myself on a dusty track with trees and fields stretching away as far as the eye could see, we cantered along for a while until we came to a small stone bridge that spanned a narrow stream, on the other side of the bridge the road forked, there was a signpost it pointed left to Slyrule Castle and right to Chingle Mount, I took the left fork Slyrule Castle.

After a short time I spotted the castle some distance away and urged the horse into a gallop, the drawbridge was down so I rode across into the grounds and dismounted. I removed the shield and strode across the courtyard and through an open door set at an angle in the castle wall into an entrance hall. Stone steps were immediately in front of me, I could also see into a large hall to the right of the steps, tapestries hung from the walls, I drew my sword and started up the steps.

The steps curved to the right, at the top I found myself at the end of a long corridor where suits of armour stood sentinel against both walls. The corridor ended in an open arch that led into another room. I walked stealthily down the corridor, shield held in front of me and sword raised at the ready.

I entered the room and stood before a circle, about twelve feet in diameter that was drawn in the middle of a stone-flagged floor. In the center of the circle stood a one-eyed giant, he was facing the arch and his malevolent gaze was fixed directly on me. He was at least seven feet tall and was wearing black leather armour; it covered his torso, his arms and his legs and there was a scarlet red cape around his shoulders. His single eye was milky white, I knew he was blind and I realised he wasn't really looking at me all but that he more sensed my presence.

In a booming voice that reverberated around the room, he announced himself as Gylanfore. He raised his right arm, his hand was covered by a pewter coloured glove, black thunderclouds began forming in the room and the giant raised his arm and lightening seemed to be drawn from the clouds and the air itself into the glove. As the lightening was absorbed the glove started to glow, it got brighter and brighter as more lightening was absorbed into it.

I could sense that power was being concentrated in the giant's hand. Just when it seemed that the power had reached saturation point, Gylanfore, in a smooth and fluid motion, hurled a lightening bolt directly at me. Instinctively I raised my shield and the lightening bolt struck it with tremendous force, knocking the shield from my grasp and driving me into a corner of the room. All I had to defend myself with now was my sword.

Gylanfore turned and looked with his milky eye in my direction, again he raised his gloved hand and again the lightening fed itself into the glove. At saturation point another bolt was released in my direction, I had no shield to fend it off this time so I strode forward to meet the lightening bolt, sword raised in the manner of a baseball bat. I swung the sword and hit the bolt as a baseball player might strike the ball for a home run.

The bolt flew off the sword and hit the giant staggering him backwards. He bellowed with rage but quickly recovered his stance in the center of the circle; he raised his gloved hand for a third time and hurled another lightening bolt in my direction.

I had retreated back into the corner but as the bolt flashed off his glove towards me, I again strode out to meet it and for a second time, I caught it perfectly with the sword and smacked it back at him. It hit him squarely in the middle of his chest and he was again staggered back by the force of the blow.

I sensed that each bolt I hurled back at him was weakening him; he continued to throw bolts, I lost count of how many but with increasing confidence I strode out of the corner to meet each of them and smashed them right back to where they came from. Gylanfore became weaker and weaker as the bolts struck him down, eventually he was drained of his strength and could hurl nothing more, he stood cowed and shrunken in the middle of the circle looking haggard, drained and well beaten.

With sword in hand I walked slowly up to him, even in his crouched position he still towered over me. I raised my sword meaning to strike the deathblow; Gylanfore turned his milky eye in my direction and leered at me.

'You haven't beaten me,' he said, 'you know I'm not really here, I'm on top of Mount Olympus where you can't reach me and even if you could it wouldn't make any difference, I can point my finger at you anytime I want…and at anyone else for that matter, no one can hide, no one is safe. Remember Eve, 1 2 3, you're dead!' His mocking laughter echoed off the walls.

Then the room began to dissolve around me and we were now outside in the castle courtyard but I still had my sword in my hand. 'It's not too late!' I shouted and raised the sword in both hands holding it aloft like the sword of Damocles ready to deliver the deathblow, before I could bring it down in its deadly arc Gylanfore began to fade; I looked on in horror as he became increasingly insubstantial. 'It's not too late!' I shouted again, 'it's not too late, please God don't let it be too late,' but Gylanfore was fading fast, I could now see right through him and the sword seemed to have caught in something, stopping me from striking at him.

I was still shouting, 'It's not too late!' when I felt something tugging at me, pulling me away, I struggled with all my might to stay in the dream but I was being dragged back to the surface of consciousness. Images of Gylanfore were rushing away from me, I tried one last time to free the sword and strike the all-important blow but I couldn't, I wept with frustration. My eyes fluttered open, the dream shredding as I fought to keep it in focus but I'd left it behind, it was gone. The dreamscape lost its substance and it blew away like fine dust in a wind.

CHAPTER 16

Later Frank told me I was kicking up a storm, threshing around in my seat, I was shouting about giants and something that sounded like 'it's not too late' but I couldn't remember a thing, the substance of the dream was gone and all I had left was an empty feeling of failure and despondency.

The mood persisted and I had a low level headache, probably from the wine, I wasn't much of a drinker especially so early in the day. Frank on the other hand was still engrossed in his book, there was so much I wanted to ask him but I figured it could wait until we got back.

I was sure the authorities would have plenty to tell us, especially if they had known about the situation for some time now as Professor Valdez had said, they must already have compiled an accurate data base of how many deaths fit the pattern; the records would show times, dates and places; state by state and the results of all medical examinations. There would be eyewitness testimonies, probably video footage (have you noticed someone always seems to be there with the camera rolling every time there's a disaster or unpleasant incident, (I was sure 'Aunt Sue' would be being filmed just at the time her lights went out), police commentary and a summary from the responsible federal agency.

We wouldn't exactly be starting from scratch and the work done to date by Oxford University and the Pasteur Institute would also be there waiting for us. We wouldn't waste our time running down dead-end streets, if our European colleagues had already explored them.

Frank had probably already formulated the initial plan of action in his mind, 'Let's see what the powers that be have to say and then take it from there.' These were the thoughts going round and round in my mind as I was swept up into sleep's welcoming embrace. I slept peacefully, no starring role this time in a full-length fantasy thriller.

I woke up feeling surprisingly refreshed, the seat next to me was empty, I thought for a second.........but then I figured Frank had probably gone walkabout, to stretch his legs or visit the restroom.

I checked my watch, we were two hours out of JFK, I wasn't happy that I would be so far away from Bill and the girls but at least we would be in the same country and that in itself was a comfort. I picked up my complimentary purse with the hand lotion, toothpaste and mouthwash and made for the restroom.

It was occupied, aren't they always? It's amazing, whenever I need to use the restroom on a plane, you can guarantee someone has already beaten me to it. I decided not to return to my seat but to stand at the top of the aisle and wait my turn. I did a mini workout whist I waited; stretched my legs, flexed my toes, a couple of quick knee bends and rolled my shoulders, just to get the circulation going and get rid of the stiffness.

I'd been out of my seat for maybe ten minutes and the door still read 'Occupied', I decided the occupant must be making out their last will and testament so I went back to my seat. Frank returned shortly thereafter and told me he had strolled to the galley at the rear of the plane for a coffee and cookies. I thought that sounded like fun so I retraced his steps and feasted on a cup of decaf and three chocolate chip cookies. They hit the spot.

When I got back to my seat I noticed the 'Occupied' sign was still lit.

'Have you seen anyone come out of the restroom while I've been gone?'

'To be honest I haven't been taking much notice,' Frank replied, 'why do you ask?'

I told him about my earlier visit and that I had waited for about fifteen minutes but no one had come out. I felt uneasy; I couldn't help but wonder if a lifeless form was now slumped against the door preventing anyone from gaining access.

'Do you think we should say something to one of the cabin crew?' I asked.

'No not yet, someone might have come out while you were getting your coffee and I didn't see them. Leave it for a few minutes and then if still no one comes out, then we'll report our concerns.

Frank went back to his book, obviously unperturbed; I sat there anxiously waiting for the door to open. Another five minutes passed and I decided it was time for action so I pressed the overhead call button. 'I'm reporting it Frank, I think there's a dead body in there.'

A steward arrived having answered my call and asked if I needed something, I was about to tell him of my fears when my answer was cut off by the sound of a flushing toilet, the door opened and a boy of about thirteen emerged looking anything but corpse-like.

The steward continued to look at me, so feeling flustered and not a little foolish, I asked for another cup of decaf. He beamed his first class passenger smile and was gone.

I touched Frank's arm and rested my head on his shoulder. 'I nearly made a fool of myself that time. I think this thing has gotten to me; I don't want to see bogeymen at every turn but at the same time this is damned serious and there's no way I'm able to trivialize the situation.'

'I agree,' Frank said 'and if you hadn't called the steward, I would have done it myself so don't fret, you were right be concerned.'

With a sigh of relief I settled back into my seat and thumbed through the in-flight magazine. There was a feature on Montego Bay in Jamaica, we'd gone there last year for our vacation and had a fabulous time, seeing the photographs of Doctor's Cave Beach and Rosehall Great House brought back some happy memories and by the time I had read the article, my spirits had completely lifted, the gloom and doom were gone, replaced by tropical sunshine and I was ready to face whatever challenges might come my way.

At long last we were being told to return to our seats and prepare for landing, I felt like an expectant child as I fastened my set belt. The landing was perfect and all three tiers of the plane erupted into spontaneous applause for the captain.

CHAPTER 17

We taxied to a stop and waited for the triple elevated skywalk to be connected, one for each cabin for simultaneous embarkation and exit, not all airports had this facility, in fact only a hand full. It greatly speeded up the getting off of the plane.

At the end of the skywalk an elevator and stairs took the two upper tier passengers down to the same level as the first cabin passengers and then it was a dash for immigration and customs.

As we stepped off the stairs at ground level we were approached by two men in suits, they each flashed an ID with their photograph and name prominently displayed; at the top of the ID it said 'Department of Homeland Security'.

'Professor Burke, Dr James, welcome home, please come with us. May we have your passports please?'

I looked at Frank and he looked as perplexed as I felt. He gave a slight nod. We handed over our passports. We walked towards immigration but stopped outside a glass door before we got to the end of the corridor. The sign on the door said 'No Admittance – Authorized Personnel Only'.

There was a touch pad at the side of the door and one of the suits punched in a number and opened the door, he invited us to step through. We were in an office, a man was sat at a desk, and his shirt said Homeland Security over the pocket. The guy with our passports approached the desk and handed them to his colleague. He took them, stamped them without even looking at them or us and gave them back to the suit.

'Would you follow us please?' he said, handing our passports back to us. He led us through the office and out through another door at the back into another office, our luggage was already there waiting for us.

'Are those bags yours professor, doctor?' We said they were. 'Follow me please, the bags will be taken directly to your hotel.'

'Deja vu I thought, just what happened to us when we arrived in Geneva. I could almost hear Dr Maier saying the same thing in his German accent, 'Your luggage will be taken directly to your hotel.'

He set off again and we followed deeper into the bowels of the airport, down antiseptic looking corridors that would have been more at home in a hospital than an airport, up two flights of stairs and face to face with a large white sign with red letters telling the world, 'Private – No Admittance Authorized Personnel Only'.

A surveillance camera mounted on the wall over the door fixed us with its one imperious eye. A faint click released the door telling us we had been cleared for entry. The suit held the door open for us and we stepped into an anti-room where an attractive lady of about thirty-five sat a desk with a laptop and two telephones displayed in front of her.

'Good morning Professor Burke, good morning Dr James, we have been expecting you, just a moment please.' Her voice was almost musical. She pressed a button on the intercom, 'The professor and doctor have arrived.'

'Please send them in Jane,' replied a disembodied man's voice.

Our attractive lady flashed a Rembrandt-white smile and bade us enter the main office.

It was some office, whoever occupied this place had to be someone pretty damned important. In fact the president of the United States would have been at home in it when the Oval Office was being repainted.

We stepped onto a lush dark blue carpet which stretched all the way to mahogany paneled walls, which were adorned with five paintings of country scenes, I think they were Constable Prints, I recognized his famous 'Flatford Mill' work.

A large grand looking mahogany desk faced us, with papers and file folders stacked neatly to one side; an ornate brass letter opener was laid on an inkpad. An empty burgundy leather-buttoned chair was pushed back from the desk and two matching visitor chairs were positioned to the front.

To the left of the room was a mahogany conference table and chairs for eight persons. The one thing about the office I didn't like was that there were no windows, it made the room almost claustrophobic; it reminded me of a luxurious 'panic room'. A man was seated at the table and he rose to meet us, I recognised him at once, his name was Sam Bartram, a senior aide to the President; the Press often referred to him as 'the shadow', as wherever the President went Mr Bartram was sure to follow. The less complimentary press referred to him as the President's lap dog.

He was a handsome man with piercing blue eyes, he wore his iron grey wavy hair in a trendy long style, his athletic frame belied his age, he must have been in his middle sixties and at about 6'3" he was a commanding presence. When he smiled, the laugh lines around his eyes suggested someone who enjoyed life.

'Hi Frank, Eve, good to see you, sorry to have to call you back so quickly but there are things happening here that need to be urgently addressed.' He came round the table and shook our hands warmly, his smile which touched his eyes, revealed a perfect set of even, white teeth. 'Hi Sam, good to see you, it must be pretty important if the President has you dealing with it.' Frank was obviously well acquainted with him. 'Eve, do you know Mr Bartram?'

'Please Frank, we're all friends here; Eve I'm Sam and I'd be honoured to be your friend, if that's ok with you?'

I smiled back at him, it was hard not to he had such an engaging personality. 'Consider us friends,' I replied.

'Is anyone else joining us?' asked Frank.

'No, later, at another meeting but not for now; we need a little privacy, the fewer persons who know what we know, or don't know, the better. In fact the reason we're meeting here and not somewhere shall we say, more official, is indicative of the need to treat the matter with extreme sensitivity.

To be honest Frank, things are developing in a worrisome way, the President is deeply concerned and it's becoming increasingly difficult to keep the lid on it. People in positions of power and influence are already asking questions, so far we've been able to field them but it can't work for much longer. There has to be a national and international strategy, we can't go it alone on this one, it's too big, the potential for a worldwide calamity is not lost on us. We need an answer to one all important question; why is it that some many healthy people all over the world have started dropping like flies for no apparent reason?

If we can come up with an answer or even something plausible, we could move to head off what will develop into an extremely ugly situation with global implications. But I'm getting in ahead of myself; please tell me what you learned in Geneva and please, won't you sit down, I'm sure your account will be a fairly long one.'

We accepted his invitation. Frank gave him the full story, leaving nothing out, everything that had happened from the time he received the request to go to the WHO, to when we arrived back home. I filled in some of the blanks but as always, Frank's uncanny ability to remember even the merest detail left very little unsaid.

Sam Bartram listened without comment and without giving away the slightest indication of what he was thinking. If he were disturbed by what he was hearing, it didn't show, he just nodded occasionally and little else. When we were finished we looked to him for his reaction but he just sat there silently evaluating what he had just heard.

After what seemed an age but was probably no more than half a minute, he stood up, walked slowly over to the mahogany desk and picked up the telephone. He punched in a number and waited, a few seconds later I heard him say, 'Mr President, I'm with Professor Burke and Dr James, I've just listened to Professor Burke's account of his trip to Geneva and it is very much in line with our own assessment of the matter, may I please proceed as suggested? There was a period of silence at his end while I presumed the President gave his response. 'Thank you,' he eventually said, 'I'll report back as soon as I can.' He hung up.

'I guess you know who I was talking to. Thanks for the briefing, it confirms some of the things we already knew and definitely adds to our knowledge. Now it's my turn to bring you more fully into the picture and tell you what we know, what we believe we know, what we speculate and what we are in completely in the dark over.

It is an absolute fact that healthy people are dying in every country on earth for reasons we don't as yet understand. We have given it the name 'Sudden Death Syndrome', or 'SDS'.

You mentioned Bangladesh and the Middle East as two places where the populations had reacted violently to these sudden death occurrences; they'd assumed it was a diabolical plot set in motion by malevolent third parties that had been responsible. Of course they had no idea as to the real reason behind the deaths.

Sadly, they're not the only places that have experienced violent reactions from their populations, there have been several more incidents that have not made the news, either because they were suppressed by the authorities or were not considered newsworthy enough. Some of the incidents were reported as old scores being settled by long standing enemies but we know the truth is much more sinister than that. For example, three day's ago Tibetan villagers attacked a regional communist party office in Lassa and butchered the entire staff of twenty because they thought they were systematically killing the villagers as part of the decades old dispute between the Tibetan people and the Chinese government and what the Tibetans saw as another dark Chinese plot to kill off the local population and replace it with one made up of ethnic Chinese, even though China took the path to democracy some years ago.

See what I mean about old scores being settled? Fortunately, because China is a Permanent Member of the Security Council, the authorities were aware of this sudden death thing and addressed the matter on a very humane basis. They're also having their own problems with some of their rural population up near the Mongolian border and here again, instead of reacting violently against the villagers as would have been the case in years gone by, they sent a high powered delegation from Beijing to meet with the village leaders and successfully defused the situation.

In South Africa, Desmond N'domby the black rights activist who is well known for his conspiracy theories concerning Uncle Sam, has too many people in that country and neighbouring countries at fever pitch, preaching that the mystery deaths occurring all over the country, can be linked to the US government's genocide policy against the black race. What a mad man.

Similar statements are coming out of some Arab capitals, although in their case it's Muslims we're trying to get rid of. All garbage but too many of their people for years and years have been fed a diet of hatred of all things American and are all too ready to believe anything they hear. Some of the mullahs are baying for revenge; they want to declare a fatwa against us. At least the new democracies in Amman and Damascus are appealing for calm but many of the fundamentalists hold positions of power in the mosques and take every opportunity to spew their venom all over the faithful. Thank God there are now more moderates than radicals.

In Pyongyang, Kim Su Il their supreme leader and nutcase or is it Supreme Nutcase and Leader, has convinced his population that the Japanese and ourselves have developed a new strain of virus and smuggled it into the country on fishing boats letting it loose in the coastal villages, it's now supposed to be spreading and slowly wiping out the village populations; when they have been decimated and those who are left are too sick to resist, our armies, helped by the South Koreans are supposed to invade from land, sea and air and take over the country. Mr Kim has the entire country on a war footing.

Every newscast shows file footage of the US, Japanese and South Korean armies massing in numbers as they prepare for the invasion. What worries us about this one is that North Korea has WMD's and wouldn't be afraid to use them, I mean, what do they have to lose?

To make matters worse it's true, people are dying and it's not going to go away because as things stand right now, people are going to carry on dying and if the computer predictions are correct, at an ever-accelerating pace. It's frightening.'

'But I, we, had no idea matters had reached this stage,' I interjected, looking at Frank, 'I'd read some of the stories you mentioned but I thought it was the usual rantings coming out of the legion of America haters; you know, those who use the age old tactic of diverting the attention of the masses from the state's own failures and unite them against a common enemy. And there's no better enemy to unite behind than good old Uncle Sam is there? '

'It actually gets screwier, let me tell you; there's more than one country that's linking the increase in its death rate to McDonald's burgers and fries, saying something's been deliberately introduced into the meat, potatoes and even the bun, that over the years, has been saturating the body with fat and has been absorbed into the bloodstream, clogging up the arteries and is now, right on time, causing strokes and heart attacks in epidemic proportions. In other words, a time bomb was planted and primed by the US Department of Dirty Tricks to explode, medically speaking, in the bodies of their populations to destabilise unfriendly governments.

They've even used evidence from our own medical studies to prove the link between junk food, obesity and poor health. Hm, some countries are even saying that McDonald's is part of the CIA. That's a new one huh?

So you see news reports and the like, that you thought were the usual run-of-the-mill anti-American garbage, have their roots in what we are here to talk about.'

I thought of Bill and the girls, I wondered if they were OK and I suddenly had the need to hear their voices.

'Mr Bartram, I need to ring home, my husband doesn't even know that I'm back in the US and... I didn't get any further, Sam Bartram raised his hand, 'Eve, what can I have been thinking of, we've already been in touch with Mr James and told him Professor Burke and yourself have been asked to return to the US for urgent consultations and that meetings have been arranged to coincide with your arrival at JFK. He knows you will be tied up for a couple of days and that you will contact him from your hotel later today. We assured him you were fine and that what you were doing was in the national interests. I can also assure you that your family is well, including your folks back home.

I'm sorry I didn't mention it earlier; I guess I got carried away with bringing you up-to-date with events. Professor, if you have anyone you would like us to contact we would be glad to.'

'No thanks, I have no immediate family, Eve and her family is about the closest I've got.' I smiled at the unmistakable warmth of his words.

'How long are we likely to be here for?' I asked

'Tomorrow I'm heading for DC, both of you will join us there the day after for about two days of meetings and then you should be on your way back home. Incidentally Eve, when you talk to your family this evening, I'm going to have to ask you to keep the nature of your meetings at WHO and our meetings strictly confidential, you'll understand why. A story's been put together that should fit for now and should address most peoples' immediate questions, I don't know how long it will hold but it should buy you research guys some time to try and get a handle on this thing.

The story is based on an actual incident that occurred in the early part of this century when a particularly deadly flu virus somehow escaped from a lab in the UK, the virus was from fifty years previous, nineteen fifty six I think, it had been referred to at the time as the Asian Flu Virus, it was virulent then and was still deadly fifty years on; it ravaged Britain and spread throughout the five continents like wildfire. There were no available vaccine and no time to develop and produce one, by the time it ran its course; it had claimed more than twelve million lives.

We're going to use a similar scenario and Russia has agreed to be the fall guy, it couldn't be the US for obvious reasons. The new Director General of the WHO Professor Yasmine Patel will address the UN's General Assembly next week, informing them that a Moscow research laboratory was studying the genetic code of a mutated strain of the influenza virus as part of a project to develop a new generation of genetically modified vaccines.

The virus got loose but because of its particular mutation, it doesn't spread rapidly in the conventional way, affecting the most vulnerable like the young and old but rather it strikes randomly and without warning across all age groups and all sectors of society. She will say that some people have a natural immunity, whilst others, who had been incubating the virus without experiencing the usual pain and discomfort and without even knowing they were infected, experience a sudden and rapid shutdown of their cerebral cortex resulting in instant death. The virus is known to have spread rapidly from continent to continent and has been identified as being the culprit responsible for many of the deaths that have been occurring throughout the world.

She will conclude by saying that after death occurs the virus dies also and is undetectable to those carrying out the autopsies and finally that the body's organs show no signs of deterioration or failure.

She will say that The Pasteur Institute, Oxford University, the Center for Disease Control and the team working on the Human Genome Project, are pooling their resources to find a vaccine to bring the pandemic under control and will assure everyone that everything possible is being done and that there is no need to panic as good progress is being made. The story must be able to satisfy all governments and be capable of allaying the fears of the world's populations.

There'll always be the fruitcakes who'll claim its part of a US inspired plot but they will be in the minority and the world will earn itself some breathing space while we try and nail this thing before it really gets out of hand.

Many governments will be happy to hear her address, as it will get them off the hook with their populations; for them, they'll accept virtually anything the UN says, let's face it, the story lends credibility to their claims that they are not responsible for the higher than usual mortality rates but there are other governments like Canada, Australia, Israel and those of the European Union that are going to need something of substance to convince them that Professor Patel's statement is the truth the whole truth and nothing but the truth'

'Do you have the slightest idea of what's going on and why, asked Frank, 'there must be a statistical base by now from the pooling of information by the countries of the Permanent Members Grouping?'

'Yes, a picture is emerging and I can tell you that it's the same picture in every country on earth, not a pleasant one either. So far all the available data is remarkably consistent; our own in the US is similar in every way to that in all the other countries represented on the Council, so when I describe what's happening here, you can be sure something very similar like it is happening in every other country on planet earth.'

'Then what is happening,' asked Frank, 'can you tell us?'

'Yes, I can and I will, you needn't take notes, before you leave I'm going to give you a specially prepared brief that pretty much describes what you're going to hear from me, it has the necessary supporting graphs, charts and commentaries; please read it this evening to prepare yourselves ahead of the upcoming meetings.'

I sat back, tried to relax and waited to hear the bad news, I knew it would be bad, I'd already heard and seen enough in Geneva and since we got back to tell me that. What I hadn't realised until I tried to relax was that ever since Sam Bartram had started his presentation, I'd been sitting with my fists clenched and my body as tight as a coiled spring.

Frank had his arms folded across his chest, I could see his jaw muscles were bunched as he clenched and unclenched his teeth and I guessed that he too was expecting the worst.

Sam produced a large burgundy leather-bound book from his official government briefcase and laid it in font of him, it had 'Top Secret, Restricted Circulation' printed on the front in gold letters, he opened it to the first page, removed his glasses from his top pocket and read the first few paragraphs in silence, as if he were familiarizing himself with its contents.

'We think whatever it is that's now underway, started about two years ago, maybe three, in truth we don't really know when it started, it could have been going on for several years unnoticed and only revealed itself when the numbers grew to a level that could no longer be ignored. It was one of those small European countries that first noticed a marked increase in the level of sudden deaths in their population. It had become a statistical anomaly and so they routinely reported the matter to the European Union's Health Commissioner.

No other country had made a report but the Commissioner was required to request all other countries within the Union if they too had noticed similar increases in their mortality rates. It wasn't long before several of the other small countries reported similar statistical anomalies; the bigger countries with their much larger populations were unable to identify anything remarkable from what were meaningless statistical samples, so their higher than usual mortality rates went unnoticed. The same was true for the US with our even bigger population.

The EU health commissioner reported the matter to the WHO and it wasn't long before more thorough analyses were underway which showed the larger countries, including us, that they too were being affected by this strange phenomenon. What was also strange was that autopsies on these sudden death cases revealed nothing. The people shouldn't have died. Whatever was killing them was no respecter of age, race, or social group; some were pre-schoolers, others were elderly; there were teenagers, middle-aged people, male, female, rich and poor. It made no difference. Of course, you know much of this from your visit to the WHO.

It's estimated that in the US there have been as many as fifty thousand of these sudden and unexplained deaths but the true figure could be much higher. The worldwide figure probably tops three million and is not just rising every day but actually accelerating. If we can't find out why this is happening and if it can't be stopped and if the death rate continues to gather momentum, the current social unrest will give way to protests and riots the like of which have never been seen before and not only in the volatile parts of the world.

We have worked out a possible scenario, it goes something like this, and the world's great economies will wobble, teeter and eventually collapse, plunging the world into a downward spiral of social and economic disintegration. The security forces couldn't even begin to think about containing the backlash; there would be looting and killing in every village, in every town, in every city and in every country on earth. But this wouldn't be human kind's final chapter, nor even close to it, not by a long way; for while the carnage had been spreading to the four corners of the earth, whilst civilisation itself was on the brink of collapse, there would have been no let up in the ever-accelerating mortality rate. Bodies would be piling up, not in the morgues, which would be full to bursting point, but in the streets, in houses, in hospitals, in prisons, in fact everywhere where there are people and there wouldn't be anyone around to collect them up and dispose of them. Disease would become rampant causing even more deaths. Hospitals would have long ceased to be places of care because there wouldn't be anyone left to run them.

The supply of electricity would soon be disrupted and then fail completely, nuclear power stations would have to have been shut down to avoid the possibility of nuclear accidents; water supplies initially subjected to disruption would eventually cease altogether, telephone services would fail as would all non-computerised data links, there would be no TV, no radio and travel by road, sea or air would become impossible; the only aircraft in the skies would be military ones as they made final but futile attempts to hold on to a semblance of authority in what would have become a totally ungovernable world.

In fact in a fairly short space of time, there wouldn't be a government, the White House would itself have become a victim of the anarchy and as the gangs broke in looting and torching every room it would soon be reduced to a burnt out shell, the same for the congressional buildings and the Senate, even the Pentagon couldn't be protected and would eventually be overrun by the mad remnants of society, who by this time might have formed themselves into marauding gangs, dispensing their own kind of justice.'

What Sam was describing was a vision right out of Hell; he made Dante's Inferno seem like a Sunday school picnic.

My initial reaction was to think that it was all a major exaggeration, the kind of overstatement you make when you want not only to make your point but to drive it home as forcefully as possible and yet, if things were as potentially as serious as he was saying, then I could see the honesty in his imagery. It was worse than every scene in every disaster movie ever made and the real horror was that it wasn't make believe, this was no Hollywood production tipped for an Oscar nomination for best picture of the year, they were scenes from a possible upcoming real-life drama entitled 'The Disintegration and Demise of Human Kind' starring each and every one of us.

Sam hadn't finished and I was brought out of my reverie as he continued with his apocalyptic tale of death and destruction.

'But that's only us,' he continued, 'what about the rest of the world. Great Britain would suffer the same fate, probably ahead of us because of their smaller population and size. London, Birmingham, Manchester, Glasgow would all fall to the fury of the anarchists, as gangs went on the rampage; looting, murder and rape would be the norm. The Houses of Parliament would be destroyed as surely as our own seat of government would be shortly thereafter. Buckingham Palace and Windsor Castle, Westminster Abby, St Paul's Cathedral and the Tower of London would suffer the same fate.

In France, the Louvre, with its priceless paintings would undoubtedly be torched; Goyas, Rembrandts, van Goghs, even DaVinci's Mona Lisa, would be reduced to a heap of smoldering ash. And oh, poor Italy, the treasures of Florence, Venice and Rome, smashed to smithereens and yes the Vatican too wouldn't escape the collapse; the Sistine Chapel, St Peter's Basilica, the sculptings, the art, ancient books and manuscripts, all a testament to humankind's progress through the centuries; gone, all destroyed. Looted, burned and smashed.

And what about China, Japan, India, Egypt and Iraq, all of them with treasures and histories that show all of us where we're coming from?

Think of it, mighty Africa, the cradle of the human race, reduced to a conflagration of tribal wars raging east to west and north to south; truly, it would make the twentieth century Nigerian civil war, when the break-a-way north declared itself the free and independent state of Biafra, seem like a Sunday school picnic. Millions perished in that futile war through starvation and the fighting that followed, until, with nowhere to turn and with the rest of the world mere spectators, a proud and defiant people were brought to their knees in abject capitulation. It hurts your head just to think of it.

What about the despots and dictators in the rogue states, do you think they'll stand idly by while their populations threaten their power bases? I don't think so. They'll send in the army, just like the Chinese did at the end of the last century when students poured into Tiananmen Square in Beijing, peacefully demonstrating for democratic reform. You've seen the news footage of the tanks being driven over the students as they lay down in protest, you've heard the guns barking and the rat-a-tat-tat of machine gun fire as the kids were mercilessly mown down. It makes you sick to your stomach.

I'm telling you; unless we come up with some answers in no time at all the streets will turn into rivers of blood. The earth will burn and life as we know it will disappear forever.

Do you think that's it, the final chapter, the end of everything we hold dear; the earth now reduced to rubble while rival gangs fight over spoils and territory like scenes from the Mad Max movies? Do you think everything will eventually settle down and in some future millennium when good sense has at last prevailed and good has finally triumphed over evil, the survivors, the remnants of humankind can crawl out of the rubble and start the long process of rebuilding? No professor, no doctor, let me tell you what the final chapter will be, not the end of the world but the end of humankind, extinction, the total death of the species, no more humans, the earth given over to cockroaches and scorpions.'

He must have seen the look of on our faces, a mixture of puzzlement and disbelief, Frank opened his mouth to say something and then seemed to think better of it and quickly snapped it shut. I wanted to protest and tell him he was off his mind and that he couldn't be being serious but I knew he was deadly serious.

Everything he had said was true but the final bit, surely not, that part had to have been for effect, how the hell could the human race end up like the dinosaurs or the dodo or the other species that had become extinct. Hell, some things are just not possible and this was one of them. I think Sam must have been reading my mind because he turned his piercing blue eyes on me.

'Do you doubt me Eve? What about you Frank, do you think I've lost it, do you think I'm just trying to put the frighteners on you, or maybe you think I'm playing it for effect? I'm not. Many species have died out over the ages, in fact ninety nine percent of all species that have ever existed since the earth began are now extinct, and why do you think humankind should be any different? Sure we posses a higher intellect than the others but so what, we are only ever one step away from savagery. For all our sophistication and achievements we still wage war on each other, we still allow our own kind to starve to death while others have too much to eat and millions die every year from treatable diseases for which we have warehouses stacked with medicines if only they could afford to pay for it.

To this day we don't know why the dinosaurs died out, sure, there are some good theories but that's all they are, theories. They ruled the earth for many millions of years, far longer than we have been around and then in a blinking of an eye they were gone, forced by something, we don't know what, to make way for the rise of the mammals.

Was it a gigantic meteor that smacked into the earth, plunging us into a kind of nuclear winter destroying the dinosaurs' natural habitat and erasing their food chain?

Perhaps it was a chain of mighty volcanic eruptions, spewing ash and dust high up into the atmosphere blotting out the sun, lowering the temperatures and upsetting the finely balanced ecology that brought about the catastrophic climate changes that wiped out one of the most successful species in the history of the world. We don't exactly know.

And what about the wooly mammoth, they were alive and well, foraging for food when suddenly they were frozen to death on the spot, literally where they were stood. Do you remember when their frozen bodies were discovered in Siberia, they still had undigested grasses in their stomachs? Stood up eating one minute and quick frozen the next, like poultry in a supermarket freezer section.

Let me put it this way, our computer models tell us that unless we can find a solution to this SDS, the human race will be extinct, have died off, will be no more, call it whatever you will, within less than five years.'

His words seem to hang in the air between us. I felt a bit nauseous and I had to swallow a small amount of bile that had found its way past the sphincter in the esophagus; a really strange feeling suddenly overcame me, as if my body, no my entire being was only a shell, completely empty and I was alone, a speck of helpless consciousness in the endless void of the universe.

CHAPTER 18

The shrill ringing of the telephone on the mahogany desk broke the moment, Sam raised himself wearily from his chair and my eyes followed him as he walked towards the desk. 'Hello,' he said into the mouthpiece. I was still watching him, his every nuance of movement and expression and I clearly saw a look of great sadness spread rapidly across his face. He was obviously listening very intently, and then he said 'Yes sir, thank you sir.' He quietly and deliberately, almost reverently replaced the receiver.

Frank and I looked at him speculatively and my eyes continued to follow him as he walked even more slowly back to his seat; he paused before sitting down, a man carrying a great and mighty weight; he suddenly looked old, the vitality had been drained from him and he seemed to have shrunk into his body. He looked ten years older.

The silence grew as if the seconds were hung together like a long paper chain. About a minute lapsed, it seemed much longer but I'm sure it wasn't and then Sam turned two watery eyes at us.

'That was the President, he wanted to tell me personally, my brother Phil, has just died, he said it was SDS, no question about it. Phil's the Governor of Oklahoma, he was speaking at a fundraiser as part of his re-election campaign; the President said he was at the podium talking when he suddenly dropped to the floor.

He said the paramedics were with him in seconds with all of their medical support paraphernalia but he was already gone, lights out, that's it, finished, not even a ten second count.

I can just imagine him stood out there in front of four hundred people, big grin on his face, probably telling one of his corny jokes, I doubt he even got to the punch line.

My God,' he said, as if he suddenly realised where he was, 'where is this thing taking us?' Not waiting for an answer he stood up sharply, knocking his chair back. 'Would you please excuse me for a moment, I have to ring Debbie his wife and my wife Peggy and then?' He strode purposely to the door, his sentence tapering off soundlessly as he went into the outer office, the door closed softly, almost reverently, behind him.

Frank and I shared the emptiness in silence, the 'Alone in the Universe' feeling had returned and with it a fear that was almost primal. I was the first to speak. 'Frank, I feel like I'm here but not really here. I keep telling myself that this isn't happening; that it's just a bad dream I'll soon waken up from. It's like Armageddon but much, much worse; I mean a bible story is one thing but this isn't a bible story, it's not a story at all. It's madness, it's like I've been given a look at tomorrow's newspaper headlines and I don't like what I'm seeing.

All this talk about extinction, isn't that a bit far-fetched? Dinosaurs became extinct, so did the dodo and lots of others but not us, we can control so much, even nature has had to bow to humankind's ingenuity. We're the most intelligent species ever. We're in charge of things, masters of our own destiny; how can we just disappear from the planet leaving it to cockroaches and scorpions and ants and worms.

No, I can't accept that, it's too ridiculous? I'm not saying we don't face a real and serious threat, obviously we do but you can't say that because a relatively small number of people and it is a small number in relative terms have died under what are presently mysterious circumstances that everyone else will go the same way. There's nothing scientific about that and it's only a mystery because the reasons for the deaths have not yet been identified and the culprit isolated; once that's been done and it will, the mystery will be no more and we can set about creating an antidote, a vaccine or maybe just a pill to be taken four times a day after meals.

All this talk about extinction; it's a hell of a quantum leap from a handful of unexplained deaths to the end of the human race.' I realised I was babbling. 'What do you think Frank', I tried to sound calmer, 'the human race extinct? Impossible!'

If I expected Frank to quickly ally himself with my take on things, I was in for a disappointment, he said nothing at first but he was thinking, that brilliant mind of his was hard at work; I could almost hear the cogs turning and his brain humming. You know, the human brain is a unique and wonderful thing, either creations' ultimate glory or evolution's ultimate achievement, it depends on which side of the fence you happen to live on; it's ability to process and analyse information, sift through it and put things in their correct order and at the same time throw in the logical, illogical and emotional dimension only a human being is capable of, that's what separates us from the machines, the human dimension is something computers are unable to copy, there is no human dimension in a machine's analysis. You know how it is, garbage in, garbage out.

He looked at me studiously, he knew me well, maybe better than anyone else.

'Eve, in most circumstances your professionalism and as a scientist your ability to be totally rational and objective, would be beyond question but you are something much more than a scientist you're a wife and mother, I know how much you love Bill and the twins and true to your maternal instincts, if you detect a potential danger to your family, you leap to their defence, your overriding thought is their protection. It's often said that mans' number one priority is self-preservation but with woman it's the preservation of her young, their survival comes before her own. It is 'she', not 'he' who is the custodian of the human race; right now you're thinking and acting like a woman, it's in your genes, you can't help it and thank God for that because if the species is ever truly under threat, it will be woman who rides out to confront the Horsemen of the Apocalypse and that would be some battle, perhaps the real Armageddon.

But let's try and remove the emotion from the equation, what have we got? The fact that people are dying is beyond dispute, the fact that their deaths can't be explained is also beyond dispute and the fact that the growth in the world's mortality rate is speeding up is also indisputable; perhaps the most important detail of all is that what is happening is happening across the planet, as far as we know every country on earth is experiencing the same wave of deaths, what did Sam call it, Sudden Death Syndrome? The final detail worth mentioning is that as far as we know this is only happening to humans and not any other species, not even our close relatives the primates.

All we have to do is find out why and stop it. If we don't or can't, in a good deal less time than Sam Bartram's five year computer projection, humankind will be well on it's way through the door of existence and into the oblivion of extinction; leaving the cockroaches and scorpions to crawl and scurry, as they have done for countless millennia, across the face of the globe, rulers of all they survey. In very little time, all evidence that there was once an intelligent race that had dominated the planet would disappear, in the following thousands and even millions of years after our extinction, buildings would crumble and fall, everyday evidence that we had once been here would rot, rust, turn to dust and eventually simply blow away.

Nature would waste no time in moving in to reclaim what had always been rightfully hers. Natural erosion and winds, along with Mother Nature's relentless pursuit of the land would do the rest.

The silence would be deafening, no sounds of war, no babies crying of hunger, no guns barking on the streets of our cities; the stillness would be unimaginable. The air would be rare and pure, the rivers and seas sparkling and clean, teaming with an abundance of marine life and with none of man's harmful emissions spewing out of millions of automobile exhausts, the hole in the atmosphere would soon heal itself and the polar caps would reform themselves into their once pristine condition.

The forests would spring back to life, lush and green and spread, covering up the scars left by man, no one to slash and burn the trees to make way for what we refer to as civilisation. An almost silent world of splendid beauty, free of pollution, no evidence that the hand of man had very nearly destroyed the planet before nature had stepped in under the guise of Sudden Death Syndrome and took it back.

Perhaps it's no more than we deserve, maybe its natural justice. Like some great celestial judge telling the human race that the penalty for the wanton destruction of planet earth is oblivion, extinction and with no possible appeal.'

CHAPTER 19

Madge Grant was a twenty six year old geneticist, she was all of five foot tall (in her stocking feet, as her mother used to say) but if she lacked height, she had no problem getting herself noticed, especially by the opposite sex because she was quite beautiful (her mum used to tell her 'good things came in small packages'). In fact her mum had a saying for almost every occasion. 'Look before you leap', she would often tell her and then follow it up with, 'He who hesitates is lost.' always delivered with stony-faced seriousness and sincerity.

'What a contradiction', Madge thought, running the two sayings over in her mind and then smiled warmly at the memory. She had been close to her mum but last year, whilst the very picture of good health, her mum had suddenly died. Madge hadn't known her to have a day's illness in her life. In fact Mrs Grant used to describe herself as 'one of those depressingly healthy people'.

The post mortem had revealed nothing and the coroner had recorded an Open Verdict on the cause of death. She missed her mum a lot.

Madge's father had died in an automobile accident when she was only four; he was driving his old Vauxhall Viva back to Bolton from Darwin, it was the middle of winter and snow lay white and thick on the high roads that traversed the moors, the police report said the tyre tracks indicated he was probably taking a bend too fast and lost control. They found the wreck at the bottom of a steep gully.

Her memories of him were insubstantial, a bit like dreams are when you wake up and no matter how hard you try to keep them in focus, they simply refuse to re-solidify and start to shred, leaving you with scraps of memory and feelings of frustration and dissatisfaction.

Madge was a native of Bolton in Lancashire, part of the old cotton mill belt of North West England. The town had nearly died from dereliction in the nineteen fifties when the great Lancashire cotton mills started to close because they couldn't produce cotton as cheaply as India and Pakistan but the town somehow managed to adapt to the new paradigm with investments turning it into a shoppers' paradise.

Bolton Wanderers, the local football team had helped to keep the name of Bolton firmly in the public domain as it did surprisingly well in the English Premier Soccer League and European competitions.

As a little girl Madge had wanted to become a super model and she might well have succeeded if she had been another ten inches taller but her genes dictated that there was never going to be even a remote possibility of that; although she had gorgeous shoulder-length chestnut brown hair, large hazel eyes, a pert nose and flawless skin, not to mention a perfectly proportioned body, it was all to no avail, her skeleton was just too small for the catwalk.

None of this bothered her, she'd been a happy child and her mum had dedicated herself to Madge's happiness and made a damned good job of it. Madge excelled at school, a straight 'A' student; she was determined to make her mum proud of her.

Her mum had been a nurse at Bolton Royal Infirmary and Madge had grown up against a background of hospitals and medical books and referred to all the doctors and nurses as 'aunty and uncle' and so it was no surprise that she when she started thinking of university she favoured a career in medicine.

She had pondered which branch of medicine she would like to pursue; Paediatrics had appealed at first but then as she thought of treating sick and sometimes dying children the idea hadn't seemed quite so appealing after all.

Then one day she had been watching the 8 o'clock evening news, there was a series entitled 'This Day in History' which showed flashbacks to stories that had made the news five, ten, fifteen and fifty years ago; the lead story had been the successful mapping of the Human Genome by scientists in the UK and the USA in 2004; there on the TV screen had been the US President and the British Prime Minister wearing ear-to-ear smiles making simultaneous announcements to the world of the success of the project.

It had struck a chord with Madge and she had wanted to find out more about it, so she went to the local reference library and read as much as she could on the topic. The more she read, the more fascinated she had become.

She learnt there had been enormous advances in medicine as a result of genetics, several diseases involving recessive genes that had brought misery and grief over the years had either been eliminated or where now treatable, there was still a long way to go but as the old Chinese proverb says, 'Every Journey Starts with the First Step.' Another one of her mum's favourites.

Madge entered Bolton Girls School on a scholarship offered by a local bakery and applied herself diligently to her studies; she was focused and her ambition was to get straight A's and be accepted by Oxford University. She did get straight A's and was delighted when Oxford accepted her.

Madge's mum was the proudest parent in Bolton when she attended her daughter's graduation. The story of Madge's academic achievement even made the human-interest section of the local rag, the Bolton Evening News, from the fuss they made it seemed that the whole town was proud of her and three weeks before her nineteenth birthday she left home for Oxford.

'Ah, sweet memories,' she thought 'and now look at me, stuck in the basement of the British Museum, looking for goodness knows what and when I do eventually find it, I probably wont even know that it's staring me in the face.'

After she graduated Madge decided to pursue a PhD in Genetics with ideas of a career in academia, she chose as her thesis 'The Genetic Sequencing of Extinct Animal Species.' The beasts that stalked the earth or flew in the skies eons ago had always fascinated her and at one point she had seriously thought of Paleontology as her chosen field, the idea of working with these mysterious creatures, of which we knew so much and yet so little, was exciting and compelling but poking into dusty crates and cupboards looking for specimens in the museum's nether regions was not her idea of fun, especially as she nursed a number of allergies, dust being one of them.

Every now and again she was seized with bouts of sneezing, they were so frequent and so lengthy she had unconsciously started counting the number of consecutive sneezes each time she was in spasm; her record was thirty-one. She knew it was silly but she did it anyway.

When she located her specimens, she would take them back to her lab (after clearing it with the Assistant Curator) and get to work. She knew she wouldn't be working with DNA from TRex or Diplodocus, it simply couldn't be extracted from fossils dating back millions of years but there were techniques that could be applied to more recently extinct species.

The pioneering scientists following the successful conclusion of the original Human Genome Project had developed the techniques and they had been successfully employed in the DNA sequencing of a species of Cave Bear. The species had been extinct for over ten thousand years. In this experiment DNA had been extracted from a forty thousand year old tooth.

She thrilled at the thought, she couldn't wait and fairly trembled with anticipation, that was the part of the assignment that really excited her and she absently hummed some nebulous tune as she moved from crate to crate and exhibit to exhibit, looking for items she could transport back to her lab in Oxford.

CHAPTER 20

Frank and I sat for a moment, each of us wearing identical blank expressions, staring off into space as if we had been put into hypnotic trances, viewing our own versions of the advancing apocalypse; the death of a species, the rebirth of a planet.

It couldn't be denied that whilst the demise of the human race was something you couldn't even get your mind around, the restoration of planet earth to its previous untrammeled glory allowed a certain morbid fascination; after all, with our own deaths we are each confronted with our own mortality, our own private extinction.

Human existence only has reality for us as long as we are alive, after that who knows what will be waiting at the end of life's rainbow of existence, a crock of gold, or a crock of something altogether different? Let's face it, although you know it intellectually, you can no more conceive of your own death than you can the extinction of the human race.

The door opened allowing reality back in, it was the lady from the outer office, the one who had greeted us on our arrival. 'I'm sorry,' she said, 'Mr Bartram apologises, he has had to leave, an emergency, he said you knew what it was and hoped you would understand. He said a driver would be here in about ten minutes to take you to your hotel, he asked me to give you this.'

The 'this' was an envelope with the words 'TOP SECRET' emblazoned across the front in large black letters, I took it from her, and it also had 'Professor Frank Burke and Dr Eve James 'typed in much smaller letters. It contained the briefing paper promised to us by Sam, a note advising of a meeting scheduled for two days time in DC, a list of attendees the list contained the names of two Nobel Laureates, the Secretary of State and the Head of Homeland Security; the meeting was to be chaired by the President's special advisor Sam Bartram. I wondered in view of his brother's sudden death whether Sam would attend.

The note, which sported no letterhead, also informed that the meeting was top secret and we should not discuss it or any aspect of the subject matter with anyone. I noted that the meeting had no title and was devoid of an Agenda. The final paragraph told us that our flight tickets and details of a one night's hotel reservation in DC would be waiting for us at our New York hotel.

I passed it to Frank who glanced at it and gave a curt nod to indicate the content had been duly noted.

We continued to share the silence, I think we were still piecing everything together and trying to put it into something that resembled a scientific and balanced conclusion. It wasn't easy.

A couple of minutes later the secretary announced the arrival of our driver, he was another one of those FBI types, close cropped hair, all suit and shoes, he introduce himself as Edward, no second name just Edward. We followed him out onto the corridor, as we went through several halls and offices we started to hear the noise and bustle of human activity, I found it strangely comforting, sort of back to reality, sweet civilization; I'd quite forgotten that we had spent the last few hours in the bowels of the JFK International Airport.

After what seemed like a marathon walk we found ourselves in a private underground car park, the cold and damp in these places clings to the many concrete pillars like a lover's embrace, this and the dim inhospitable lighting that fails to penetrate the deeper shadows creates a most unwelcoming ambiance and I always feel compelled to glance furtively every which way, just in case some undesirable is lurking in the gloom ready to pounce on me. On this occasion we walked unmolested to our waiting Ford LTD.

As I opened the rear passenger door I wasn't sure whether I should be worried or relieved that unlike Geneva, we only had the one driver and also unlike Geneva, the vehicle was fitted with only one set of pedals. It would have been nice to think that my milky-eyed nemesis couldn't fling his lightening bolts at the US as easily as he could at Geneva, after all isn't Geneva and Mt Olympus both in Europe and we were six thousand miles away? 'Wishful thinking Eve,' I told myself, 'there isn't a country on earth safe from his deadly intentions.' This was an enemy without any discernable weakness and threats of retaliatory action would simply go unheeded, assuming we had such actions available to us.

We exited the car park and drove into a dark and dismal early evening, we were greeted by heavy traffic on the freeway with a myriad of white lights stretching off into the distance to our left, heading slowly in our direction and an endless river of red lights immediately in front of us, we pulled in behind a large tanker and joined the queue, I couldn't help but remember my flight of fancy involving a tanker that played the lead role in its own version of 'Demolition Derby.'

'Have you heard the newsflash?' asked our driver.

'What newsflash is that?' I enquired.

'The King Airlines crash.'

'No, what's that about?' To be honest I didn't think I wanted to hear.

'It only happened within the last hour, it seems the plane was on it's final approach to Hong Kong airport, the report said the flight deck didn't respond to instructions from air traffic control, it just kept coming on in too fast and at the wrong angle, it didn't make any attempt to reduce speed or take precautionary measures or anything like that; it overshot the runway and ploughed into the sea.

The reporter said rescue teams were already on their way to the accident site and that a helicopter was over the spot where the plane came down but all they could see was wreckage, the view was that it was unlikely they'd find any survivors. Two hundred and eighty one passengers and eleven crewmembers were on board. Right now no one knows what caused the accident; the authorities say they're not ruling anything out at this time. I guess they'll be looking for the black box to give them the answers.'

Frank and I exchanged glances. 'Had the flight been normal up until that time?' Frank asked.

'Don't know,' said the driver, 'news was still coming in so I suppose the later bulletins will have more details.'

I had a pretty good idea what the cause of the crash was, what was particularly worrying was that there must have been at least two experienced pilots on duty; one fatal heart attack is always a possibility but two? I didn't think so.

'They say bad news always comes in three's,' the driver continued. I was reminded of what happened to purveyors of bad news in the olden days, they used to shoot the messenger.

'Why, what else has happened? I asked.

'The Nicks beat the Bulls in the playoffs.'

'Really?' I said, my spirit suddenly soaring out of all proportion to his jokey response, 'that is bad news.' I stole a look at Frank and he returned it with a wry smile.

For the rest of the journey our friendly doomsayer had nothing else to share thank God, and Frank and I observed the commandment 'Thou Shalt Not Discuss the Subject of the Extinction of the Human Race,' to be honest, at this stage I didn't need any encouragement.

Eventually we left the river of red taillights and headed for the hotel. Checking in was quick and efficient, no sign of paramedics running about the place dealing with 'Blight' victims, just the usual hustle and bustle you expect in a busy international hotel.

Frank asked if I wanted dinner, I declined, telling him I needed to speak to Bill and the twins and then to take a long hot shower, I told him I would probably call room service if I got hungry. He said he would probably go down to the bar for a beer and sandwich.

My room key told me I was in 508 whilst Frank was in 810, three floors up. We collected our envelopes containing the airline tickets and DC hotel reservation information. Flight departure time was noon; an official car would pick us up at the hotel at nine thirty and take us out to the airport, we would be met at Ronald Regan and taken to the meeting, which was scheduled for a three o'clock start.

I told Frank I would call him in the morning at about eight thirty and we could chat over breakfast. We rode the elevator, me to the fifth floor and Frank I guessed, to the eighth.

'Good night Frank, I hope we'll see each other in the morning,' I said, at an attempt at dark humour.

' I know what your feeling Eve, nothing seems the same anymore, from what we've learned these past few days no one can be certain of surviving even the next second never mind the entire night. To be honest I find the whole damned thing frightening and I have no family to worry about, except for you, Bill and the twins, you're the closest I've got to real family, I imagine it must be absolutely terrifying for you. Just pray that there is an answer to this somewhere and that we find it soon.'

I smiled at him weakly and stepped out of the elevator and made for my room, I hoped I would hear the voices of the three most important people in the world when I dialed the number in Raleigh.

'Hi Bill, hello honey, how are you?'

'Who's calling please, this is Bill James speaking?'

'Bill it's me Eve, what do you mean 'Who's calling?'

'Eve, Eve who? I don't know anybody called Eve. Oh wait a minute, I used to know someone of that name but it was a long time ago, I'd forgotten all about her.'

'Daddy daddy, is it mommy?'

'Mommy, what mommy, you mean you have a mommy?'

'Bill come on, all right I should have called but honestly sweetheart I couldn't, I'm sorry really I am. Did you not get a call from some government person telling you I was incommunicado?'

'Incommunicado you say, that's a hell of a word. Yea, all right we did get a call so you're forgiven but didn't you once say you would crawl on your hand and knees over broken bottles just to get to me?'

'Yes I did, I can't lie but broken bottles are one thing and the government is another thing altogether.'

'Daddy, we want to speak to mommy.'

'Ok guys, here she is. They're fighting me for the phone and they're too strong for me so here they are, it's my turn next.'

'Hi mommy, this is Wendy, I love you. Here's Suzanne. Ok, stop pulling the phone, here, you can speak to her but give the phone back to me when you've finished.

'Mommy, mommy, hi it's me. I love you too mommy and we've all missed you. When are you coming home, are you coming tonight, please say yes?'

'Hello sweetie, I've missed you so much too, I wish I could be there right now but I'm with Uncle Frank and we have to go to some more meetings and then I can come home. Have you been a good girl for daddy? If you have, I have something special for you.'

'Yes mommy, I've been real good, ask daddy if you don't believe me. Here daddy tell mommy I've been good.'

'Me too me to, I've been good as well mommy.' Wendy wrestled the phone from her sister.

'I know you have both been good and as soon as I come home I will have something special for both my beautiful little girls. Let me speak with daddy now please.' Bill came on the phone.

'Hi darling, quiet at last, the girls have gone to watch TV that should keep them occupied for the next thirty seconds. What's going on hon? The phone call said what you were involved in was of national importance or something; sounds serious.'

'Bill I love you so much, I want you to know that I say it with all my heart, you were and still are my dream come true, you have always made me so happy, there is no better husband or father anywhere. I mean it Bill, every word of it.'

'Whoa, slow down, you make it sound like your giving a eulogy. What brought that on? You've not been gone that long. Something has happened, what is I?'

'Bill, when they told you what I was involved in was of national importance, they weren't kidding, it is, so much so that they have instructed Frank and me not to discuss the matter with anyone, not even you, I can't tell you a thing, not even who else is involved in the discussions and meetings. Believe me Bill, if I could I would.'

'You're not joking are you? I guess it must be something different from what you went to Geneva to discuss.'

'Bill I really can't say, please help me by showing a little understanding, you know how I hate to keep things from you but this thing is way outside of my jurisdiction. Frank and I have a meeting the day after tomorrow in DC and then we should be on our way home. I think they wanted to give us a day to recover from the flight before involving us in the next meeting and I must say I'm grateful to them, I feel quite exhausted.

You know as soon as we came off the plane, we were met by immigration officials and given special clearance before being whisked straight into a meeting and as soon as it finished we were brought to the hotel and here I am. I'm not even sure I should have told you that much. Oh God, what have I got myself involved in.'

'Hey, don't please, you worry me, I'm not used to hearing you talk like this, it's kind of scary. Listen Eve, I'm here for you, whenever you're able to share, then I'm here, I don't know what it is that's going on but I'm sure proud that you're country has told you it needs you. You're one great lady and I 'm a very lucky guy. I love you Eve, I love you with all my heart.'

I had to choke back the tears; I offered a quick prayer for our safety and then told him I would ring again as soon as I could. I said goodnight to my terrible twosome and replaced the receiver.

CHAPTER 21

I walked to the window and looked out over busy streets, ordinary people living ordinary lives, I tried to imagine the myriad of thoughts that were going round and round in their collective minds; some exciting, some sad, others harbouring secret hopes and fears and I suppose a few of them dangerous and nasty but all of them alive and all of them unsuspecting, not knowing that the thoughts they were thinking could easily be their last. Automobiles crawled along the streets like long undulating multi-coloured snakes amidst a cacophony of every day sounds; the same scene was being played out in thousands of cities across the globe, could life really be so fragile, it seemed so unfair, it might have been different if we could exercise a measure of control but in the final analysis we were nothing more than hostages to fortune, at least there was no favouritism the only criteria for dying was that you were alive.

I was reminded of the adage 'ignorance is bliss when it is folly to be wise.' I was wise and wished it were not so but you can't unknow what is already known and it was there and then that I realised and accepted not just the enormity of the problem but also the role that fate had cast for me and I accepted the role and promised whoever was tuned in to my thoughts, that I would do everything I could to what, save humanity, 'why not,' I thought with a chuckle, as if saving humanity was a job for superheroes, 'someone has to do it?'

I remembered the driver's air crash story so I switched on the TV to CNN to see if there was an up-dated report. Ads again, as I said before always ads, then a filmstar-type face appeared on the screen. 'And now the accident involving King Airline's flight 202 from Bangkok to Hong Kong, for the latest update we're going live to Jeremy Parker in Hong Kong. Jeremy what's the latest on the crash, has anyone indicated the likely cause?'

'No, not yet, a spokesman for the airline stated but added that there was no immediate indication that the crash had been as a result of terrorist activities, he said they were still trying to locate the flight recorder, the Black Box as it's more commonly known and wouldn't speculate on the cause of the accident until the recorder had been recovered and the data analysed.

Eyewitnesses said there was no explosion and no flames, we managed to obtain some footage shot by an amateur photographer, you can clearly see the aircraft on its final approach, notice how it doesn't change its angle of approach nor does it appear to slow down, the wing flaps have not been adjusted for landing, it looks like a guided missile intent on hitting its target, in this case the sea.' The plane overshoots the runway and crashes into its target.

The spokesman confirms there were no survivors, two hundred and ninety two people perished, two hundred and eighty one passengers and eleven crew.'

'We heard earlier that the airport tower claimed the pilot didn't respond to instructions and that they had received a transmission from the aircraft that the captain was incapacitated due to a heart attack. Is that true?'

'There's nothing official but one of the air traffic control officers did report a message was received from the aircraft regarding the captain, apparently he did suffer what seemed to be a heart attack about three hundred nautical miles from the destination but the second-in-command took the controls without any hitch and was bringing the plane in. As of now the cause of the crash is something of a mystery, we will have to wait for the recovery of the Black Box to shed some light on it.'

'Thank you Jeremy, we'll keep watching this one.

President Cooper was meeting with….'

I didn't hear the next report I was still playing the air crash report over in my mind. It seemed pretty clear to me what had happened, the captain had fallen victim to 'The Blight' as had the second-in-command, and there was no one else who could fly the plane so the flight co-ordinates programmed into the onboard computer by the second pilot would have remained unchanged. The plane had simply followed the programme and flown into the sea. I tried not to think of what it had been like on that plane, the final minutes ticking by as it neared its destination, the realization by the cabin crew that the plane was on a path to destruction, the mayhem in the cabins as the passengers finally understood what was happening, the helplessness, the naked fear, perhaps some final goodbyes, a few prayers and one or two 'I love you's.'

I realised my heart was pounding in my chest and my mouth had gone dry, I prayed none of that had happened, that the passengers were unaware of the problems and that the end had been mercifully quick. I sank to the floor and wept silently, in truth I wasn't sure who I was weeping for; the victims, the world or perhaps the tears were for me and all I could lose if this damned thing should ever come knocking on my door.

I resisted the impulse to pick up the phone and ring Bill, I could tell from our earlier conversation that he was more than a little concerned, and there seemed no good reason to add to his discomfort. I decided the hot shower I'd mentioned to Frank sounded good, so I stripped out of my clothes and turned on the shower.

I waited until the steam started to rise before stepping into the hot water spray; I stood there feeling the water driving the heat into my body, penetrating my skin through to the muscles and down to the bone itself, sluicing the tension down the plug hole.

I was right, it was cathartic, the bathroom had become filled with billowing steam, like a Turkish Bath, my skin was as pink as a new born babe's from the hot water jets and I luxuriated in the feeling of being vital of being alive. I stood there naked and felt invincible, dangerous I knew but good nonetheless 'Come and get me if you can,' I said defiantly to no one in particular, no one answered nor challenged my invincibility. It felt like a small victory of sorts, I knew it was foolish, even childish but I didn't care and it felt good.

Before turning in I picked up the briefing papers provided by Sam but I was feeling real tired, or perhaps exhausted would be more accurate. I leafed through it quickly and I didn't notice anything too far removed from what Sam had already told us, the several statistical tables, graphs and charts didn't seem important enough to linger over, at least that's what my increasingly weary brain told me so I just skipped over them figuring I would have time the following day to pay them a closer respect. Eventually, with my mind meandering down paths that were largely unrecognizable, I decided enough was enough for one day so I put the papers on the table and crawled into bed, I must have been asleep before my head hit the pillow and I slept the sleep of the dead (no pun intended), deep and dreamless.

A shattering noise, like a fleet of fire engines with bells ringing and roaring through the bedroom brought me instantly back to consciousness, I shot up in bed totally lost, didn't know where I was, wondering what the hell was going on, it was the telephone next to the bed sounding like the bells of Notre Dame Cathedral calling the faithful to mass.

My heart was about to burst through my rib cage as I grabbed in a barely concealed panic for the phone, I lifted it from the receiver and instinctively put it to my ear, the offending din was suddenly cut off in mid ring. I was still feeling disorientated, disconnected from reality when I heard a man's disembodied voice tell me to turn on the TV and put CNN on. It was Frank.

'Frank,' I managed to say through my fugue, 'what the hell is going on?' I couldn't keep the annoyance out of my voice.

'I'm sorry Eve, just put the TV on.'

I somehow worked the remote and the newscaster-cum-film star appeared, 'no adverts this time,' I thought. Behind the handsome face was a file photo of Harry Hewson the Senate Majority Leader and across the bottom of the screen was a red ribbon with large white writing on it, it said 'BREAKING NEWS.' I'd missed the earlier part of the announcement, the anchor was saying '.... he will best be remembered for his work on environmental issues and to his friends he will always be the perfect golfing companion.

Senator Harry Hewson, who died of a heart attack today at his home in Chattanooga, would have celebrated his sixtieth birthday next Monday. He was a true American.'

I hadn't realised I was still holding the phone to my ear, gripping it so tight that I had cramp in my fingers. 'Eve, are you there, Eve, say something?'

'Yes Frank, yes I'm here.'

'Did you see it, the newscast about Hewson?'

'Yes I did.'

'Are you thinking what I'm thinking?'

'Yes I am and even worse, I'm thinking it was the same thing that brought down the King Airlines plane.'

'Did you see the later bulletins?'

'Yes I did and I think there can be little doubt that both pilots were victims of Sudden Death Syndrome, except on this occasion it brought down a plane-load of people as well.

Can you imagine how many Joe Blows are dying all over the world every day and we don't know about it. Each death carrying its own tragedy, someone loses a wife or a husband, a brother, a sister, a mom, a dad, even a best friend? The shock, oh my God, healthy and well one minute, I mean second, and then poof, gone, dead.

I'm still having difficulty with it, even though I know it to be so. I feel trapped, helpless and useless, like I should be doing something, anything.

Frank I'm sorry, forgive me, I feel like I've had enough for one day, I'm going to try and get back to sleep. Good night.'

I didn't even wait for his response, I just hung up, not angry but dejected I think that best describes how I felt. I turned off the TV and glanced at the bedside clock, the numerals told me it was eleven thirty, I'd only slept for about two and a bit hours. I lay my head down, sleep wasn't so fast coming this time but eventually, like a thief in the night it crept stealthily up on me and pulled me gently into oblivion.

I was in a plane, a big commercial airliner, it was full of passengers and everyone seemed to know each other; there was a great deal of noise, people were talking and laughing and generally having a good time, it was almost like there was a party going on but I didn't know anyone and no one knew me, no one spoke to me, I felt so alone, so terribly lonely.

I tried to engage some of the passengers in conversation but no one took the slightest notice of me, they just looked through me it was like I wasn't there. I was close to despair and felt my frustration turning quickly to anger. Just when I thought I was ready to blow a gasket an authoritative sounding voice came over the public address system, 'This is the captain speaking. All passengers must return immediately to their seats, fasten their seat belts and be quiet.'

The cockpit door opened and the captain emerged looking cool and confident in his crisp white shirt with the captain's black and gold epaulettes on the shoulder, I couldn't see his face as it was wreathed in shadow. I felt uncommonly grateful to him, the chattering and loud laughter had really started to get me down, now there was only a deep abiding silence as everyone had obeyed his instructions by returning to their seats, belting up and being quiet. He strode purposefully down the aisle and try as I might I was still unable to see his face. He stopped next to me and said, 'I have a message for passenger Mrs Eve James.'

'I'm Eve James,' I responded.

'I know.'

He hunkered down at the side of me, now I could see his face and I found myself looking directly into a single milky white eye and the face that surrounded it wore a hideous expression, somewhere between a smile, a leer and a grimace. Strangely, I didn't feel the least bit afraid and I said, 'Shouldn't you be on Mt Olympus?'

'Never mind that, look who I've brought to see you.' When I looked past him I saw Bill with the twins standing outside of the cabin door, they were all holding hands. I started to rise from my seat to go to them but Captain Cyclops put a restraining hand on my shoulder.

'Let me go,' I said, 'I want to go to my family,' and I tried to brush him aside but his grip was resolute, he just held me down tighter.

'Don't worry Eve we're all going to be together very soon.' He started to laugh, his laughter grew louder and louder until it filled the entire plane.

With his head thrown back still bellowing, he returned to the cockpit slamming the door shut behind him. Bill and the twins hadn't moved, I wasn't sure whether he had walked round them or through them. Their expressions remained unaltered, I started to get up out of my seat again but suddenly the angle of the plane dipped violently, the nose pointing down.

The plane's speed increased and I was pinned to my seat by the G force, Bill and the girls still didn't move, the new angle of the plane and its increased velocity had no effect on them. It seemed as if the plane was flying at an impossibly steep angle of descent, we were obviously on a collision course with the ground or the sea or a mountain or something.

I expected the passengers to have been screaming in panic by now but there was only silence, with effort I managed to turn my head and look around the cabin, everyone was in their seats with their eyes shut, as if they were sound asleep, I looked up at Bill and the girls, they were stood in the same place, their eyes were shut too.

I felt confused and disorientated, fear gripped my mind and I was close to panic, my breath was coming in short sharp gasps and I was clenching and unclenching my fists. Captain Cyclops' laughter, which now had a distinctly hysterical sound to it, as if it were issuing from someone on the threshold of insanity, was still booming out of the cockpit. It was the only sound on the plane. And then the realization, the passengers were not sleeping, they were all dead; Bill was dead, so were

Wendy and Suzanne, 'But how could they be dead and still standing?' I calmly debated with myself. They were all dead; everyone was dead except for Captain Cyclops and me.

I managed to free myself from the seat, I leaned over the 'dead' passengers on my left and pressed my face to the cabin window, I couldn't see anything, only white billowing clouds like mountains of cotton wool towering all around us, pressing menacingly against the fuselage and then we were through the clouds; like a precision thrown dart we hurled unerringly towards our final destination. Captain Cyclops bellowed with renewed lunatic frenzy and I braced myself for the anticipated impact.

The ground was a long way below us and at this altitude I couldn't make out any of the details on its surface, it just looked flat, even the colours looked smudged, nonetheless, the ground rushed at us as if it couldn't wait to envelop us in its deadly embrace.

I staggered to my feet and lurched like a drunkard to the front entry/exit door, I grasped the handle and tried to yank it upwards, it didn't budge, I tried again and the handle moved a fraction, I could feel icy-cold sweat trickling down my back and my hands were slick, I wiped them on the front of my shirt, in my panicked state my adrenaline level had soared and I was determined to get that door open, although I had no idea what I would do if I were successful.

Still Captain Cyclops roared like a loon, I braced myself, feet apart and got a good two-handed grip on the handle and pulled for all I was worth. What happened next was like something out of an old Arnold Schwarzenegger movie, the handle flew up and the door cracked open, the furiously rushing air caught it and ripped it off its hinges tossing it like a weightless leaf into space.

Before I had time to think, I was sucked out through the opening where the door had been and was in free fall as the aircraft plunged past me on its path to destruction with a cargo of dead passengers for company.

I plummeted to earth and with the wind howling in my ears, I could still hear the sound of his mad, mocking laughter echoing back to me but it must have been in my head because by now the plane was little more than a speck below me.

I didn't see the plane hit the ground, it just got smaller and smaller until it disappeared from sight; it seemed that I was at an impossibly high altitude, maybe somewhere up in the stratosphere far higher than the average sky diver is when he makes the leap from plane to nothing and as I hurtled after the plane, and just before I was due to keep my own appointment with death, the dreamscape suddenly shifted to something entirely different.

I was stood on a hillside clutching a bunch of daffodils; the sky was cornflower blue with white fluffy clouds hung in clusters. Apart from birdsong the earth was quiet and for some reason felt empty, it was as if I were the only one left alive, the air was impossibly clean and intoxicating, like vintage wine and I knew that the answer to the 'Question of the Ages' was about to be revealed to me. I was standing on the threshold of discovery with my face turned towards the sun and just when I had opened my mind to the knowledge about to be bestowed upon me, a force beyond my understanding plucked me from sleep's clutches and dumped me back in my bed. The questions remained unanswered.

CHAPTER 22

When I was fully awake I had a lingering memory of both dreams and felt strangely exhilarated, as if Captain Cyclops really had tried to kill me and failed, it could only have been a great victory for me. The second dream filled me with a hope I had no right to feel, if the dreams were prophetic and in some way related, I had an idea where it left me but what about Bill and the twins, where did it leave them? I decided not to think about it.

I switched on the TV to see if there were any new developments from the King Airlines crash but it was only the weather report, I switched to BBC World just in time to hear the announcer giving a reprise of the news headlines.

'The Black Box flight recorder from the ill-fated King Airlines flight has been recovered, investigators from the Chinese Civil Aviation Authority are studying the data, a spokesman for the C. C. A. A. said an announcement would be made as soon as possible. The Australian Civil Aviation Authority with whom King Airlines are registered has sent a representative to assist with the investigations.'

I looked at the clock, it was a quarter past ten, I'd slept longer than I expected, I decided to ring Frank's room before I showered. Frank answered on the third ring.

'Hi Frank, good morning, did you sleep well?'

'Good morning to you, boy do you sound different today. When I didn't hear from you I figured you must have quit the hotel and started to hitch hike it back to Raleigh.'

'I'm sorry,' I said, 'I was feeling kind of down last night, what with the flight back from Switzerland and then the meeting with Sam Bartram, the air disaster and chatting with Bill and the girls, I guess everything just caught up with me. I didn't mean to take it out on you Frank, I'm real sorry.'

'Hey, don't worry about it, it's OK, I know it's been rough on you. I can't even tell you everything is going to be fine because as things stand now they're not going to be fine at all. Look, why don't we get out of the hotel and take a cab downtown, we can get a coffee and some breakfast, maybe at Rockefeller Plaza, what do you say? We can walk for a bit and stretch our legs, boy that should feel good after all the sitting on the plane, then in the office with Sam and then to the hotel in an automobile, it's so long since I walked any distance I think my muscles might have atrophied.'

'I think that's a great idea Frank, give me half an hour then meet me in the lobby.'

'You've got it,' he said and hung up.

I was down in the lobby in twenty minutes; Frank was already waiting for me. I thought both of us looked much better than we had the previous evening, I guess we had both needed a good nights sleep. Frank went to Reception and ordered a cab.

We rode in companionable silence looking out of the cab's windows as we headed for Rockefeller Plaza, it was nice to be alive and seeing so many people out on the streets, it was hard to take in Sam's five-year computer projection. New York City has a life of its own, like it lives and breathes and has a heartbeat, you can almost hear it and feel it reverberating through the sidewalk. I love New York, my spirits had steadily lifted and by the time we were walking up Fifth Avenue things didn't seem half so bad in the winter sunshine.

We passed the day doing nothing more than enjoying our surroundings and each other's company; we studiously avoided the subject of 'Sudden Death Syndrome'. We walked down Fifth Avenue and then up Sixth, we window-shopped and generally kept the conversation light, preferring to talk about the girls and our next vacation, which we planned to spend skiing in Colorado. Neither Bill nor I had ever taken a skiing vacation and we felt it would be great fun to introduce the girls to the simplest beginner slopes now that they were older and could appreciate that type of holiday.

As I said, Bill and I had never been on skis and we figured we would probably spend most of the vacation in a prone position in the snow, I was scared to death that the girls in a careless and unsupervised moment, would go careening down the slopes flopping over and over like rag dolls, wrap themselves around a tree and in the process sustain multiple broken limbs finally coming to a stop in a deep snow drift at the bottom of the ski run. Bill had pointed out that the girls would not be attempting to establish Olympic records at their first time out and it wasn't an Alpine ski run they would be on but rather a flat, little beginner's slope.

We had lunch at a wine bistro, Frank ordered pastrami on rye and a glass of sweet white wine, I think it was Sauternes, for me it was a hot roast beef sub with horseradish sauce and a glass of ice-cold lager beer. It was delicious; food had never tasted so good.

We returned to the hotel by taxi and arranged to meet for dinner in the hotel's Olympus Grille Restaurant (I couldn't imagine the floorshow would feature a one-eyed Cyclops fresh from a successful stint at 'The Top of Mount Olympus,' for which the restaurant had been name).

Once in my room I debated whether to put the news on, I mean my spirits had fairly soared during the trip to Manhattan and although they had since slipped a little from their perihelion, I didn't think I wanted to hear about anymore airline disasters, riots in Bangladesh, or wars in the Middle East.

I thought one of the sit-com re-runs might keep my spirits on a high so I turned to the Golden Oldies channel and was rewarded by an ancient black and white episode of 'The Beverley Hillbillies,' even a hundred years on, the antics of the Clampet family, Jed, Granny and the rest, are still uproariously funny. This episode featured Mr Drysdale, the President of the First National Bank of Beverly Hills, trying to persuade Buddy Ebsen not to withdraw his millions from the bank to finance another one of Jethro's hair-brained schemes. It was genuinely funny, even refreshingly funny in an uncomplicated way; no violence and no sex (unless you counted Ellie May in her tight hillbilly garb), it reflected a time when America was still desperate to cling to its innocence, in spite of the Vietnam war which was raging at the time the series was being shot, the assassination of President Kennedy in Dallas Texas and the cold war with the Soviets, which had reached new heights with the Cuban Missile Crisis.

The events of 9/11 had still to be written and were forty years away, the Oklahoma bombers were as yet unborn. I realised my musings had done nothing to sustain my feelings of 'bonhomie,' my thoughts had already turned to the dark and threatening world of 'The Blight,' SDS or if you preferred 'The Imminent Destruction of Human Kind.' 'Now there's a subject to get you in a party mood,' I thought sardonically.

CHAPTER 23

Madge picked up her notes, she actually enjoyed reading this stuff, to her it was the very bedrock of her existence, while her friends were out on dates or just chilling out in the pub, Madge preferred to curl up with her research material. Not that she didn't have plenty of offers; the truth was she had to field a never-ending stream of invitations. She liked guys and had dated a few but after a couple of weeks they always wanted to get heavy into it, while she had not the slightest intention of settling down yet.

She had set herself a number of goals and entering into a serious relationship was not one of them. Those things would have to wait until she had achieved her academic ambitions.

For some reason, tonight she seemed to be having difficulty concentrating, she had read and re-read the paragraph several times over but the words were not sticking, they entered her consciousness but couldn't maintain a foothold and slid right out again. A teacher once told her that if she should ever have problems absorbing information, she should read the words out loud instead of to herself, it was a sure fire way of registering the data. She decided to take the advice, so repeated slowly:

'In genetics, the gene is either identified with the cistron, or the unit of selection (a Mendelian gene that determines a particular character on which natural selection can act). Genes undergo mutation and recombination to produce the variation on which natural selection operates.

The Human Genome Project which started in1988 was the largest research project ever undertaken in the life sciences, over $1.5 billion was spent over the first five years.

Genes account for only a small amount of DNA sequence. Over 90% of DNA appears not to have any function, although it is perfectly replicated each time a cell divides and is handed on to the next generation. Many higher organisms have large amounts of redundant DNA and this is probably an advantage as there is a reservoir of DNA available to form new genes if an old one is lost by mutation.'

She thought that was pretty basic stuff but relevant nonetheless, and then always the age old question of why do species become extinct? She knew that some were hunted out of existence by man, like the dodo from the island of Mauritius and the passenger pigeon of North America but then there were other species that had disappeared with more than a hint of mystery surrounding their demise; in the scale of things, the extinction of the dinosaurs and wooly mammoths had been virtually instantaneous.

The current thinking on the extinction of the dinosaurs was that a massive comet had collided with earth, so massive that the impact caused enormous changes in the earth's climate, killing off much of the vegetation and in the process depriving the enormous plant eating dinosaurs of their food supply. When they died out there was little or nothing left for the meat eaters to get their teeth into, so they died out as well?

She had never been impressed by that particular theory it left too many questions unanswered, why, she wondered, would all types dinosaurs in every corner of the earth be affected in the same way and at the same time. Why did every dinosaur become extinct, why not some, or most?

And what about the mammals, there were plant eating and meat eating mammals all over the world, why didn't they die off too but they didn't, they survived just fine and not just survived, they became the rulers of the earth and no one more so than the most successful of all the mammals, man himself?

The mammoths were something all together different; in the early twentieth century villagers in the frozen Siberian tundra discovered a number of complete mammoth carcasses preserved in the permafrost, they were still covered in their shaggy woolen coats. The villagers removed some of the carcasses, dragged them away and thawed them out, they were hungry and probably couldn't believe their luck, so without further ado they cut up the carcasses and cooked the meat. It was still edible after tens of thousands of years.

Fortunately for science, the authorities learnt of the discovery and sent a team to investigate. Several carcasses were removed to Moscow for examination, the autopsies produced some very interesting data, the stomachs of the mammoths contained undigested grasses and leaves, the only conclusion that could be drawn from that was that the mammoths were feeding by the river one minute and then inexplicably they keeled over dead and fell into the river. They would soon be frozen solid, entombed in blocks of ice for the next twenty thousand years or so.

Madge looked up from her notes and rubbed her eyes, she had always found this aspect of the subject particular fascinating; these species had taken millions of years to evolve and yet disappeared in the virtual blinking of an eye and in circumstances not the least bit compelling. She thought she might return to it in her thesis.

'That's enough for one day,' she said to no one but herself. She stood up and stretched, gave an uninhibited yawn, laid down her notes and headed for the bedroom, what was it her mum used to say, 'Early to bed, early to rise, makes a man healthy, wealthy and wise.' She smiled warmly at the thought of her mum and her famous sayings.

As she lay in bed hovering somewhere between sleep and consciousness, her mind paying visits to disparate locations and none of them making cohesive sense, she remembered something reported on the ITN eight o'clock news and suddenly her conscious thought was sharp and focused. 'What had he said?' The Government denies there is any link between nuclear power stations and the apparent increase in the coronary death rate.

A Downing Street spokesman said that attempts to blame nuclear power stations for deaths amongst the population is old hat, he said it used to be claimed by opponents of nuclear power that cancer was more prevalent amongst people living in close proximity to the power stations than the rest of the population and that that particular myth had long since been debunked. He further said that it was a mistake to assume there had been any increase in the incidence of heart attacks; it was unfortunate he said, that some persons had experienced coronaries whilst driving their motor cars and that the subsequent crashes had themselves produced fatalities, which had added to the tragic nature of events. It was only natural that these unfortunate occurrences would be subjected to greater scrutiny.'

Her mind started to loose it's grip on reality as Madge was gently lowered into the Land of Nod but before she was completely under, her mind remembered that in the past week there had been at least six of these tragedies, it seemed something more than unfortunate and coincidental. Anyway she didn't believe in coincidences.

She made a mental note to check this out in more detail in the morning but before it could be stored in her 'things to do' memory file, she had succumbed to sleep's enticement and been transported to that other existence, the 'Land of Dreams' where events seem just as real as those we experience in our waking state.

Madge dreamt of a world populated by fantastic beasts, a world where she alone was privileged to walk amongst them.

In her dream the air was hot and humid, the vegetation thick and lush, ferns with gigantic fronds and vines as thick as an elephant's leg hung from the fabulous trees and the ground shuddered as giant sauropods lumbered by out of sight, lost in the dense foliage. In the distance she spied a herd of Meglasaurus traveling slowly under the immense weight of their bulks across the endless veldt, grouping themselves close together should a ravenously hungry Tyrannosaurus Rex select them for attack; a Pterodactyl as big as a light aircraft swooped and dipped on the thermals. Madge sighed with satisfaction knowing that here were all the specimens she would ever need.

CHAPTER 24

Eve had set the bedside alarm to seven and now its insistent ringing suggested she might want to wake up, she did but only with great reluctance. Sleep had acted as a cocoon from reality and she was in no doubt she preferred the cocoon.

She lay there for a time savouring the new day; she thought how nice it would be if the events of the past week and all this talk of people dying and airplane crashes had been nothing more than a bad dream. 'No such luck,' she told the room, 'this one is for real and the sooner we can get to Raleigh and start work on finding the cause and then the answer, the better I'm going to feel.'

Her spirits still felt pretty buoyant and she fairly sprang out of bed went into the bathroom and turned on the shower, she thought she would ring Frank just to make sure he was up and getting ready for breakfast, in truth she was ringing for a different reason altogether but she didn't want to articulate it.

She counted eight rings and then the answering machine kicked in, she hung up quickly, as if the telephone had suddenly become too hot to hold. She conjured up a dreadful vision of Frank lying lifeless in a tub of cold water; eyes wide open staring into eternity, 'The Blight's' latest victim.

She wondered what she should do, call the front desk, call the FBI, she realised she was quickly sliding into a state of panic; a loud rapping on the door snapped her out of her fugue of indecision. 'Hello, who is it?' She called out.

'It's me Eve.'

'Thank God,' she thought, it was Frank's voice, he was OK, 'where have you been, she shouted at the door, I have been ringing you?'

'Are you going to keep me stood outside of your door, while you holler at me from inside your room? I only came to see if you were up; I woke early and went down to Reception for a cup of coffee.'

'I'm sorry Frank, I didn't mean to be mean, and I'll see you in the breakfast area in twenty minutes.' She breathed a sigh of relief and chastised herself for being overly paranoid.

Twenty-two minutes later she was walking into the breakfast café. Frank rose from his seat and warmly greeted her with a hug and kiss on the cheek.

'You look fresh and well-rested,' he said.

'Thanks, I did get a restful night's sleep, how about you?'

'I did OK,' he said, 'it took a little while to drop off but when I finally did I slept the sleep of the dead, no pun intended. You sounded a little strange when I came by your room, what was going on?'

'Oh nothing much,' she tried to sound casual, 'I rang your room earlier and got your answering machine;

when you didn't answer the call I started to imagine the worse, it was a tremendous relief when I heard your voice outside the room. Sorry if I was sharp with you,' and then quickly changing the subject, 'what do you think today will bring?'

'I'm not sure, there are a few heavyweights attending so I guess we can expect some decisions to be taken.'

'Do you know them, the heavyweights I mean, I've read some of their papers and I actually went to California State when they debated 'The Use of Embryonic Stem Cells in Medical Research,' Professor Lindo was a member of the discussion panel. It was still a sensitive topic back then and elevated many people's passions. Didn't he get his Nobel Prize for his work in that area, embryonic stem cell research?

'Yes he did. The man's a genius, absolutely one of the top people in his field. The other Laureate is Professor Michael Banbury; he won his prize for his work on Evolutionary Biology. Again, he's the best there is in his field, I've met them both and know them reasonably well, I can't imagine they are going to the meeting just to make up the numbers; they'll be looking for decisions to be taken, so I don't expect it to be a talking shop.'

'What do you think of the Secretary of State being there? I was bowled over when I saw Frieda Lindt's name on the list of attendees?'

'I've never met her but she's a sharp cookie and a close confidant of the President. Look how she handled the crises last year in Argentina and Brazil; it's common knowledge that it was only her skillful intervention and personal standing that defused the confrontation between both civilian governments and their military.

I remember the TV pictures showing everyone smiling and shaking hands like good friends with Secretary Lindt in the middle of it all. It was only days previously that the armies in each country were threatening to undo decades of democracy with military coupes.

Her presence is pretty significant; there can be no questioning the seriousness of the meeting. It obviously has the President's personal endorsement.'

'I was shocked to see Miriam Carter's name on the list, why do you think she's there?'

'I was surprised too at first but when I recalled Sam Bartram's scenario for the end of civilization, I guess the Director of Homeland Security is a good choice to have around the table, after all, there must be a plan for what will have to be done in the event that we're unable to stop this thing in its tracks.

If people continue to die and at an ever-increasing rate, what will be the consequences, is there a timetable of events for the disintegration of the human race? It seems to me that the crises we face will be much more domestic orientated than international. I think her job is the hardest of all, I mean, if the scientists identify the reasons behind SDS and how to deal with it, then that's it, we've won and we can all go home but what if we don't, what if the deaths go on and on and on, what happens then? I would hate to even have to contemplate that but it's exactly what Miriam Carter will have to do.'

'I have to say Frank I'm feeling more than a little overawed at the thought of being in such exalted company, you're pretty big news yourself I mean, the Head of the Human Genome Project is a big shot by anybody's estimate while me, I feel I'm really only there to make up the numbers. I'm way out of my depth on this one.'

'That's not true Eve, your work on the Genome Project has been ground-breaking, you probably know as much about gene sequencing as anyone, you'll have a major contribution to make both at the meeting and then afterwards when we get back to the lab.

Don't worry yourself; don't you think a lot of thought went into who should attend the meeting? The President himself would have been consulted and would have given his personal approval. Without question you're there on merit.'

We finished breakfast and agreed to meet back in Reception in forty-five minutes for the arrival of our driver.

CHAPTER 25

Jamaica should have been a tropical paradise; it nestled in the beautiful turquoise Caribbean Sea ninety miles from Cuba and only an hour and a bit flying time from Miami. Its climate was close to perfection, the coastline trimmed with white sand beaches and the interior of the island consisted of mountains, tropical rainforests, rivers and waterfalls. Exotic flowers and fruits were in abundance and grew just about everywhere. The Jamaican people were amongst the friendliest anywhere. So why wasn't it paradise? The slums of Kingston the capital city bred some of the most vicious criminals imaginable and like a cancer they had spread their sickness throughout the island infecting rural and urban areas alike.

They formed gangs and dominated the life of entire communities literally dispensing their own brand of justice; the gang bosses were known as 'dons' or if a politician were talking about them he would probably refer to them reverently as 'community leaders.'

The dons were extremely powerful and had accumulated great wealth from their nefarious activities; their gangs controlled the drugs trade, extortion, kidnapping and prostitution. They had underworld connections throughout the Americas and Europe. They also controlled too many of the local politicians and affiliated themselves to one or other of the two major political parties. They were ruthless and well organized and their firepower was superior to that of the Jamaican Police Force or Jamaican Defence Force.

From time to time gang warfare erupted resulting in the loss of many lives, and all too often the lives belonged to the wrong people, non-gang members who happened to be in the wrong place at the wrong time, or the poor unfortunates often found themselves the victims of reprisal killings. The gangs fought over turf, drugs, politics and anything else that interested them. Sometimes they killed just for the sake of killing and to demonstrate that they held the power of life and death.

They had no interest in the lives of others and many didn't care about their own lives, they were content to live by the gun and die by the gun. The dons only had to give the word and death and destruction would rain down on one community or another, the resultant reprisal killings would be answered with more tit-for-tat murders from the other side, and so it went on.

The police and army were powerless against them and the political parties who had spawned a good many of these gangs, were now themselves being eaten alive by the very monsters they had created. Ordinary Jamaicans fearful for the future of their country and their lives demanded action from the authorities but things had gotten so far out of hand it was difficult to imagine what if anything could now be done. The one thing that had stopped the island from falling into total anarchy was that the gangs were constantly at war with each other; the common enemies were the security forces but killing them was sometimes less important than killing each other.

The Chief of Staff of the Jamaica Defence Force and the Commissioner of Police lived in constant fear of the gangs finding something to unify them, something that would result in them joining forces, turning their hatred and collective firepower on the security forces.

None could have known the role that fate would play in the drama that was about to unfold.

A joint police/army initiative involving a number of excursions into the ghettos netted lieutenants and senior members from several gangs and they were taken into custody. The dons immediately saw this as a direct challenge to their position and authority.

Retribution was swift; fifteen policemen and six army personnel were shot dead in the following two days. The response of the security forces was to step up their joint patrols with more forays being made into gangland territory. High-powered weapons and stacks of ammunition were found and seized in house-to-house searches and more gang members arrested. It seemed that the police and army had at last captured the initiative. Then disaster struck, four lieutenants, two from each side died whilst in police custody. The police said the men had died from natural causes but the gangs and their sympathizers claimed the police had executed the men in cold blood; it wasn't the first time the police had stood accused of carrying out extra judicial killings. In this instance though the real culprit was Sudden Death Syndrome (SDS aka 'The Blight') but at the time the Jamaican authorities had no knowledge that there was any such thing as SDS. To them the men really had died from natural causes. The truth was still some distance away.

The human rights monitoring group 'Jamaicans For Justice' (JFJ) demanded a full judicial enquiry into the deaths of the gang leaders, the government refused; the JFJ then asked for independent autopsies to be undertaken on the four men by a pathologist nominated by a leading human rights advocate and additionally for the results of the government's own autopsies to be published. The government agreed to publish the results of the autopsies carried out by its own pathologist but not to the request for independent autopsies.

The authorities were at pains to point out that the men had died in cells which were at the time occupied by other men and that there were no marks on the bodies of the dead men, indicating that they had not been attacked by the police or anyone else.

The Jamaican police and their political masters were not liked, trusted or respected by the population at large, the force had often been accused of carrying out extra-judicial killings so its pleas of innocence fell largely on deaf ears.

The following day three more policemen were murdered and that same evening there was a co-ordinated assault on the Cross Roads police station with six policemen being killed, another two shot and in critical condition and the station torched after the assailants had removed the station's supply of weapons. The government decided that the deteriorating situation was likely to get worse and start to spread across the island so they hurriedly declared a State of Emergency.

The security forces planned response to what the Daily Gleaner's morning headline proclaimed a 'Declaration of War By the Gangs,' was to send armoured vehicles and troop carriers with heavily armed soldiers and police marksmen into the gangland strongholds of West Kingston, Grants Pen, Olympic Gardens and Mountain View Avenue in Kingston, Spanish Town, Flankers and Glendevon in Montego Bay.

The government's plan was simple, to take the gangs by surprise by hitting all the major gangland strongholds at precisely the same time.

The gangs, through their well-placed and well-paid informants in the political parties and security forces, were told of the intended assault including the detailed planning arrangements. The security forces taking advantage of curfew restrictions imposed under the State of Emergency regulations and under the cover of night fanned out across the island and in the early hours of the morning they were in place having thrown a noose of vehicles and manpower around each of the communities.

Just before dawn the joint force of police and army personnel moved deeper into the targeted communities tightening the noose.

The gangs were ready, their members lying in ambush waiting for the lawmen, they occupied strategic vantage points in all the communities, their guns trained on the various entry and exit routes, there was no sign of the usual neighbourhood activities as the dons had ordered the people to stay off the streets.

As the force penetrated deeper into gang-held territory the lieutenants waited for the command from the dons, when it came it was a single word, 'Fire!' The element of surprise was too much; the security forces were caught in a terrible crossfire and were cut down before they ever had a chance to respond. High velocity rounds punched holes in the forces' vehicles, stitching lines of death across the bodywork and spilling the occupants into the road where an executioner's bullet waited for them.

It was clinical. It was efficient. It was slaughter. The army and police made a feeble attempt to return the fire but the bullets were coming at them from every angle and all they could do was shoot haphazardly at the buildings and rooftops. The security forces were so exposed that to the mobsters it was little more than target practice and they fell like ducks in a shooting gallery.

The air was filled with the smell of cordite and the screams of the wounded and dying but the mob was in the grip of a bloodlust and had no intention of stopping firing until every last law officer was dead.

The force commanders called for backup and helicopter support but it was all too late, the carnage was over in about thirty minutes. When silence returned to the communities, almost seven hundred police and army personnel lay dead in the streets.

By the time reinforcements did arrive it was all over. As well as their fallen comrades they found several bodies that they assumed were gunmen and twenty more that probably belonged to civilians caught in the mayhem. The gunmen had simply melted away. It was a disaster of gigantic proportions. Observers at the scene reported that it looked more like something from a Balkan massacre, or the aftermath of several devastating Baghdad car bombs.

The gangs were gleeful and emboldened by their successes, when news spread about how the security forces had been out-witted and routed they realised how more effective it would be if they made peace with each other and concentrated all their efforts on confronting the security forces instead.

They harboured no thoughts of taking over the country in some kind of quasi- paramilitary coupe, they realised there had to be at least a façade of respectability and normalcy in the country if they were to effectively operate internationally, especially in narco-trafficing, so they hatched a plot with their political cronies to put their own people in positions of political power.

The gangs would wreak havoc on the island by targeting all police posts and police personnel, those in positions of power who were genuine in their fight against the gangs and all they stood for would be disposed of. The plan was that when it became obvious that the island was sliding inexorably into anarchy and teetering on the edge of civil war, their political puppets would offer themselves to the frightened and war-weary masses to negotiate an end to the hostilities and at the same time put themselves in line to assume the mantle of political power once they had successfully delivered the peace. Once done, the gangs and government would be as one, locked in an unholy alliance and 'peace' would reign where war was before.

Gang wars and the shattered lives they left in their wake would be a thing of the past, there would be an end to murdering of security force personnel and on the surface Jamaica would be appear to be on the road to social and economic recovery but inside it would still be rotting from a malignant tumour that would eventually drain the life-force from the island, reducing it to the status of a pariah in the eyes of the international community.

The plans were carefully laid and would likely have worked but as the dons prepared to call their summit meeting three of their number were struck down by 'The Blight,' this time there were many people around who witnessed the deaths and would later confirm that 'dem jus' dead, jus' like so.'

At the same time both political parties lost several of their stalwarts and all sections of the population continued to experience rising levels of unexplained deaths.

No one believed that the deaths or the unusually high death rate had anything to do with the authorities; the deaths were talked of as if they were something of a worrisome mystery but in a society where violent death was commonplace and life was cheap, a few more deaths were nothing to get overly excited about.

There were those, especially amongst the members of the newer 'cult' churches who felt it was all down to God's punishment on Jamaica for the creation of such a corrupt and violent society.

It wouldn't be long before the same people would be offering up the island's first human sacrifices in another insane attempt to placate an angry God, but this had nothing to do with God and yet at the same time had everything to do with God but in any event nothing could stop Jamaica from drowning in the quick sands of lawlessness and terror not brought on by gang warfare or narco-trafficking but rather the relentless march of Sudden Death Syndrome.

CHAPTER 26

Eve and Frank were enjoying a second cup of coffee in the hotel lounge when the public address system told them their driver was waiting for them in reception. Their luggage was already in the car when they saw their man; he was the same who had brought them to the hotel a couple of days before.

'Hi,' said Eve pre-empting his greeting, 'it's Edward isn't it? I hope you have no more items of news for us today.' She was wearing a slightly crooked smirk so it was obvious she was not being entirely serious. 'You know that in the good old days recipients of bad news would shoot the messenger.'

'In that case I'd better not tell you the latest then.'

'Ok,' said Eve, playing along with the game she had initiated, 'you're safe, I don't have my gun with me today.'

'Then I guess it must be ok. Here it is, I was listening to the car radio while I was driving over here when the programme was interrupted by a newsflash, two rail accidents, they said, one on the London subway, dozens dead and the other on the Kyoto to Tokyo rail link in

Japan, again dozens of fatalities. The announcer said that details were sketchy but they would get back as soon as more information was available.'

Frank and Eve listened to him not sure if he was joking with them, and then,' You're serious aren't you?' Eve said.

'Totally, from the way you raised the topic of the news I thought you had already heard. It's really shocking though isn't it, first the King Airlines crash and now these two rail disasters? I know there have been other incidents that were perhaps not so high profile and didn't make the headlines but there have been quite a few reports of automobile accidents lately, they all to frequently seem to feature some dude who's had a heart attack or something while he's driving and the car suddenly becomes an unguided missile that unerringly finds its target anyway.

I have this uneasy feeling that there is something out there, something that isn't quite right, I don't know what it is but reading between the lines I'm convinced there is something going on.

It's not just the reports of accidents that worry me, haven't you noticed the number of reports regarding anti-government demonstrations, street protests, old wounds between old enemies being opened, unrest in India, Bangladesh and tribal confrontations in Africa?

I'm not the proverbial rocket scientist but I'm not stupid either and I know that when all these reports are taken in isolation, they just amount to another shitty day on planet earth but when you piece them together then a different picture emerges, it's like the whole damned world is on edge, as if we're waiting for something to happen, something bigger and more important. In fact the more I think about it, 'frightening' would be a more appropriate word to use than 'important.'

I liken the situation to a snowball sitting on top of snowy mountain, something dislodges it and it starts rolling down the mountain side, trouble is it's gathering speed and the snowball is getting bigger and bigger as it goes faster and faster. You don't have to be a genius to imagine what will happen when the snowball finally gets to the bottom of the mountain? I reckon there's going to be one hell of a mess.'

I could tell from the expression on his face that Frank was fascinated by Edward's take on the situation. 'What do you put it all down to?' He asked.

'I honestly don't know but I'll say this much, I figure it has something to do with the way people keep dying for no good reason. Look at the King Airlines crash; according to the news the theory is that both pilots died pretty much at the same time, I guess the black box flight recorder will soon confirm if that's true or not.

What do you think the chances are of both pilots having heart attacks at the same time? Pretty remote wouldn't you say? A hell of a tragic coincidence but I'm not buying it, I don't believe in coincidences.

There's been too many of what I've come to think of as a mysterious plague of heart attacks, I say mysterious because all of a sudden there seem to be so many more of them and nobody wants to admit it and no one seems to want to speculate as to why it is. I'm also willing to bet that the train accidents in London and Japan will have something to do with human error occurring because yet again some driver or controller has had one of those mysterious heart attacks, just like the automobile drivers, or Frank Kruger or even Mr Bartram's brother.'

He paused as if to catch his breath, it was like he had wanted to get it off his chest for some time. 'Well you did ask and as crazy as it sounds that's my take on it. I'm sorry if I spoke out of turn but I'm not the only one expressing these kinds of misgivings, I know a number people who believe things are not quite the way they seem.

If the Government knows something they had better start to share it with us, if on the other hand there is nothing to share then they should tell us that as well. It's not too late to stop the rumour mill.'

Frank looked thoughtful. 'What you say is interesting and I think you are being very perceptive in linking together what appear to be disparate events, it makes for interesting conjecture; I can't say I know any better than you what is going on if indeed anything is going on but I do agree that if someone knows the score then they should share it with the rest of us. What do you say Eve?'

I understood where Frank was going, there were ordinary people out there who suspected that something was amiss and as is usually the case, they suspected the Government was keeping them in the dark and ultimately that could prove to be dangerous.

People often made a quantum leap to a Government-inspired conspiracy and cover-up when something happened that was disturbing or they didn't understand. There was the so-called UFO cover-up, the crop circles cover-up, and perhaps the most famous of all, the Kennedy assassination cover-up and conspiracy.

This was something to take to the meeting, ordinary people were getting suspicious of recent events and the authorities would be wise to take note and come up with an action plan before things started to escalate and get out of control.

I didn't get a chance to answer as we were already approaching the airport. Instead of heading for 'Flight Departures' we took a sharp left and stopped at a security barrier. Edward flashed his ID and we were allowed to drive to a second barrier.

One of the new Homeland Security Guards invited us to step out of the car and into an adjacent building. We were asked for our flight tickets and instructed to step through the metal detector, our luggage, which had been brought into the building, was sent through the X ray machine. With all procedures seemingly satisfactorily completed we returned outside and got back in the car.

I asked Edward what was happening; he said that we were not going on a scheduled flight to DC but on one of the State Department's executive jets. Frank smirked at me, 'what did you say about being in exalted company? I wonder how many of the attendees will be arriving on a private jet.'

'Maybe it's a race see who gets us first, them or SDS,' and then whispering, 'I hope they have more than two pilots.' The look in Frank's eyes said it all.

Edward took us right up to the plane, Frank recognised it as a Jet Stream 5, he said he'd once flown on one when he'd been asked to attend an urgent meeting in Pittsburgh last year.

We thanked Edward for his services and conversation, shook hands and climbed the steps to the cabin.

There were twelve seats six on each side arranged so they faced each other, with a work desk in between them. The cabin was decorated in earth-type colours, to provide a relaxed ambience I guessed; the seats were large and comfortable as I discovered when I slid into one, Frank of course took the seat facing me.

I looked around, I was still having difficulty digesting all the things that had happened to me in such a short time, my life had turned upside down and was changed forever, or at least until 'The Blight' stepped in.

Frank and I retrieved the briefing documents given to us by Sam Bartram and were deep into their content when our concentration was broken by the appearance of a man in uniform. He introduced himself as Captain Harris and he would be taking us to DC, he told us his co-pilot was Captain Reid and Corporal Simms would be in the cabin with us to look after our safety and serve us with snacks and beverages. He advised us to 'belt up' as we were taking off in a few minutes.

The flight was fine, we didn't fall out of the sky and Captain Harris didn't swap his identity for that of Captain Cyclops. I had just about finished reading the brief when Corporal Simms told us we would be landing at Ronald Regan in fifteen minutes.

Twenty minutes later we were on the ground and getting into another of those unmarked, non-descript Fords and on our way to a location somewhere on Capitol Hill.

CHAPTER 27

'Are you nervous? asked Frank, 'don't be, you certainly won't be out of your depth, these people might be excellent at what they do but so are you and the fact that you have achieved so much in your career in such a short time says a lot about you. So just relax.'

'Thanks Frank, I was feeling a little bit nervous, well alright, more than a little bit but I'm fine, don't worry I won't clamp up or anything like that, I'll be ok.' He gave my hand a re-assuring squeeze.

I'd only been to DC a couple of times, basically as a tourist and therefore, I wasn't too familiar with the place. We drove past The Smithsonian and The Lincoln Memorial; even I recognised them, made some left and right turns before stopping outside a two-story building. A solid-looking twenty-foot wall topped with security cameras at defined intervals prevented any proper uninterrupted view of the building, which was set well back from the perimeter wall. Access to the building was through a large ornate metal gate.

The driver stopped the car and waited, the gates clicked open and we drove forward to a heavy-looking security barrier. A sign next to the barrier read 'RESTRICTED AREA NO ENTRY ALL VEHICLES MUST STOP'. In somewhat smaller letters at the bottom it said 'Department of Homeland Security'.

The barrier was manned by four military personnel, young men in their twenties sporting the traditional short cropped haircut, very athletic looking, each wearing a sidearm. I thought they might be Marines.

There were several remotely operated security cameras in evidence around the security point to ensure there was full coverage of all entry and exit points. They constantly panned the area as if they suffered from a nervous disposition and were unable to stay in one position for too long.

Two of the Marines scanned the Ford with electronic gadgetry whilst the other two dealt with the driver, everything must have been in order because we were allowed to proceed to a parking spot at the front of the building.

Two more Marine-types stood guard outside the front door, this time as well as side arms they also displayed automatic rifles, I didn't know much about weaponry but the rifles looked more than capable of laying down maximum fire-power should the need ever arise.

They snapped smartly to attention when we approached as if we were a couple of five star generals and the door swung inwards to allow us entry. Once over the threshold the door closed noiselessly behind us.

We were in a foyer although in truth it was more like an enclosed steel cube; a disembodied but pleasant female voice invited us to remain still while we were scanned. I detected a faint humming sound; I guessed it came from whatever machinery was employed to look into our darkest secrets.

A door slid open in the steel wall in front of us and the same pleasant female voice bade us enter.

As we stepped through the door a man was hurrying down the corridor, hand outstretched to greet us; he wore a worried look and was slightly stooped as if the troubles of the world rested on his shoulders. They probably did. I recognised him immediately, it was Jim Garland the Vice-President of the United States.

'Frank was first off the mark. 'Mr Vice-President, what a surprise and an honour to see you.' He grasped his hand and shook it warmly.

'Frank, the honour is mine, there's nothing much I am able to do about stopping the progress of this killer thing, that's down to the people who really matter. People like you and Eve.'

He turned to me, on his face the worry lines were now smoothed out and a smile had replaced the frown. 'Doctor Eve James I presume,' he said in a classic Stanley/ Livingston parody.

I smiled up at him and took his proffered hand. 'Hello sir, I'm flattered you know who I am.'

'No need to feel flattered, Frank will tell you that I take a personal interest in the Genome Project and he has spoken of you often on the occasions when we have met to discuss the project's progress, funding and the like. I'm familiar with your work and in fact Frank and I not only discussed you joining the Project but I was the one to suggest to Frank that it might be a good idea for him to take you along to Geneva.'

'On that basis I feel even more flattered,' I replied as I shot a confused look at Frank who favoured me with a knowing smile.

He put an avuncular arm around my shoulders and led us down the corridor variously apologising for the liberties they had taken with us and enquiring if the flight to DC was ok.

We stopped outside an open door and he stepped aside to allow us to enter. We found ourselves in a fairly typical conference room, long table down the centre and chairs down each side with one chair positioned at the head of the table. Water, juices, tea and coffee were strategically placed.

The table was set for seven persons. The Vice-President lowered himself into the chair at the head of the table, the place reserved for the Chairperson I assumed; the VP noticed my somewhat quizzical look and explained he would chair the meeting as Sam Bartram had personal family matters to deal with. Frank and I nodded our understanding.

He motioned for us to take the places to his right. Frank started to open his mouth to say something when the other attendees entered the room; the first to enter was Frieda Lindt the Secretary of State followed by Miriam Carter, Director of Homeland Security; the two Nobel Laureates Professors Michael Banbury and Jack Lindo came in together seemingly locked in deep conversation.

They all gathered just inside the door, the VP invited them to take their seats, he suggested the Secretary of State sit to his left, then the Director of Homeland Security and next to her Professor Lindo, Professor Banbury to sit next to me.

'The meeting should be considered informal,' the VP intoned, 'if anyone requires to be addressed by their title that's ok but please refer to me as Jim, due to the sensitive nature of the discussions I don't intend that anyone should take notes but I do intend to make a recording of the proceedings and you will all receive personal copies of the recording under high security cover.

He removed a micro-recorder from his coat pocket, placed it on the table and pressed the start button.

Everyone is aware of Sam Bartram's personal tragedy and since he now has important domestic matters to attend to the President asked me to take the chair. Although most of us know each other, for the sake of courtesy we should all introduce ourselves, starting with me.'

Once the intro's had been completed the VP paused as if he was wondering where he should start, everyone looked at him expectantly. 'Ladies and gentlemen, he said at last, 'I don't want to sound alarmist but it is not an exaggeration to say that the world is faced with a problem of incalculable proportions, you've all read the brief so you're aware of the position and this time there is no East – West divide, no North versus South situation, no Jewish - Muslim – Christian conflict and so far there is no indication that a nation's wealth can purchase any comfort for its citizens.

I need not repeat the high profile deaths nor the disasters that have occurred as a direct consequence of this thing we call Sudden Death Syndrome or SDS. For your information we were advised this morning by the Chinese government that the flight recorder from the King Airlines crash confirmed beyond any doubt that the cause was definitely due to both pilots falling victim to this damned scourge. Can you believe it; their deaths were a mere ninety seconds apart?

SDS has claimed Harry Hewson, Sam's brother Phil and more than a million more across the globe. As well as the deaths that can be directly attributable to SDS there have been thousands upon thousands more indirectly, as a result of disasters, accidents and civil unrest.

You saw and heard what happened recently in Jamaica, our people on the ground tell us that SDS was responsible for engineering the whole mess when it snuffed out the high-ranking mobsters and then by a quirk of fate stopped what would have been a bloodbath across the length and breadth of the island by harvesting more victims from the gangs and this time in full view of their cronies.

The Jamaican Government is still trying to understand exactly what happened and as another twist, many of the corrupt officials have been weeded out and although the drug situation is still serious the authorities are actually gaining the upper hand in their efforts to reduce narco-terrorism and the high murder rate.'

I looked around the table; everyone was listening intently as if he were delivering the world's final news bulletin.

He continued. 'It is pretty obvious where we are heading if we can't find a way to stop or slow this thing down, the nation will fall apart in a nightmare scenario that beggars the imagination. Everything this country has ever stood for will be lost as bodies pile up in homes, in workplaces and on the streets. We are literally only months away from the disintegration of civilisation, not just ours but throughout the world. Unless SDS can be brought under control every country on earth will become one big repository for rotting corpses.

With respect to you Miriam and your wonderfully dedicated staff, your department will be rendered powerless to handle the situation; oh for a few months at most you'll struggle to maintain a semblance of order as you put in your various survival plans but as your own people fall victim along with the rest of the population, those of us who remain will simply give up and seek to ensure our own survival until we too join the legion of the dead.'

'Is it really as serious as you are telling us?' asked Miriam Carter, the Director of Homeland Security. 'I'm not suggesting there is anything trivial in what we are facing but I did hear a story from a reliable source to the effect that a deadly and virulent strain of virus had escaped from a top secret lab somewhere in Europe and that it had spread from continent to continent like a Californian bush fire, fatalities very quickly followed and as the virus spread there was a concomitant increase in the numbers of deaths. The more it spreads the worse the situation becomes; it was now a case of finding an effective antidote before it develops into a full-blown pandemic.

If the report is true or close to the truth we should waste no time in closing our borders, closing the ports and airports to stop further cases being brought in, bring in the CDC for them to trace and contain whatever infections are already here and put the scientists to work finding the antidote.' She looked confidently from face to face, convinced she had the problem identified, sorted and fixed. A smile played delicately around her lips giving her a self-satisfied almost smug look.

Frieda Lindt, the Secretary of State was a glamorous lady of about forty-five, her blonde hair was cut in the latest short style, her steely blue eyes suggested an agile and incisive mind, she hadn't been appointed America's chief diplomat for nothing; she was as sharp as a box of knives. 'I've heard the same story myself Miriam and I regret to have to tell you that the truth is much, much worse than the story you heard, if it were that simple it wouldn't be necessary to have us all sat round this table today. The Vice President is not exaggerating at all when he describes the scenario we are facing; I can tell you that the consensus from those experts who are in the loop is that we face nothing less than the total extinction of the human race. Is that a fair statement?' She asked turning to the VP.

Miriam Carter squirmed a little in her seat and looked almost embarrassed with her own naiveté as Jim Garland nodded his concurrence.

'Don't feel bad Miriam,' said Garland, 'to anyone who hasn't been dealing with this thing, the truth would always seem stranger than the fiction.' And then addressing the meeting generally he said, 'and for reasons that must now be clear to you, knowledge of the existence of SDS and where it's leading us has to remain on a strictly need to know basis.' Turning back to Miriam he said. 'It never ceases to amaze me how these stories start and where they originate because the story you heard is actually very close to what has been agreed will be told to the UN's General Assembly by the Director General of the World Health Organisation. The intention is to assist those governments trying to head off trouble that has brewed or is brewing in their respective countries. Some of the countries will be only too happy to believe the story, it gives them something to tell their populations and the source is the UN, whose pronouncements are trusted more than most of the member governments. Other governments will not be taken in by the explanation and they will suspect something more sinister is being kept from them.

'Who exactly is in the loop?' asked Professor Lindo.

'Would you like to take that one Miriam?' asked Garland.

'The Ambassadors representing those countries which are Permanent Members of the UN Security Council; the Presidents, Prime Ministers, Foreign Ministers and Heads of State of the same countries; the Secretary General of the UN; the Director General and Deputy Director General of the WHO; Professor Jacques Rombert the Head of the Pasteur Institute; Professor Ron Davies the Head of Genetics at Oxford University; Prof Burke and Dr James, myself and now the rest of you around this table.'

' We believe that confidentiality has held so far,' said Garland,' but two things in particular are quite worrying to us; firstly, and very soon, we'll probably have to say something closer to the truth to some of those countries that just won't buy the preferred story, like Canada, Australia and the EU countries and secondly the credibility of the story will be short-lived because of the speed at which SDS is moving. The 'escaped deadly virus story' probably has a shelf life of about six months, so if the scientists fail to get a handle on this thing soon we will all be overtaken by the inevitable developments and God help us because the alternatives are simply too frightening to contemplate.'

'Do you have an immediate plan of action?' asked Frank. 'And is it something that has been agreed with our partners?'

'Yes there is of sorts, although you'll understand that with a situation as dynamic as this, when things could change almost from one minute to the next, different countries are going to experience developments at different times; for example, the more undeveloped and volatile the country, the quicker they'll experience breakdowns in law and order and dislocation to what passes for normalcy in their neck of the woods.

It's likely that the response from the authorities will be swift and cruel but it won't last for very long, their army and police force won't be able to sustain any lengthy suppression of the population because their numbers will become progressively depleted rendering them incapable, panic will inevitably rear its head, first in the cities but then spreading everywhere and whatever passes as cohesion in society will quickly disintegrate and the country will experience a very painful death.

We expect that countries like our own where generally speaking there is respect for law and order, will manage to hang on to its sanity for only a little bit longer but we too will eventually succumb to the same panic in our population, our security forces likewise, will be unable to control the deteriorating situation, the law of the jungle will preside across the nation and ultimately we will suffer the same fate as the rest of the world, we will become a country totally devoid of human life.'

The words were heavy and I inwardly winced and their meaning was all too clear and in the silence that immediately followed the Vice-President's statement, they still commanded the attention of us all.

'But returning to your question Frank, regardless of all I have said, yes we do have a plan for going forward and we will follow it as best we are able. Let me tell you what it is because that's the real reason we're all here and the fact that each of you has an important part to play in it.'

I thought that this was how the generals must have felt in the Second World War as they waited for General Eisenhower to brief them before going into battle. I was tense, alert, even afraid but ready and willing to do my duty. It was a strange feeling for me and I realised I had unconsciously sat up straighter in my chair, had I been stood I was sure I would have been at attention. We all waited with bated breath.

'On Wednesday, that's tomorrow, Professor Yasmine Patel, Director General of the WHO will inform the entire General Assembly of the escaped virus story, for your information, Moscow has agreed to be the fall guy. The Professor will tell them that it causes instant death and is undetectable at autopsy..........' He gave them the same story Frank and I had got from Sam Bartram two days previously but I still listened intently, hoping I might convince myself to believe the lie because as horrendous as it was, it was infinitely preferable to the truth.

'Remember,' he continued, 'the real purpose of this story is to give the scientists some breathing space to do their work before,...well you know what. Also we hope it will buy some time for those governments with baggage. Not that we have an interest in propping up corrupt regimes but right now instability anywhere in the world is to be avoided, the ground is already fertile in too many countries for militant groups to take up arms and believe me it would take very little to light the fuse that would plunge large parts of the world into all out war.

As for Uncle Sam, this is what we're going to do, first we'll establish a 'Monitoring and Co-ordinating Group' chaired by me; the membership will be the Chairman of the Joint Chiefs, you Linda and you Miriam, Professors Banbury and Lindo,' he nodded in their direction, 'the Head of the CDC and Sam Bartram.

The Joint Chiefs will advise the committee on what is happening in the armed forces both from a military perspective and from an internal perspective; Linda, your job will be to keep your finger on the world's political pulse, you'll provide an update on the international situation, we're particularly concerned at what the North Koreans and Iranians might be tempted to try; Miriam will report on what's happening at home.

And now our three professors, I want you to form yourselves into a sub group, Professor Banbury will liaise with those scientists in France and England who are working on this project, he will keep the sub group informed of what is happening across the pond, Professor Lindo will liaise with Professor Burke and his team and meet with Prof Banbury to compare notes and provide status reports to Prof Burke.' He paused as if to collect his breath before continuing, 'Frank, as the head of our scientific team you carry the hopes of the nation on your shoulders; you will devote all your time and energies to finding a solution to SDS, if you need anything, whether it's funding, equipment, supplies and the like, please submit your request directly to me, I'll make sure you don't encounter the usual red tape and you get what you want without any delays. I think that's everything, are there any questions?' He looked expectantly from face to face.

'How often will this committee meet?' asked Ms Lindt.

'Initially, every two weeks and we'll meet here but time place and frequency could change as the situation develops.'

'If I might just add,' said the Secretary of State, 'all our partners on the Security Council are aware of our plans as we are of theirs. We are all working together in an unprecedented show of co-operation. No one is holding anything back, we all realise that our future survival, in fact the survival of the human race depends on absolute mutual trust and co-operation. We have systems in place to ensure a swift and smooth flow of information.

Professor Banbury will have a counterpart in Paris and London who will feed back information to their respective monitoring groups and we will all exchange minutes of our respective meetings.'

'Thanks for that Linda, just two more things before we end the meeting, first the need to maintain absolute secrecy, no one must know of the existence of this group and what it's working on and second, recognising the reality of the situation, we will need to identify a successor for each of you, if you have any suggestions on who this could be please let me know. You will be advised within the next two days of whom that person is but they won't be informed or given the slightest indication of the work we are involved in, should the time arise when their presence is needed they will be given a dossier that will explain everything. Of course we understand that we should also nominate a successor for them as well, and another and another but…' he gave a shrug of his shoulders and an imperceptible shake of his head. 'Is there anything else anyone wants to say?' We looked almost furtively at each other hoping for a reaction, a protest that things were not half as bad as was being suggested but I think we were all aware of the truth and no one was in the mood to make platitudinous statements. 'No?' 'OK, let's get to work, Frank would you and Eve wait a minute please?'

Everyone silently filed out leaving the three of us at the table.

'What do you think Frank, any ideas?' asked Garland.

'I've thought of little else since Eve and I arrived for our first meeting at the WHO, I've run a thousand programmes through my mind based mainly on what Sam Bartram told us and the video-linked meetings we had with Paris and Oxford. Eve and I were also given a graphic and harrowing account by Valdez's assistant Maier of the deaths of his wife and son. Of course, I haven't seen any clinical reports regarding autopsies and the like and I haven't had the opportunity yet to examine tissue samples and do any genetic sequencing analyses at Duke but regardless of all that we are obviously dealing with a unique situation here, something I haven't been able to get my mind around. What about you Eve, any first thoughts?'

'I've been giving it a little thought as well, I haven't tried too much to speculate what might be causing it, I mean, if Pasteur and Oxford haven't come up with anything yet and they've had the opportunity to do a bit of what Frank and I need to get into to, then I figured it would be an exercise in futile speculation for me to hypothesize on what the cause and solution might be. Instead I've been trying to find a different angle, see if there were any parallels we could draw on.

At first my mind kept couldn't get out of the present, It kept returning to what was happening in the here and now and every time I chased it down I kept coming up against a brick wall and I couldn't get around it.

Something told me the problem was not unique and that I needed to open my eyes because I wasn't seeing the wood for the trees and then it hit me, like Paul on the road to Damascus. Of course it had happened before, in fact thousands of times before, it came to me that the human race was treading the same path thousands of species had trodden before us, the path to extinction.

Think about it, more than ninety percent of all the species that have ever existed have become extinct, some, like the dodo were hunted to extinction by man whilst others became victims of such things as climate shifts or environmental changes that affected their habitat and the food chain but literally thousands of species have simply disappeared from the face of the earth for no reason we know of, they just died out as if it were part of the natural scheme of things.

Maybe that's what's happening to us as a species, we're dying out, our time has come, we are on the same path many others have gone down before. I mean why is it that we should be different from any other species? We're mammals with a genetic make up that is basically the same as our fellow creatures, sure we have a more developed intelligence and intellect than any other species that have been before us but that doesn't mean of itself that we have anymore right to survival than they had.' I was suddenly aware that Frank and the VP were regarding me intently and I felt uncomfortable under their gaze.

'That's an interesting idea Eve' said Garland, plainly discomfited by my contribution 'but not something we would want to share with our colleagues either here or elsewhere. What do you say Frank, a story like that might not strike the right chord with some others?'

Frank shot me a look that suggested I should keep such fanciful stories to myself and maybe change my bedtime reading habits. Even so, like a knight of old, he rode to the rescue of his damsel in distress. 'Eve was only indulging in lateral thinking; a rich and inquisitive mind is an essential tool of all scientists. We must never dismiss a notion just because it's unpleasant, if we're going to beat this thing we will have to consider every possibility; even if Eve's musings were true, given our higher intelligence and superior intellect, we could well discover a way to halt the march of SDS and either neutralise it or reverse its progress. Eve's original thinking, or something very much like it, will in all probability forge the key that eventually unlocks the problem.'

I was grateful to Frank for his intervention and support but disappointed that it was necessary; I had expected better from the Vice President, his response had been almost petulant and childlike.

'Yes I see what you mean and of course you scientists must consider every angle and every option but I'd be grateful if at this stage you would confine those kinds of discussions to meetings of the scientific intelligentsia. I can already sense the tension in some of those people who are privy to the information, as time goes on and no solution is found, with the inevitable consequences, I can see the defensive facades some of us have erected beginning to crumble and then what?'

He didn't pause he wasn't expecting an answer. 'Now let's get down to the real business,' another jab at me I guessed, 'let me have a list of all the things you need for you to do whatever it is you need to do. Whether its equipment, staff, access to people, files or reports; just about anything you want you can have. The President is very clear as to the threats we face and the timeframe we must work with, he has personally instructed that nothing must stand in your way, there must be no impediment to you finding a solution.'

'Well Jim the first thing I need to do is get back to Duke and get together with Eve to work out a game plan, which will include that list of further needs. One thing is certain, I will have to call an early meeting of the team probably immediately after Professor Patel has made her presentation to the General Assembly, what she says and when she says it will enable me to provide a convincing cover story and define my expectations without raising any suspicions. This is particularly important if we are not to waste any precious time in fielding difficult questions, after all we don't need any alarm bells ringing because there is a change of direction in our focus and endeavours.'

'Good, yes I like that, you were always one for not standing on ceremony, you never did waste time on generalities and niceties, just wanting to get on with the job, that's the kind of attitude we need right now. Let me give you both my private, secure telephone number, the person who answers your call has already been given your names and will patch you straight through no matter where I am or what time of day it is.

You're both booked on this evening's flight to Raleigh, the flight leaves at seven. I've arranged for a car to be outside to take you to the airport, no private jet this time I'm afraid, you'll be traveling with the plebs; he stood and held out his hand. 'good luck Frank, you too Eve, I know it's been said before but never with more truth and feeling, your country is depending on you, perhaps even the entire world.'

We shook hands and left the room, I stopped in the doorway and half turned meaning to leave him with some reassuring words but he'd walked to a window and was stood motionless seemingly lost in his thoughts, staring through the glass into nothingness. He looked shrunken and not a little afraid. Perhaps he'd had a premonition that he would be President Garland in just a few short weeks.

CHAPTER 28

Madge opened her eyes and for one fleeting moment thought she was still somewhere in Jurassic Park watching a herd of Diplodocus traverse a lush tropical plain, their small heads slowly dipping and rising on their long slender necks, which were a perfect balance for their tails. Diplodocus means 'double beam'. Even though they were gargantuan in size they appeared graceful as they strode purposefully through the tall waving grass. The sun felt warm on her face and she could smell the richness of the vast unspoilt vista and the sounds of prehistoric earth were strange yet comforting to her ears.

But as is the case with all dream images they were all too quickly elbowed aside by reality intent on reasserting itself. Her dreamscape was quickly shredded as her bedroom wall swam into focus. She rubbed her eyes and sat up in bed, her memories of a land of fabulous creatures fading fast. She stretched her five foot two inch frame to its absolute limit and then throwing back the covers she swung her legs out of bed and onto the carpeted floor.

She thought of the things she had to do shower, dress, and breakfast then out to the British Museum to identify her specimens. Once she identified what she wanted she would give the information to the Assistant Curator's office and they would arrange delivery to her Oxford University lab.

The bathroom was soon filled with steam as Madge stepped under the hot water spray; she hummed one of her non-descript tunes as she luxuriated in the warmth. Her mum had always referred to her as a hothouse plant, a tropical flower and she smiled at the memory. She decided she was feeling good today, impulsively she snatched her yellow plastic duck off the soap tray, she called him Quackers and they had been inseparable after her dad had given it to her for a fourth birthday present and gave him an exaggerated kiss on his faded blue beak. 'Who loves ya baby?' She asked the duck. He didn't respond. 'Well no time to waste, needs must when the Devil drives,' she told herself as she toweled herself dry, 'cornflakes and then out.'

She shrugged into an old pair of faded jeans and a tee shirt that said 'Ask Me I Might' on the front, donned a pair of ankle-length socks, slipped into her sneakers and felt ready to face the world. She looked gorgeous; she would have in sackcloth and ashes.

Madge made her way to the museum by way of the underground. She loved the area of Bloomsbury where the museum was located, it had many lovely old Victorian properties, some surrounded a small park that was like an oasis in middle of this great English metropolis; walking through this old and lovely part of London she could easily imagine a door opening and there would be Eliza Doolittle, Professor Higgins and Colonel Pickering coming out onto the doorstep. 'Ere, dawn't you be sow saucy!' She could almost hear Eliza addressing her ageless protagonists.

She was soon walking through the museum's entrance and making for the admin office where she would collect her security badge that would allow her access to the museum's hinterlands.

'Hi Percy!' Madge cheerfully called out to the elderly security guard.

'Mornin' Miss,' he replied, you're lookin' real nice this morning, truth is you look real nice every mornin'.'

'I'll bet you say that to all the ladies.'

'Naw Miss, only them what's as pretty as you.'

Madge pressed the button outside the Admin Office door and spoke into the speaker grill to announce her presence. There was an audible click and she pushed the door open and went in. 'Good morning everybody, lovely day today,' she said as she breezed in. The response from the office staff, or more appropriately lack of it, suggested they were less ebullient than Madge on the merits of the day so far.

'Here Madge take your ID and go cheer up someone else,' Sally admonished. Sally was the Office Supervisor. She handed Madge a clip-on badge that said 'Unlimited Access'.

She took the badge and exited the room as breezily as she had entered.

CHAPTER 29

The nether regions of the museum were reached via a staircase that led from the ground floor to a basement containing dozens of rooms of various sizes; fortunately she was armed with a list of the contents of each of the rooms that would be of interest to her, the task of identifying her precious samples would have been impossible without it.

She now knew exactly what she was looking for and once her friend Percy opened the door to the staircase for her, she would home in unerringly on the targeted samples.

Her first port of call was Room 3; it contained many fossilized remains of species that no longer graced the land and oceans of the world. Madge thought it extremely depressing to think that so many creatures that had once called the earth home, sometimes for tens of millions of years, now no longer existed, had for reasons no one knew disappeared from the planet for good. This unhappy thought occurred to her as she descended the stairs, it blunted the good feelings she had had since kissing Quackers earlier in the day.

Room 3 was the second room on the left and from where she was standing the interior was dark and gloomy but as soon as she crossed the threshold the lights automatically came on bathing everything in a soft yellow illumination.

A walkway ran down the middle of the room with hermetically sealed display cabinets running down the two side walls. Each cabinet was numbered and contained a fossilized specimen; the number identified the type of fossil and which animal it had come from. Madge could cross-reference the number against her list.

She scanned the cabinets on her left looking for number 77. It was located about half way into the room, second cabinet from the bottom, she peered through the glass window, checked the number again and looked at her list to make sure everything corresponded, it did, she had just located her first specimen.

The fossil was part of the jawbone of an Auroch, a long-horned breed of wild cattle; it had been depicted in numerous cave drawings and had survived in Poland until 1627 then it disappeared from sight, presumably becoming extinct. Having satisfied herself that the specimen was the one she needed, she ticked a box against the number on her list and left the room. The lights went out.

She checked her sheet again and confirmed she was now looking for Room 15. There it was, a little further down, which was where she would find her second and third samples. She entered the darkened room and was greeted with light; she quickly made her way to cabinet numbers 3 and 4.

Cabinet 3 contained fossilized specimens of a Wooly Mammoth and Cabinet 4 those of its close relative the Mastodon. These cousins of the modern day elephant had disappeared after the last Ice Age, about sixteen thousand years ago.

What was interesting about the Mammoth was that some of these beasts had been found frozen in the Siberian Tundra with food still in their mouths and with undigested food in their stomachs. This suggested that they had been eating grasses by a frozen riverbank when they all had spontaneously died on the spot and fell down dead, as if their lives had suddenly been switched off.

Their carcasses would have frozen very quickly in the sub-zero temperatures and then stored in Mother Nature's vast deep freezer. Why they had suddenly died no one knew.

She again ticked the appropriate box on her list and moved on to Rooms 18 and 22. Room 18 contained the fossilized specimens of a Great Auk, a marine diving bird from Northern Europe; the last one had reportedly been seen in 1844. Room 22 housed the fossilized remains of a Smilodon, better known as the Sabre-toothed Tiger. These creatures resembled modern day tigers but were gigantic in size with long curving, wickedly sharp canine teeth; many of them had died in the California Tar Pits thousands of years ago.

Feeling extremely happy with her haul Madge ticked the final two boxes on her list. Now it was just a case of returning the list to Sally in Administration for processing, the museum would arrange for the specimen to be delivered to Oxford and then the real work could start.

Her good mood had fully re-asserted itself by the time she was climbing the steps to the upper floor and in keeping with her mood she unconsciously hummed another of her non-descript tunes.

She pushed the bar on the door at the top of the stairs and exited into the museum proper, Percy was nowhere to be seen. She made her way to the Admin Office and paused at the door before pushing the buzzer, she could hear someone crying. She pushed the buzzer. The door lock clicked and she went through. Sally was sat at her desk silent and as white as a sheet, Betty, one of the clerks was stood with her arm around the shoulders of a colleague who was sat in a chair weeping. Madge was alarmed.

'What's happened?' She asked.

'It's Percy.' Sally responded in robotic fashion.

'What about Percy, what's happened to him?' The seated woman sobbed louder.

'He's dead,' intoned Sally.

'Dead, how can he be dead? I only spoke with him not an hour ago.'

Betty took up the story, as Sally seemed to lose focus. 'He, Percy that is, came into the office for his usual eleven o'clock cup of tea, you could set your watch by him, never a minute early, never a minute late, always eleven o'clock on the dot.' Madge shifted her feet impatiently wanting Betty to get on with it. 'He was stood next to Hilda,' Hilda was obviously the lady sobbing because Betty silently mouthed something and nodded in her direction, 'talking about his family he was, I think it was something to do with his granddaughter starting a new school and how he was worried about her settling in.'

Madge had to make an effort to restrain herself from telling Betty to stop prattling and get on with it. Betty continued, 'you know how he was, Percy, he adored his grandchildren, I think he had five, yes that's it he did have five, two granddaughters and three grandsons, he talked about them…' It was as much as Madge could stand.

'Betty, stop prattling and tell me what has happened to Percy? I don't need to have a blow-by-blow account of his relationships with his grandkids. Now please get to the point.'

Betty looked hurt and Madge could have bitten her tongue for showing her frustration but she needed answers not a sermon. Thankfully Sally found her voice. 'It's like Betty says, Percy came in for his cuppa, he was stood cup in hand talking, when the cup and saucer suddenly crashed to the floor and Percy crumpled in a heap to the floor as well. Just like that,' she snapped her fingers, 'one second he was telling us about Suzie's new school, the next he was on the floor dead.' Madge was incredulous. 'We called 999 and they sent an ambulance, it was here in quick time but it was obvious he was a gonner. The medics took one look at him and knew, they felt for a pulse, I suppose they have to but we could all see he'd gone.'

Madge was speechless, her friend Percy dead? It seemed unreal. She managed to recover her voice. 'Had he been ill?' She asked. Sally and Betty just shook their heads and Hilda continued to sob.

'No,' said Sally, 'I've been here at this job for the past five and a half years and Percy was already here when I arrived and I don't remember him having even a day's sick leave.'

'There was the time he hit his thumb with a hammer when he was knocking that nail in the ladies loo so we could hang a little picture on the wall,' Betty couldn't help herself, 'it always looked so bare in there just plain white walls and they show dirt so easily. I suggested they change the colour to…'

'Oh do be quiet,' said Hilda finding her voice at last, 'who the hell wants to know about the colour of the walls in the ladies loo?'

'Alright I'm sure,' said Betty, determined to have the last word, 'I was only trying to say he had had a day off but I suppose it doesn't count because he wasn't sick.'

Madge's feelings of bonhomie had by now totally evaporated and all of a sudden her specimen list didn't seem quite so important. Percy dead, she could hardly believe it and yet there had been several news reports of people dying suddenly. There had been two senior American politicians who had suddenly died only the other day and then there was the plane crash in Hong Kong when both pilots had suffered heart attacks at about the same time. Even her own mother had gone the same way. She wondered sparingly if there could be a connection but how could there be, and Percy was getting on and had probably suffered a heart attack, nothing unusual in that, especially at his age. 'Still'… Her thoughts tapered off without becoming properly formed and defined.

'I'm devastated,' said Madge. And she was.

'Sally, I realise my timing could be better but I have deadlines to meet and I'm already behind with my project, I don't mean to be disrespectful to Percy or anything like that but can I leave my fossil specimen list with you and ask you to arrange for them to be delivered to Oxford?'

'Yes love, of course you can,' Sally had recovered her equilibrium 'you not finishing your project won't bring Percy back. Here let me see it.'

Madge passed it to her and she quickly glanced through it. 'This is fine my love, let's see, today's Tuesday, I'll try and arrange to have it to you by, hmm, Friday. How will that suit you?'

'That would be great Sally,' Madge said with a smile of gratitude, I'll tell the college reception to expect them. Listen, let me know when and where the funeral is, I wouldn't want to miss it.'

'Will do Madge and try not to get too depressed, Percy wouldn't approve.'

'Thanks Sally. Hilda, Betty, I'd better be off, bye everybody.'

She walked out into the reception area of the museum; the place seemed diminished without Percy. Her mood had turned sombre, Bloomsbury didn't look half as nice and the sounds of London were strangely muted. 'Is it my imagination,' she thought, 'or is there some connection between these sudden deaths, and is mom's death part of some strange pattern that's just starting to show itself?' Madge determined to be more alert to reports of sudden and premature deaths, she realised only the more prominent members of society would have their demises reported on but at least it was a starting point.

The more she thought about it, the more convinced she became that there was something that didn't quite ring true and she was not stupid enough to believe that the politicians were always forthcoming with information they'd rather keep from the masses and if that were true she thought she might not want to know what it was.

CHAPTER 30

THE NEW YORK TIMES – Wednesday 30 November.
NEW STRAIN OF FLU VIRUS ESCAPES MOSCOW LAB, MANY PUT AT RISK HEAD OF W.H.O. SAYS NO NEED TO PANIC.
By Desmond Willerby, Medical Correspondent.

Professor Yasmine Patel, Director General of the World Health Organisation addressed the General Assembly of the United Nations in New York yesterday. She told them that the number of sudden deaths that have reportedly occurred recently in different parts of the world have been attributed to a mutated flu virus that escaped from a laboratory in Moscow several months ago. Apparently several viral samples were in the process of being made ready for sending to labs in California, Geneva and Paris when the security of one of the samples was compromised resulting in the virus escaping.

She said she wanted to stress that the incident was not terrorist related but a genuine accident; new measures have been put in place to ensure there would be no repetition in the future. She gave no further details on how the accident happened.

The virus is the same as the one that had caused more than half a million deaths in the nineteen fifties pandemic when it had been known as the Hong Kong flu virus, however, it had now been genetically modified in the Moscow lab to enable a new generation of flu vaccines to be produced. The labs to which the samples were being sent were working on this new vaccine. She said that the WHO had been responsible for the supervision of the project.

Influenza remains a major cause of death throughout the world, attacking especially the elderly, the infirm and the very young. Because of the virus' ability to mutate naturally, the challenge to medical science is to try and keep one step ahead in order to identify new vaccines as a defence against the new mutated strains. The WHO-inspired project was designed to produce a new super vaccine that would be able to respond to any mutation by being able to mimic the virus' genetic code and kill the virus before it was able to infect the host.

Professor Patel stated she had no wish to trivialise what had happened and commiserated with the families of the victims but she stressed that there was no need for panic as the WHO would be working in close collaboration with health authorities in all member countries to contain the spread of the virus. She said indications were that there was a slowing down of reported incidents of what was now referred to as 'Sudden Death Syndrome' or SDS for short.

She stated that the virus had a short incubation period and victims didn't always exhibit the usual classic flu symptoms, infection was not always debilitating and was rarely fatal; nothing in fact to compare with the tens of thousands of deaths that result from the usual annual influenza outbreaks.

She stressed that many infected persons had made speedy and full recoveries having suffered only mildly sore throats and slight rises in body temperature. Some of those who had died had appeared to do so without warning, they had seemed fine one minute, and then had died the next, this was tragic and distressing but was not untypical of the pattern that followed exposure and initial infection.

Many governments from developing countries can now breath collective sighs of relief because although the situation is worrying in the extreme, at least the rise in sudden deaths that they have been experiencing can now be attributed to natural causes and not to some sinister government-inspired plot as had been claimed by opponents of the regimes.

Prime Minister Yussuf Mohammed of Bangladesh responded quickly to Professor Patel's statement by saying his government felt vindicated, as rural opponents of his regime had accused the his government of targeting the rural population by amongst other things, poisoning their water supplies because they had been vocal in their opposition to government policies regarding controversial legislation on land ownership and crop selection and production. This had led to riots throughout rural townships and protest marches in the capitol Dhaka.

In a joint press release the governments of Israel and Palestine reaffirmed their 'Friendship Pact' after relations had reached breaking point following claims by Palestinian leaders that the Israeli government had encouraged settlers to do whatever they deemed necessary to protect their water supplies. The claim was that settlers had added poison to the supply.

The Israeli government and the settlers had always strenuously denied the accusation and subsequent tests on the water supply supported the denial but some militants had refused to accept the findings of the UN chemists who carried out the tests saying it was a US contrived result.

The joint release said both governments were of the view that their refusal to react to the militant's claims had been vindicated by the Director General's statement to the General Assembly.

In yet another release the Australian government said they welcomed the Director General's statement but felt there were still gaps that needed to be filled in. They said they looked forward to working with the WHO to stop the spread of SDS and pledged their country's assistance in the quest to find the super vaccine referred to in the presentation.

Edmundo Rostronio, a spokesperson for Argentina's Department of Health said they wanted to study the content of the presentation in more detail before commenting

The New York Times feels the Government of India, not to mention a clutch of African dictators, must have slept a little easier in their beds last night given the levels of social unrest they have been experiencing.

See Editorial comment on page 10.

THE CHINESE PEOPLES' DAILY – Thursday 1 December

SUPER BUG ESCAPES MOSCOW LAB, W.H.O. SAYS NO NEED TO PANIC.

By Y. Lieu

Professor Yasmine Patel WHO's Director General, reported to the UN General Assembly on Tuesday that a new strain of influenza virus had managed to escape from a lab in Moscow and had infected a number of people across the world. She said there was no need for undue alarm as her staffs were working with the health authorities of member states' to stop the spread of the virus.

The Peoples Congress passed a motion endorsing the WHO's handling of the matter and pledged to co-operate in any way appropriate.

CHAPTER 31

Frank and I climbed into the back of the automobile and were soon on our way to the airport.

I sat there, my body tense and as tight as a coiled spring, thoughts racing around my head at a thousand miles an hour, I didn't feel in control of the situation and I didn't like the feeling one bit. 'I can't believe how my life has turned upside down in such a short space of time,' I said, 'it seems like one minute I was in the familiar surroundings of my lab enjoying life to the full, every second of what I was doing was precious and fulfilling and the next, I'd been catapulted into a story more appropriate to a science fiction thriller with me as one of the central characters. The trouble is I didn't like the plot and the villain of the piece had no name and no face and it threatened not only my family and me but also the very existence of the human race. That in itself sounded outrageous, I mean how is it possible, everything inside of me screams it can't be happening but on an intellectual level I know that it is. Worst of all there is nowhere for me to run. I mean how do you confront an enemy you can't see or touch and don't know where it will strike next?'

Frank didn't answer immediately, he well understood the seriousness of the situation and weighed his words carefully before responding. 'In my experience the answer to these types of problems is often staring you in the face but you're so intent in looking for a complex solution to what you believe to be a complex problem, you end up not seeing the wood for the trees.

The thing about this particular problem is that with Pasteur, Oxford and ourselves all working on it we won't be in any danger of ploughing a lone furrow, thinking it's taking us ever closer to the solution when all the time we are getting farther and farther away, as might have been the case if we were the only ones involved. Because the others are in it too, we'll be able to think laterally and pursue lines of thought and experimentation we might otherwise feel was a luxury or worse, a waste of time.

The other good thing is that thanks to Prof Banbury's co-ordination efforts, we'll be keeping each other informed of what we're up to and won't run the risk of chasing down dead end streets that one of us has already travelled.'

'You know Frank, that's one of the things I like about you; you always seem unflappable when the problem appears to be insoluble and you're able to put things into a scientific context and identify the way forward. I'm sat here worrying about all kinds of things and you've already established your vision as to how we'll set out our stall. I bet you've decided which members of the team will undertake what tasks and what you hope to achieve in a given timeframe, I'd even wager that your first report to the Vice President is all but written in your mind.'

'Eve, you make me sound almost machine-like. The only thing I have more than you is age and with age comes experience and with experience comes ability to handle things that you've basically been exposed to before. Time will equip you just as well as it has me.'

'That's one of the main things that worry me Frank; time is something we may not have. And that brings me to my next point, what about Bill and Wendy and Suzanne, what's going to happen to them? Suppose they die before I do, I can't bear even to think about it? The situation itself is bad enough but the randomness of the victims is something else again. I know I've said it before I'll say it again, I'm frightened; no not frightened, I'm terrified. In fact I'm so damned terrified I don't even know whether I can be any use to you. Maybe you need some one who is stronger than me.'

'Listen to me Eve, let me tell you why you are perfect as my right hand, firstly, because of Bill and the kids you have a major vested interest in finding a solution to this thing and you'll leave no stone unturned in your quest for answers; secondly, if anything should happen to me, there is no one better qualified than you to carry the work forward and if something happens to both of us, then God help us.'

I put my head on Frank's shoulder and wept silently. The tears ran hot down my cheeks.

I used to think that the worst thing I could ever imagine happening to me was to be buried alive, I had shared that morbid fear with Poe for as long as I could remember but the thing that confronted me now was infinitely worse. I wanted to kick and scream and claw at something, to fight until I could fight no more but then fight again anyway. But there wasn't anything or anyone to fight; this thing wasn't made of flesh and blood but it was good to give it substance, to think of it in terms as a cowardly being, unwilling to confront me face to face. O f course I realised it was silly of me to think in these terms but giving it enemy status, something tangible I could almost grasp, made the concept of dealing with it that much easier.

I figured Bill and the twins had to be OK because I was certain a 'change in their status' would have been reported to me. I wanted to ring Bill so badly, I needed to hear his voice but I was afraid, I'd never been good at lying, especially to Bill but I would have to become an expert now because it had been made very clear that talking about Sudden Death Syndrome to unauthorised persons was way off the radar screen.

Frank seemed to read my thoughts. 'Eve, why don't you telephone Bill you must be desperate to hear his voice, talk to the girls; you're not being deceitful when you tell him a story that differs slightly from the truth; in fact I don't believe you'd tell him the entire truth even if you could. Why would you want to put that horror story on him, you know how you feel about how this could affect them, well Bill would feel no different, he'd only worry himself to death over something that neither of you have the slightest control over?

And in any case he will have heard about Prof Patel's speech at the UN, so just tell him that your new task is related to what she had been talking about, that way you wouldn't be telling a lie because you are working on that very same issue.'

I realised the truth of Frank's remarks so I decided to make a brief call to Bill, just to satisfy myself that he and the girls were fine but before I could the car was pulling up at 'Departures', I would have to wait until we were in the Departure Lounge.

It took no time to check in and we wasted no time in going straight to the Departure Gate. We had an hour before the flight time so I made my way to a quiet corner of the airport and keyed in our home number on my cell phone.

'Hola,' it was Wendy, she'd just started Spanish at school and wanted to impress at every opportunity. The sheer innocence of her voice brought a lump to my throat.

'Hi darling,' I said, 'my what a clever girl you are speaking Spanish.'

'Mommy, Mommy,' she yelled, Spanish suddenly forgotten, 'where have you been, why haven't you telephoned, when are you coming home?'

'Daddy, daddy!' chorused another voice behind the first. 'It's Mommy!' 'Let me speak to her Wendy.'

'Don't grab the phone when I'm still talking.'

'Girls, girls, where are your manners? I thought you were ladies, and ladies don't behave like two dogs fighting over a bone; you'll both be able to speak with Mommy but let me say something to her first.'

'OK,' said Wendy.

'Alright,' said Suzanne.

I guessed the phone was being surrendered but only with great reluctance. And then he was there Bill, wonderful Bill, and his voice sounding strong and very reassuring.

'Hi honey, we've missed you; I thought maybe you'd been kidnapped by the CIA to keep you from spilling State secrets. How are you, or maybe the question should be, where are you? But before you answer I just want to tell you that I love you so very much.'

I wanted to throw my arms around him and hug him and kiss him and tell him how much I loved him, the moment was so intense it frightened me. The truth was I was scared to death of losing him. For the first time in a long time I thought of King Cyclops, leering at me from the top of Mount Olympus with a look on his face that suggested he knew a lot more than I did.

'Banish the thought!' I mentally yelled at myself. 'Bill, I'm real sorry I haven't been able to talk to you, it wasn't intentional but unbelievable things have been happening, so much so that I've hardly been able to keep pace with events and I was told that the authorities would assure you that I was fine but I'm coming home now and I'll tell you about it when I get there. For now you'll just have to be satisfied with your wife telling you she thinks you are the most wonderful man in the world and loves you with every fibre in her body. Oh Bill I do, I love with a passion I can't wait to show you.'

'Whoa, what's this, telephone sex? Hm, I love it when you talk dirty.'

'Bill!' I admonished, 'don't let the girls hear you.'

'Hey don't panic, they're not around.'

'Listen honey, Frank and I are at Ronald Regan and we'll be boarding the plane for home in about half an hour. If you can wait that long for me I promise to make the wait well worthwhile.'

'For you I'd wait till hell freezes over.'

'There's no need to wait that long, I'll be there before you know it. Until then just know that I love you more than life itself.'

'I know they say that absence makes the heart grow fonder and I guess this just about proves it. OK I'll wait but if you're not on the flight then I'm gonna send out the search parties to track you down and bring you in.'

'We have a deal, see you soon, tell the girls I'm on my way.'

We said a few more I love you's and then I disconnected, the silence in my ear was deafening.

On my way back to where I'd left Frank I stopped at the Newsstand to pick up a magazine, there were two young women of about twenty stood next to the magazine rack, one was in a real state of agitation talking loudly and excitedly, throwing her arms about in all directions, I couldn't help but overhear her.

'Three people Sadie, three, that's what she said, two on Concourse A and one on C. She said she saw the one on C, said she was at the check-in when this woman at the next counter just crumpled to the ground, she was stood talking to the check-in girl one second and the next, dead on the ground. She claimed she saw it with her own eyes.'

'She must have had a heart attack,' said Sadie.

'Well I suppose that's possible but what about the other two, did they have heart attacks as well?'

'Who told you about the other two?'

'The same woman, she said one of the check-in girls told her that the woman who'd just died was the third in an hour. Third in an hour? Sorry, I don't believe in coincidences, I mean, have you ever heard of three people dying of heart attacks all at the same time and basically in the same place. Let me tell you what I think, I think they'd been exposed to something, maybe something like anthrax or some other highly toxic substance, perhaps a poison that seeped through the skin.'

'Well let me tell you what I think, I think you should have been one of the stars in that movie with Mel Gibson and Julia Roberts, what was it called, Conspiracy Theory, that was it. I mean, if they were on different concourses and were probably strangers as well, where did the substance come from that killed them? No, I'm willing to go along with the heart attack story, it makes a lot more sense; tragic yes but not impossible.'

All thoughts of 'People Magazine' left my head; whatever it was it was coming, it's assault on humanity was already well underway, I could sense its presence, feel its nearness, almost smell it and it was getting closer, moving faster, gaining speed, randomly planting its kiss of death with total impunity on victim after victim.

I walked back to Frank in something of a fugue, totally wrapped up in the conversation I had just overheard, I was so engrossed that I collided quite heavily with a well built man who was heading in the opposite direction to me, I went down like a sack of potatoes, I figured this must be what it's like to meet head on with a Mack truck. I was surprised to see the man was also in a heap on the ground, as I started to recover my senses I was dimly aware of a crowd of people staring down at the two of us. My face burned with embarrassment.

'I'm so sorry,' I started to say, realising that the collision was my fault for not looking where I was going. The man lay quite still. I raised myself up on one knee.

'Are you OK?' I asked getting to my feet. There was still no movement from my victim.

'You alright luv?' said a lady with a British accent. 'I saw the whole thing I did. That bloke just walked right into you, or maybe fell into you would be a better way of describing it. Such a big fella and you being so little, I was sure you would be hurt.'

This only added to my confusion. The man still hadn't moved, I bent down and felt for his pulse, there wasn't one. I put the side of my face to his nose and mouth area, nothing, he wasn't breathing.

'What's happened Eve?' it was Frank. 'Are you OK?'

'I'm fine Frank but he's not, he's dead.'

'Oh my gawd,' said the British lady, addressing the entire airport, 'she says he's dead. Poor geezer, I saw it all.' She had quite an audience by now. 'He must have died just before he walked into you,' she was addressing me again; 'err fell into you I mean. What a terrible thing, poor man, it's a shame that's what it is.'

'Frank, you'd better find security and have this poor man's body removed from here.'

To the lady I said. 'Can you wait here a minute, you'll need to give a statement to the airport authorities?'

'Alright luv, I'm not rushin' to get back to England just yet.'

A detachment of airport security personnel was soon on the scene having been alerted by Frank, I identified myself to the supervisor and quickly gave him my story, I also pointed out the British lady and he invited the three of us into an airport security office where we both gave and signed formal statements. I explained that my flight to Raleigh would be boarding soon but he could speak to me at the university if he needed anything else.

Frank was waiting for me outside the office and we made our way to the Gate, most of the passengers were already boarding so we just joined the queue.

Frank and I were both in reflective moods, hardly surprising given the circumstances and the flight home was accomplished in relative silence.

When we exited the airport I was delighted to be greeted by Bill and the girls. Bill was stood there wearing a big grin and the twins couldn't contain themselves, they broke free from Bill's grasp and ran hell-for-leather towards me screaming, 'Mommy, Mommy!' I caught them both and hugged them so hard I was afraid I might hurt them.

'Hi darlings, it's so good to see my two little angels I've missed you so much,' I bent down and hugged and kissed them; I felt desperate and didn't want to let them go. I was paralysed by fear for their safety but I couldn't show it, Bill was sensitive to my moods and actions, the last thing I needed was to arouse his suspicions by acting out of character after all I had only been away from home for a relatively short time.

I wanted to scream with anger and frustration, how was it possible I thought, that something as horrific as this thing called SDS could enter my life unbidden and unannounced and threaten everything that I held dear. And worse, I was powerless to stop it or take any action to protect my family from it. I looked into the faces of my daughters and saw two beautiful little girls looking back at me with love in their eyes, as innocent as a brand new day and as guileless as newborn babes. I fought back the tears but I couldn't stop one single teardrop escaping and running silently and slowly down my cheek.

'Hi hon,' it was Bill, 'hi Frank, thanks for returning this most precious of packages home to me.' He slipped his arm around my waist and I snuggled close to him.

'It's good to see you Bill and in truth, I'm not sure who brought whom home, ever since we left for Switzerland, Eve has talked about nothing else but how much she was missing you and the girls and how much she was looking forward to getting home, I've never felt so neglected.'

'Yea right, since when did Eve not enjoy spending time with one of her most favourite people?'

'Alright,' I said, 'I admit, it was great being with Frank but as much as I love Frank and love my work, the thought of you guys here waiting for me to come home was a feeling beyond compare.'

'Aren't you the serious one,' said Bill, I wondered if I'd been over- reacting and Bill suspected something was amiss, 'a beautiful young woman like you should be glad to leave the old man and the kids behind now and again.' I was relieved he hadn't noticed anything.

'Where are the old man and kids you're talking about? I asked 'When I see them I might have to agree with you but in the meantime give me a big kiss and tell me you love me.'

He did, tenderly and lovingly, right there outside of the airport in full view of the world and neither of us was aware of anyone else in the cosmos.

'You are coming home with us aren't you Frank, I have a lasagne in the oven, garlic bread in the microwave and a good bottle Rose Anjou?'

'Yes Frank do come, Bill's lasagne is well worth turning up for.'

'Listen guys I really do appreciate your invite but I must take a rain check, I have to get home and start preparing for tomorrow, there's a lot of work to be done and I don't have two precious kids and someone who's been counting the minutes to my return to take my mind off things. So if you don't mind I'll decline this time but you can drop me home, I would very much appreciate that.'

Frank lived about twenty five miles from the airport and we were about another ten miles further on. The twins chatted on and on without drawing breath, I had to hear about how lonely Fred the goldfish must be and how much he needed a friend in his bowl to talk to, and that Miss Edgar the grade teacher, had told Suzanne she was very clever for being the only one in class who could spell 'chatterbox' and how there had been a hailstorm yesterday and, and, and......... Frank made all the right comments in the right places, he was great with the kids, I felt a great surge of love for him at that moment and had to catch my breath as I thought of my malevolent one-eyed god lining up his lightening rod on Frank. I physically flinched and quickly banished the thought from my mind.

'See you guys soon,' Frank called to Bill and the girls, as he retrieved his luggage, 'see you in the morning Eve.'

'Sure thing Frank.' I responded.

'Bye Uncle Frank,' the girls chorused.

'See yah Frank,' called Bill and then we headed home.

CHAPTER 32

We chatted about this and that on the way home, we seemed to have such a lot to catch up on, Bill talked about the new project he was working on and the girls gave me a blow by blow account of all that had happened in their lives during the time I'd been away. It amazed me how easily and quickly life moves on without you. I suddenly felt sorry for the parent who is separated from their children following a divorce, as much as they might want to remain a part of the day-to-day lives of their kids it simply isn't possible, life is mainly a routine and if you're not there, you can't a part of that routine no matter how hard you try. Thank God I was part of their routine but I couldn't help but wonder for how long that might be.

CHAPTER 33

It was getting quite late by the time we finished dinner, the twins were visibly tired and there were none of the usual protests when bedtime was announced. They asked for a bedtime story and I was only too happy to oblige, I got as much fun out of reading the stories as they did from listening. They chose The Gingerbread Man; it was one of my favourites as well.

Their eyes were drooping long before I got to the end so I carefully closed the book, tucked them in with a gentle kiss on their foreheads, they mumbled an inaudible 'nighty, night,' and slid silently into the Land of Nod.

I found Bill reading the newspaper in the living room. I smiled at him.

'Come over here honey,' he patted the seat next to his. I dutifully obeyed.

We sat in companionable silence for a while; I was content to feel the warmth of his body next to mine.

'Do you want to tell me about it?'

Bill's question startled me. 'Tell you about what?' I asked.

'About what it is that's troubling you that you don't want to share with me?'

I knew I couldn't fool him, I hadn't even offered him a story and he knew there was something I was hiding. I had to think quickly because I was really caught off guard this time.

I decided to stick to the story Frank and I would be giving to the team tomorrow morning, I hoped it would sound convincing. I took a deep mental breath.

'I am worried Bill, the Director General of the World Health Organisation is delivering a speech to the General Assembly of the United Nations today, she's going to report that a mutated flu virus has escaped from a lab in Moscow, the virus is particularly virulent and has been responsible for causing widespread deaths throughout the world. It's the same virus that killed the two airplane captains on the King Airline's flight that crashed into the sea on its approach to Hong Kong airport. It's also been responsible for many of the deaths in Bangladesh, India, the Middle East and Africa that caused widespread riots and lots of fatalities, there were even accusations of genocide against some of the governments.

Infection doesn't follow the usual pattern, in fact victims are often unaware that they're infected at all, they appear to be fine one second and then dead the next.' I was sticking to the Party line and I hoped that Bill was buying it; my emotions were a mixture of regret and relief.

'Hold on, back up, let me get this right; this virus is everywhere, it strikes at people randomly, they don't know they've been infected, they're fine one second and then dead the next?'

'Yep, that's about it; nastiest little thing around.' I tried to sound flippant.

'How widespread is it?'

'It's pretty much everywhere.'

'Is it here, in America?'

'Yes it is, it's on all the continents.'

'How many deaths have there been?'

'No one knows, in truth they don't have a clue but on a worldwide basis it probably runs into the tens of thousands,' I couldn't tell him the real figure was more likely in the millions. 'The presence of the virus is undetectable, even when an autopsy has been carried out, so a Medical Examiner who was unaware of the virus' existence would find it impossible to identify the cause of death but after the DG's report today, they will be able to tell that it was Sudden Death Syndrome, or SDS for short. The give-a-way is how death is observed to have occurred, as I said previously, here one second, gone the next, only SDS behaves that way.'

I looked at Bill and could tell he was stunned, after a while he found his voice. 'That's one of the most frightening things I've ever heard, it really is, it creates hostages to fortune of all of us; if I understand what you're saying we're helpless against the virus, there are no warnings that tell us when we're in close proximity to it, unless of course we happen to see someone suddenly drop down dead in front of us and finally there's no protection from infection. Have I got it right? Oh, and there's every likelihood that it's here, in our neighbourhood.'

'Yes Bill you're right; as I said previously I'm worried, when you hear of something like this you have to be. I've been to several meetings over the past few days, all of them about SDS; in Switzerland Frank and I talked by video link to two teams of scientists, one at the Pasteur Institute and the other at Oxford University, they're both working on the problem but without success so far. That's where we come in, the World Health Organisation wants us to join the effort in finding some answers that will hopefully lead to the identification of a vaccine.'

'What about the Human Genome Project, will that continue in some other form or another?'

'No, all the resources will be channelled to finding answers to the SDS problem. I haven't been able to tell you and in fact I'm not even sure I'm supposed to but when Frank and I got back to New York we were immediately taken to meet with Sam Bartram, the President's good friend and special advisor and while we were talking with him the telephone rang and it was the President, he had rang to tell him that his brother had died at a fund raising dinner.'

'Yes I read about it.'

'Well apparently it was SDS. From there we were taken by private jet to Washington where we attended a meeting chaired by Jim Garland…'

'THE Jim Garland, the Vice-President?'

'The same, there were several others there as well including the Secretary of State and the Director of Homeland Security.' Bill looked incredulous; I'd started so I decided to press on. 'Frank is to head up the scientific input of our side of the project with me as his deputy, they've also appointed a Nobel Laureate who'll be our scientific liaison with Paris and Oxford, whilst on the instructions of the President, Frank will report directly to the VP. Jim Garland said that nothing must be allowed to stand in the way of our work, and that anything we needed would be made available.' I wondered if I'd said too much but I figured it was better to drag in what was really only window dressing which hopefully would side-track Bill and deflect his attention from the more searching and for me, worrying questions.

'Tell me Eve, is there reason to panic over this SDS thing, I mean how infectious is it and is death inevitable once you're infected?'

This was a tough one, I couldn't tell him the truth but I wouldn't treat him like a child either.

'Concern is a much more appropriate word, panic suggests an out-of-control situation and we haven't reached that point yet; the rate of infection is hard to gauge, for example it isn't inevitable that because you are around someone who dies from SDS you will contract it yourself, on the other hand the number of infections can only increase until we have a treatment for it. As to the mortality rate, since in the first place you don't know you have the disease you can't know you've survived an infection, having said that, the evidence, based on viral exposure and statistical analyses, suggests that there have been many survivors.'

Bill pondered all this and I worried what his eventual reaction would be. I knew initially he would be thinking of the girls in particular and us as a family in general, then there would be the dawn of realisation as he saw the wider consequences possibly involving the US, thereafter it wouldn't be a quantum leap to recognise the worldwide implications of SDS. Finally the thought of what the consequences would be if no cure were found would worm it's way into his thought processes, at that point 'concern' would end and 'panic' would begin.

Bill's a pretty bright guy and all this would have flashed through his mind in quick time, I could almost hear the synapses in his brain connecting at the speed of light, like a super computer; eventually he said.'What do you think Eve, will a cure be found in time, or will this virus die off, disappear like Ebola or Sars as lots of other viruses do?'

'Crunch time,' I thought, the question I didn't really want asking, what I would say next would be profound in more ways than one.

The truth or a lie, that was my simple choice; if it were possible to find a cure then I had no doubt one would be found, or if not a cure at least a way of slowing the thing down, if a cure did elude us then the consequences were simply too terrible to contemplate. I decided to follow the line of least resistance, stick to the party line and make good on my promise not to divulge the full and true nature of the problem, what good would it do any way for Bill to know the truth? There was nothing he could do and he would only worry himself sick.

'With all the resources the French and British governments will be throwing at it and now our own as well, it's hard to believe a cure not being found and if not an outright cure then certainly a way of controlling the onset and progress of the disease. I feel proud to be part of the team and in Frank we have someone who has no equal in the world of genetics, if that's the avenue to be followed in the quest for a cure, Frank's the best equipped of anyone to lead the drive.'

'I'm proud too Eve, proud of you, I can only imagine the enormous responsibility that rests on your shoulders; Frank's the luckiest guy in the world to have you by his side, after me that is.'

I felt simultaneously elated and guilty; I'd managed to convey the gravity of the situation without putting the fear of God up him and without compromising my promise of maintaining strict confidentiality to the Vice President.

'Come on Bill, let's have an early night,' I said as I took his hand and led him towards the bedroom, Sudden Death Syndrome didn't seem half so important anymore. I put a mental blindfold on Brother Cyclops, what he couldn't see he couldn't harm.

Making love had never felt so good and when at last we had greedily satisfied the need and Bill's breathing told me he had journeyed to another dimension, I lay quietly by his side and cried silently. I cried for my children, I cried for my husband, I cried for my country and for my world and unashamedly, I cried for myself.

CHAPTER 34

Madge read with interest the report in the Sun newspaper, of the Director General of the World Health Organisation's presentation to the General Assembly of the United Nations regarding a mutated virus causing widespread deaths without the victims having the slightest knowledge they were infected; it made disquieting reading at the best of times but when the description of the victims' deaths read like a carbon copy of her mother's, then her attention was total. The Sun, a popular daily tabloid newspaper she had delivered every morning, referred to the disease as 'The Blight', it seemed appropriate. 'THE BLIGHT RAVAGES THE HUMAN RACE', screamed the headline. She re-read the report except more slowly this time, digesting every detail.

She never had been completely satisfied with the coroner's report on the cause of her mother's death; it was officially listed as an 'Open Verdict', which meant the autopsy had failed to identify the reason her mother had died and had left it open to speculation. At the time she had felt a great deal of pain and had been hoping the autopsy would have provided the answers she needed, she recognised that knowing the cause wouldn't have lessened the pain but at least she would have known why her mother had died and that would have helped her to accept the finality of it all but it wasn't to be. 'Open Verdict', it didn't mean a thing.

A warning bell had started to ring when Percy the guard at the British Museum had died in what had appeared to be similar circumstances as her mother. The coroner had recorded an 'Open Verdict' on him as well. Then as Madge thought more about it she remembered the newspaper reports of people dying in mysterious circumstances in a number of different countries and had even resulted in anti-government demonstrations and riots. She also remembered reading of car crashes happening as a result of drivers experiencing fatal heart attacks whilst at the wheel of their cars. And more recently there'd been the King Airline crash; the plane had come down because both pilots had fatal heart attacks at about the same time. Were all these stories just simple coincidences?

By themselves the stories amounted to little more than a string of tragic and unfortunate events but put side by side a different, even sinister picture emerged. Or did it?

'Am I on to something?' She thought, 'or is it shades of paranoia creeping in?'

She decided it had to be paranoia; after all if the World Health Organisation had identified the culprit as an escaped rogue virus, who was she to challenge their findings and yet she felt there was something sinister here, something that filled her with unease and that left her feeling dissatisfied with the explanation. Maybe it was because she was linking her mother's death with this virus when in reality no such linkage existed. It was probably part of her ongoing crusade to find an answer that would make some sense out of the tragedy, something more acceptable than 'Open Verdict'.

'I'd better not let this virus thing dominate my thoughts,' she admonished, 'I can't afford to let myself become side-tracked by paranoid thoughts, my main focus has to be the thesis and that means getting to work on the specimens when they're delivered to the lab tomorrow.'

The thought of her specimens actually being in her possession released a surge of adrenalin that sent a tingling sensation of anticipation coursing through her veins; fanciful ideas of rogue viruses were soon deposited in her mental filing cabinet and the drawer slammed shut. Instead she started to plan for the following day when her precious package would arrive.

She had already been allocated lab facilities so her first job would be to organise her research area and. set up her equipment in readiness. She had already prepared reams of research and preparatory notes, the lab work, which had a much more practical element to it, was what she was really looking forward to. She left for the university with an air of anticipation but still wearing a cloak of unease.

CHAPTER 35

THE MIAMI HERALD – Saturday 10 December

RIOTS IN CUBA THREATEN TO TOPPLE COMMUNIST REGIME

By Jamie Alvarez, Cuban Affairs Correspondent

Cuba's communist government was on the verge of collapse last night as more than an estimated two million demonstrators rampaged through the center of Havana. The Cuban armed forces were reduced to little more than spectators as they were overwhelmed by the sheer weight of numbers.

The unrest started two day's earlier as a protest against the high number of deaths that had recently occurred in the poorer areas of downtown Havana, something the authorities had been powerless to deal with. Rumors had been rife that the deaths were as a result of the ongoing crackdown on human rights activists.

Sylvia Gomez a government spokesperson strenuously denied the charges, preferring instead to put the blame on Cuban activists in Miami who have long been a thorn in the side of successive governments on the communist ruled island.

The Miami Herald has learned that the entire island has been experiencing higher than usual mortality rates and not just the more heavily populated areas of downtown Havana. Instead of playing politics by laying the blame at the door of the Miami Cubans, the government would have been better to point to the recent speech by Professor Yasmine Patel, Director General of the World Health Organisation to the General Assembly of the United Nations, when she told of a new super bug that had escaped from a lab in Moscow and was the cause of an unspecified number of deaths throughout the world.

The US is keeping a close watch on developments on the Caribbean island and has warned the left leaning Venezuelan regime not to use the unrest as an excuse to further brutalise its own people.

CHAPTER 36

I left home for the university with mixed feelings, our love making the night before had reached new heights and we had both fallen asleep exhausted but very, very happy. This morning reality had reasserted itself and I found it impossible to respond in like manner to Bill's flirtatious mood, I could tell by his sulking that he assumed I'd become absorbed in what the day held in store for me and by extension relegated him to a lesser position in the scheme of things. I'm convinced men are only boys wearing grown-up clothes, anyway what should have been a continuation of the warm and romantic feelings we'd shared only hours before, now settled into something less satisfying somehow seeming to devalue the moment.

I found it difficult to ignore the mental weight I now had to carry, I wanted desperately to share the burden, preferably with Bill, I couldn't of course and in a way I guess I begrudged him his ignorance. What do they say, 'Ignorance is bliss when it is folly to be wise'?

It was time for me to leave and given the circumstances I didn't intend to delay my departure; the twins were still sleeping and I didn't want to disturb them so I told Bill I had to be on my way, I gave him an especially hard hug, a sweet kiss on the lips, told him how wonderful he had been last night and made for the door. I'd just put my hand on the handle when Bill called my name, I turned and looked enquiringly at him, he blew me a kiss and mouthed 'I love you.' I smiled and opening the door mouthed back that I loved him too and then I was gone.

Driving down the freeway my mind was filled with many and varied thoughts, none of them particularly pleasant but there had never been anything less pleasant than SDS. I still couldn't get my mind round the fact that the human race was in danger of fading away, following so many other species into oblivion The unthinkable had become thinkable and for the umpteenth time in the last few days, fear raised it's ugly head in the pit of my stomach and sent multiple shivers up and down my spine.

I was soon driving through the gates of Duke and made for my allocated parking spot as if it were just another day, I went straight to Frank's office and found he was already sat behind his desk preparing for the meeting we would be calling with the team.

'Good morning Eve,' he said without looking up from his notes'

'Good morning Frank,' I responded, 'what do you want me to do?'

'Go and organise the team, tell them that a meeting has been called in the small lecture theater for say, 9.30. If anyone asks what it's about, tell them it has something to do with the DG's report to the General Assembly; that should be sufficient for now. Agreed?'

'Yes no problem, do you want me to say anything to the team?'

'No but I want you stood with me so I can formally announce your new position as my deputy.'

'Is that really necessary Frank, I mean Gordon has been around for a lot longer than I have and while he does treat me with respect, I think he sees himself if not as your deputy, certainly as your next in line.'

'I agree and that's why we need to ensure there is no confusion as to who is responsible to whom for what.' Frank was back in the driving seat, in his favourite habitat, confidence oozed from him, he was the boss and most definitely in charge. He returned to his notes and I went in search of the staff room to tell them about the meeting arrangements.

CHAPTER 37

THE TIMES – Date Line London, Thursday 15 December

WORLD ON THE BRINK -- United Nations To Hold Emergency Debate.
By Denby Wheater, Foreign Affairs Editor

In the face of ever increasing mortality rates across the world's continents, which are being blamed on Sudden Death Syndrome (SDS), the United Nations General Assembly will debate the deteriorating socio-politico situation on Tuesday of next week.

It is thought that as many as twenty countries are sliding into anarchy as their governments struggle to cope with an increasingly difficult situation.

Cuba has already fallen to the forces of anarchy; before the radio and television stations went off the air a government spokesperson said internal terrorists supported by covert US forces had launched a series of co-ordinated attacks against public buildings. A spokesperson for the US State Department hotly denied any US involvement saying whatever was happening on the Caribbean island was a spontaneous event and probably reflected that the peoples' patience with the communist authorities had finally evaporated. Attempts to make contact with our man in Havana were unsuccessful as all telephone links have also been severed.

A US air force recognizance plane over-flying the island reported seeing thick black smoke rising from the downtown area of Havana and satellite imagery showed many cars and buildings ablaze. The Parliament Building appeared to be one of those on fire.

Many Cuban-Americans are urging the US government to intervene but the US is reluctant to be drawn into what could be a bloody and protracted conflict with a subsequent high loss of life.

Other countries said to be on the brink of social collapse are:

Burundi
Ethiopia
Zambia
Zimbabwe
The Congo
Peru
Columbia
Uruguay
Guatemala
Panama
Jamaica
Slovenia
Bangladesh
Uzbekistan

Azerbaijan

Mongolia

There are also reports of serious unrest in parts of Russia, China, India and Iran.

Reports have also reached us that in an act of desperation the King of Nepal ordered the army to use unrestrained force on rioters. Indications are that many thousands have died in the carnage that immediately followed the order, eyewitnesses tell of thousands of dead bodies littering the streets with armed gangs battling the army for control of Kathmandu.

The electrical supply system in this Himalayan kingdom is said to have failed almost a week ago leaving the entire nation without power supplies at a time when temperatures at this time of year rarely rise above freezing. It is feared that all semblance of civilisation has now probably collapsed with an incalculable loss of life.

Surrounding countries are expressing fears that the anarchy that has gripped Nepal, might spread across their borders into their own territories.

A check with the WHO revealed that the centres working on finding a cure for what has become commonly known as 'The Blight' are making some progress in defining the virus' genome, which is an essential step in combating its unique ability to attack only human cells which has left the animal kingdom free of infection.

Whilst most of the present trouble is concentrated in third world countries, wealthy industrialised nations are also experiencing significant rises in their death rates placing an intolerable strain on health care facilities. There are reports of large demonstrations having taken place in Sydney Australia, Hong Kong and Singapore, the demonstrations were mainly peaceful although at one time it did appear that a confrontation between police and demonstrators in Sydney might erupt into an ugly incident but it passed off peacefully when the police made a tactical withdrawal into nearby streets.

Closer to home, Withington Hospital in South Manchester was besieged by protesters yesterday after rumours swept the area that hospital authorities had refused to dispense medication that was thought to afford some protection against SDS infection. A hospital spokesperson said he was baffled where the rumour had started and denied any such medication existed. Eventually the protesters dispersed and went home peacefully.

Unless there is an early breakthrough in the search for a cure, the situation can only deteriorate with more countries going the same way as Cuba and Nepal.

CHAPTER 38

The team assembled in the small lecture theatre at 9.30, there was an air of expectation when Frank entered, I took my place at his side; they obviously anticipated some kind of major announcement.

'Good morning, I have some important matters to bring to your attention,' that was Frank, straight to the point, 'most if not all of you will have heard or read about the report to the UN General Assembly by Professor Patel the WHO's DG, I don't doubt that the gravity of the situation wasn't lost on you. I'll be issuing you with a full text of the report for you to read.

To get to the nub of the matter, we have been asked by the WHO to be one of three research centres whose task will be to try and identify a cure, or at least a method of treatment for this Sudden Death Syndrome. This means that our present project will be put on ice for the entire duration of the new project. The two other research centres are the Pasteur Institute in Paris and Oxford University in the United Kingdom.

The government has appointed a high-ranking team under the direct supervision of the Vice-President to oversee our activities. I am responsible for directing this aspect of the project and Eve with immediate effect, will be my deputy; in my absence she will have exactly the same authority as I do.

To ensure there is no duplication of effort between the three research centres and to co-ordinate activities and research direction where appropriate, each centre will appoint a liaison person, ours is Professor Jack Lindo,' there were several murmurings of recognition at the mention of Jack Lindo's name, 'how it will work is that I will meet at regular intervals with him and brief him as to what is happening at our end of the business, he in turn will tell me what's going on in France and England, this will ensure we're all kept in the loop. Obviously, if there's something urgent to report, then we'll communicate at a moments notice; the main purpose of the arrangements is to pool our resources whilst at the same time pursuing our own line of investigations and to be in a position to collaborate in a meaningful way should one of the centres make a breakthrough; any questions?'

'Is there anything we need to know additional to what was in the WHO's report?'

'Not on the report itself, what was said was a simple statement of fact; our task is simple, we must find a cure or at least an effective treatment in the shortest possible time. Our investigations will centre on the genetic profile of the virus, we need to strip it of its mysteries and learn exactly what it is that makes it behave as it does but before we can do that we have to find it and isolate it and that's the problem, once it infects the host and kills it, it then somehow disappears.

This is part of what baffled those medical examiners that undertook autopsies on the earlier victims; their examination of tissue samples and toxicology analysis revealed nothing, to all intents and purposes the victims had been perfectly healthy people right up to the second of their death; we now know that the virus dies when the host dies and is thereafter totally undetectable.

Our task is to find the virus; it will be like looking for the proverbial needle in a haystack except this haystack is gigantic and the needle invisible. For starters we'll examine soft and hard tissue samples from victims as well as blood, we'll be looking for anything unusual, no matter how slight that might help us to home in on our target.

While we're getting organised we'll be receiving position statements from Oxford and Paris, we'll be able to see what lines of investigation they have been following and their findings to date, we will be able to identify the blind alleys they went down and this will ensure we hit the ground running.

The lab samples will arrive within the next seventy two hours so you have a little time to wrap up whatever you are doing on the present project and prepare yourselves for the new thrust.

I can't overstate the importance of what we are embarking on; it's no exaggeration to say that the whole world is depending on us to come up with the goods and I don't intend that we should let them down. There is no finer research institute anywhere and no finer research team so let's get to it and show them what we're made of.'

I hoped that Frank's clarion call would have the desired effect but in truth the team were so dedicated and their loyalty to Frank unquestioned that there was no way they could ever give less than a hundred and one percent.

'One final word, I'm going to have to spend a lot of time, probably too much time on admin matters so Eve will lead the sharp-end effort, I know you will all give her the same respect and co-operation you give me. If there are any other questions, please direct them to Eve. Thanks.

I was grateful to Frank for how he'd handled my introduction; he had made my position clear and unambiguous and had dealt with any perceived challenge that might arise from any of my more senior colleagues. When I thought of the daunting task facing us I felt more than a little overwhelmed and I couldn't help but feel guilty that we hadn't told the team the truth, the whole truth and nothing but the truth but on second thoughts we couldn't, because none of us knew what the truth was. It was anybody's guess what was causing the deaths, in fact the virus story given by the WHO could be true, we just didn't know but putting the team to investigate the tissue samples was the correct decision whichever way you looked at it. We had to hope that with their expertise and sharp enquiring minds they would see something that struck a chord, something that had no right to be there and by a process of investigation the killer would be cornered and exposed, we'd strip it of its mysteries and find a way to destroy it, before it destroyed us.

CHAPTER 39

BBC 9 0'clock Evening News – Friday 9 February

The centre of Rome was brought to a standstill at noon today as an estimated half a million people took to the streets of Italy's capitol city to protest their government's impotence in dealing with the effects of Sudden Death Syndrome, more often referred to as 'The Blight'. The police threw cordons around the city's famous historical sites to protect them in case violence should erupt.

The demonstration had passed off peacefully until several of the participants fell victim to the very thing they were protesting about, death by SDS. The news of their deaths incensing the crowd and the demonstrators began charging the police lines. Some members of the police force themselves became victims of the mystery virus but in the ensuing confusion, word spread through the police ranks that crowd violence had been the cause of the officers' deaths. The police reacted with force and this led to pitched battles developing between the opposing groups. Reports are that gunshots could be clearly heard across several areas of central Rome. Calm was eventually restored but not before hundreds had died with many more injured, some of them seriously. The Ministry of Culture said the historical sites had suffered only superficial damage.

Senor Sylvio Rossi the Italian president went on television and appealed for calm, he said the government understood the fear and frustration felt by many persons and that the government was working with the United Nations to ensure everything was being done to find a solution. He pointed out that Italy was suffering along with every other country and regrettably at this time there was no government anywhere which was in a position to insulate its citizens from the effects of the virus.

The impact of SDS continues to be felt globally with violence erupting in many developing countries and the already nervous financial markets reflecting the general uncertainty by closing at their lowest levels for more than a decade.

Factory output continues to fall as productivity is badly affected due to the cumulative impact the virus is having on workforce numbers. Reports reaching the BBC also suggest that many homes and factories are increasingly without power in several far eastern and sub-Saharan African countries as supply becomes ever more erratic due to dwindling fuel supplies and a lack of skilled personnel to man the power stations. The situation has also led to violent street protests, which the authorities are finding increasingly difficult to contain.

The picture in the UK and the European Union is of equal concern with SDS taking its toll in all areas of life. It has now become commonplace to see family and friends die in front of your eyes and to see people walking in the street suddenly drop to the ground dead. The authorities admit to being at a loss as to how to deal with these traumatic situations, initially there was a proposal to provide support counselling but this had to be abandoned due to a shortage of counsellors and the rising number of victims.

The number of accidents arising from drivers of motor vehicles falling victim to the virus whilst at the wheel is also worrying the authorities, even though the maximum speed limit on motorways has been reduced to thirty miles an hour and twenty in populated areas, accidents continue to occur and often with fatal results.

Another area of great concern is air travel, ICAO, the organisation responsible for the regulation of civil air traffic operations currently insists on four qualified pilots being on board every flight whether domestic or international, the number of qualified pilots available is insufficient to maintain current service levels, which are already only a fraction of their pre-SDS levels. A British Airways spokesperson said it was inevitable that services would have to be cut further. British Airways is currently only able to fly about twenty five percent of its scheduled services.

On the military front, all countries are limiting their activities to essential flights and then only with planes with at least two cockpits, this follows the tragic accidents in Germany and Japan when air force planes plunged into populated areas after the pilots fell victim to the virus. The US and other major air forces are making increased use of pilot-less drones.

At Cape Canaveral in Florida, a NASA spokesperson announced the US manned space programme had been suspended pending progress on finding a cure or effective treatment for the SDS virus.

In the UK a memorial service will be held next week Thursday for the Duke of Kent, the Duchess of Gloucester and Princess Mary, all of whom have succumbed to the virus in the past several weeks. The King, who will address the nation next week Tuesday on the crisis, is said to be distraught at the deaths of his close family members but is determined to put on a brave face and continue to undertake his duties as an example to the rest of the population.

Finally, the WHO's latest bulletin issued at 1300 GMT advises that satellite labs have now been established in Australia, Brazil, China, India, Japan and Russia, they will work in close liaison with the original scientific core centres of investigation in Paris, Oxford and Duke University in Raleigh North Carolina.

Work on identifying the virus and how it spreads and infects has centred on establishing a process of elimination that involves the mapping of the virus' genome, the harmless genes are then systematically identified and stripped away until only the salient genes remain. Once this has been achieved it will enable the scientists to devise a specific designer-type treatment, probably in the form of an oral medication that will literally hide in the body's cells lying in wait for the virus to enter the host and once detected by the body's natural immune system, will seek and destroy the virus before it is able to cause infection.

The world's deadliest pandemics are considered to be The Black Death that killed an estimated 20 million people in the 1300's, seven Cholera epidemics in the past two hundred years, Spanish Flu that killed 25 million in

1918 and HIV, which has accounted for over 20 million deaths to date. However, according to experts, Sudden Death Syndrome constitutes the gravest threat the human race has ever had to face and they say the plagues of the past pale into insignificance at the side of this one.

In other news, the severe drought conditions in Southern Spain are causing grave concern, although the region no longer has to cope with the water massive requirements of millions of tourists, the region's farmers are reporting significant crop failures as once fertile land now resembles a gigantic dust bowl. The Iberian Peninsula has suffered more than most from the impact of global warming.

CHAPTER 40

It didn't take long for the Vice President's instruction for deputies to be named for the principal players to be shown to be prudent; Frank was dead the following day. I received the news from Mrs Longworth his housekeeper; she telephoned me in an advanced state of distress, her words tumbling over each other as she sought to explain how she had arrived at her usual time of seven thirty in the morning and instead of finding Frank up and about, busying himself before setting off for Duke, the drapes were still shut and the door locked. She said she had repeatedly rang the bell and eventually decided to call Frank on his mobile phone, apparently he had given her the number in case she needed to urgently contact him, the phone had just rang and rang without answer. Then she'd remembered he had given her a spare key in case of emergencies so she had hurriedly returned home to collect it; when she let herself in she'd called out his name but there was only silence.

She had found him in his bed, at first she thought he was still sleeping, he looked so peaceful but when she had gingerly touched him and he had felt unnaturally cold, she then realised he was dead.

I didn't go to pieces as I thought I would have done, I'd replayed this possibility several times over in my mind, always fearful of receiving the news and in every instance I'd panicked at the thought of being alone but I felt strangely calm, Frank would have expected better from me, I would grieve, of that there could be no doubt but right now I didn't have the luxury, it would have to wait.

I told Mrs Longworth to wait there while I called his doctor, I told her he would make the necessary arrangements for the body to be taken away, I then went upstairs to tell Bill, he was in the bathroom shaving.

'Bill, that was Mrs Longworth on the phone, it's Frank, he's died, it sounds like SDS.' He was visibly shaken and for one brief second I thought he was going to break down, I hoped he wouldn't. He sat down heavily.

'What, how, I mean…?'

I gave him the details. 'Frank had already named me as his successor should this very thing happen; I'll have to contact the Vice President and inform him, in fact I'd better do it right now.'

'Eve, what in heaven's name is going on, have you told me everything or is this SDS thing much worse than you've made out?

I felt as if I'd matured ten years in ten minutes. I looked Bill squarely in the face.

'Listen Bill, I'm not permitted to tell anyone exactly what is happening, those of us involved at this level have undertaken an oath of secrecy, believe me the fewer who know the truth the better. You've already seen what's happening in other parts of the world; civil unrest, accusations flying around everywhere, even governments being toppled and things will get worse, we have to come up with some answers quickly because right now we only have questions.'

'There is no virus is there, the story's nothing more than a fabrication to cover up the real reason for these deaths? I bet it's some terrible government experiment that's gone hopelessly wrong and it's set a chain of events in motion that now threatens our very existence?'

'I've told you Bill, I can't talk about it, I've probably said more than I should have, trust me and please don't put more pressure on me than I've got already, I'm going to need all the support I can get.'

I went to him and put my arms around him. 'Hold me Bill; tell me everything's going to be OK.'

He smoothed my hair and cupped my face in his hands, he looked at me intently and smiled a sad lopsided smile, and 'It's going to be OK darling.' I wondered.

I retrieved the VP's private telephone number the one he had given me when we had met in Washington and punched it into my mobile, it rang twice. A woman's voice answered.

'Yes?'

'This is Dr Eve James.'

'One moment please.' Perhaps twenty seconds passed, it seemed more like twenty minutes; then a man's voice.

'Hello Dr James, I guess you called about Professor Burke?'

'Yes sir I have.'

'I got the news about ten minutes ago, terrible and shocking but regrettably not a shock, if you know what

I mean? I knew Frank well, known him for years, Frank was brilliant, one of the best, I'm going to miss him and I have a good idea what he meant to you too. Unfortunately we're not able to give him the recognition he deserves, we would if circumstances were different, I hope some day we can. Well how do you feel Eve, can you handle it, do you need anything from me, do you want me to send somebody in to help you?'

'For now I need to evaluate our position, I want to nominate Dr Gordon Walker as my successor and I need to draw up a plan of action as a matter of extreme urgency. I've worked long enough with Frank to be familiar with his approach and I've been with him on this particular subject almost from the beginning, so I feel as competent as I reasonably can be in the circumstances.'

'Frank told me he had absolute confidence in you and who am I to argue with his judgement, so I'm perfectly content for us to work closely together on this thing? Undertake your evaluation by all means but make it quick and let me know what it is you need.'

'Thank you sir, I'll report back as soon as I have everything in place.'

I felt eerily confident, in command of the situation, ready for the responsibility that had been thrust on me. Oh I was frightened, I can't deny it but not so that I wanted to run away and hide, I was ready to take over and I knew that Frank would have expected no less of me.

CHAPTER 41

I left home with Bill not quite knowing how he should relate to me, things had changed between us, I hoped it wouldn't have a negative affect on our relationship but there was no questioning that he now viewed me in a different light. It wasn't difficult for me to understand; after all I had just been in conversation with the Vice President of the United States of America and was now in charge of something so secretive that he was not allowed to be privy to what it was. Poor Bill, his life had been turned up side down in just a few minutes and there could never be any going back.

As I drove to Duke my mind was in overdrive and I found myself seemingly able to analyse a multiplicity of topics at the same time, one of the major challenges was how I would break the news of Frank's death to the team, it would be traumatic so I decided I would first have a private word with Gordon and make sure he was fully on board and then meet with the rest of the team. It was important that whilst we grieved for Frank we didn't lose valuable time in our quest for a solution to SDS.

Dr Gordon Walker was a 'boffin' in the truest sense of the definition; he was tall with slightly stooped shoulders and had thin bird-like features, his small, dark, close set eyes seemed to dart here and there and his thick black horn-rimmed spectacles were forever sliding down his long thin bony nose, to be pushed back up to the bridge by the middle finger of his right hand, his hair lay in thin flat strands across the top of his head and he always wore a long white lab coat. I found him in the lab reading a paper entitled 'Cloning of Aquatic Species' by Professor Skimmer Simm.

'Good morning Gordon.'

'Good morning Eve,' he replied, in that almost shy reserved manner of his.

'I'm afraid I have some distressing news for you.' He looked up from his ruminations not quite sure what to expect. 'Professor Burke died sometime last night; his housekeeper found him this morning.

'Was it SDS?' His response to Frank's death was not intended to be disrespectful but rather what one would expect from Gordon.

'We think so; it bears all the hallmarks we've come to associate with the disease. There'll be an autopsy of course but I wouldn't expect it to identify the cause of death, that's always the case with SDS. I've spoken with the Vice President, he knew of the death before I rang him, he was most upset, Frank and he go back a long way, they were close personal friends.

As you know Frank had already nominated me as his deputy and I gave the VP your name as my deputy, if anything happens to me you will assume direct responsibility for the project.'

He weighed my words very carefully before finally responding.

'The news isn't only distressing it's also devastating. Frank was someone I respected and admired both as an academic and as a person. He was a great intellectual and a great leader, I'm going to miss him personally and I know for sure that the team will be traumatised by this terrible news.' I realise the show must go on and I will lend my every support to you personally and to the project in general. When you say you spoke with the Vice President, do I assume that you mean the Vice President of the USA and not the Research Institute?'

'Yes Gordon you assume correctly and he personally accepted that you be my named deputy. He also urged that we waste no time in seeking a solution to our problem, so as you say, the show must go on. Let's get the team together right away and give them the bad news, after the meeting I need to brief you on several aspects of the problem that you are not familiar with.'

The meeting was held twenty minutes later and a pall of anxiety hung over the proceedings like a San Francisco fog. The team were shocked and distressed but I told them of the VP's request that we should waste no time in seeking a solution to SDS, they all agreed that the last thing that Frank would have wanted was for us to lose focus and waste our energies on mourning his death instead.

After the meeting I met with Gordon.

'Gordon,' I started, 'before I brief you on the matters at hand you are required to sign a copy of the Official Secrets Act promising amongst other things, that anything you learn from your involvement in this project cannot be discussed with any unauthorised person and that you could face charges of treason if you fail to observe the conditions put on you. Do you fully understand what I have just told you?'

'I most certainly do and I must also tell you that this thing gets scarier and scarier by the second.'

'Are you prepared to sign the document? You can still back out of the project but you will be required to honour the secrecy of this conversation.'

He agreed to sign, I figured he really didn't have much choice, I produced the document and he signed on the dotted line.

'Thanks Gordon, I'm pleased to have you working closely with me and now, I have to tell you that the situation regarding SDS is infinitely much worse than you were first led to believe. The intention was never to keep you in the dark for the sake of it but a decision was taken at the very top that the fewer persons who knew the truth the better it would be for the public good. Here it is, we don't know what is causing people to die this way, it's not some super genetically modified bug that escaped from a Moscow lab, as I said, we don't know what is causing the deaths. That's not to say it isn't an as yet unidentified organism, it might be, we simply don't know.

That in a nutcase is our task, to find what is causing people to die this way and to find the answer quickly, before we run out of time.'

'Do we have any idea at all what it might be, are there any leads that are being followed either here or in Oxford or Paris, is there anything at all that we know?'

'Let me tell you what we do know. One, death from SDS has no boundaries, in other words the elderly are dying and so are the young. The healthy are dying just as much as the sick. The rich are dying as fast as the poor and they are dying just as fast in the US as they are in the Sudan. I think you get the picture.

Two, thousands of autopsies carried out on victims have failed to identify any reason why these people have died.

Three, many tragedies and accidents, on a worldwide scale resulting in the loss of thousands of lives are as a result of SDS.

Four, the rate of death through SDS is increasing, probably daily, hence the need to find answers quickly.

Five, the work that has been undertaken so far by the Pasteur Institute in Paris and Oxford University in England has produced no results to date.

That I think puts the matter into perspective. Obviously we will have the benefit of knowing what paths Paris and London have been following and that will help us to devise our own programme but we don't have a moment to lose, as the VP said to Frank when we met the other day, the country truly depends upon us and we can't afford to let them down and it's not just our country, the world is depending on a solution being found.

Sorry to be brutal Gordon but in the circumstances…' I let it taper off. I looked at him and I could almost hear the cogs and gears whirling around in his mind, his thin features had become gaunt and a nervous twitch was playing around his left eye.

'I believe I fully grasp what it is you're telling me, if no solution is found and the death rate follows its present trend, in a relatively short space of time the human race will cease to exist.'

'Yes,' I replied, 'but I think the appropriate term is extinct.'

Gordon stared off into space as the full import of what we had been talking about settled in. 'I guess I can assume that the talk there has been of people recovering from the virus is not true.'

'Yep,' I said, 'no virus, or then again we can't rule out the possibility but certainly no recoveries as far as we are aware. The view so far is that whatever is causing these deaths is somehow linked to the human genome and that's where we come in, the state of our research is cutting edge and more advanced than other institutes. That's the angle we will investigate from. We will look for any clues in the genome that could conceivably provide us with a lead.

Now that I'm in the hot seat the responsibility for the investigative legwork will fall to you so let's decide on our line of approach and do it.'

CHAPTER 42

Snow had started to fall in the night and by the time Madge left for the university a two-inch white carpet already covered the ground. Madge loved the snow, it reminded her of the good times she had spent with her mom, making snowmen in the back yard and fashioning a small snowball and rolling it on the ground so it got bigger and bigger until it was as tall as she was. Then going home with warm ruddy cheeks and a cold red nose, her mom would make her a piping hot cup of drinking chocolate and she would sit in front of a roaring log fire sipping her drink and fairly bursting with happiness but today her thoughts were on something quite different, try as she might Madge couldn't shake off the feelings of dark foreboding that had come over her as she made her way to her lab. The more she thought about it the more she had become convinced that there was a link between her mother's death and the number of sudden deaths occurring across the globe. 'What did the Sun call it, 'The Blight' yes that was it, 'The Blight?'

Her specimens had now arrived courtesy of MailPack UK and she had already set up her equipment with great gusto, she could hardly wait to get stuck into the task and she had her notes and reference journals spread out before her but every time she sought to determine how the thesis was best approached, her thoughts would return to 'The Blight.'

Until she saw the BBC News the other night she had thought she had got this feeling of a connection between her mother's death and SDS out of her system, it was compelling stuff, frightening and fascinating at the same time.

The situation had deteriorated since the news broadcast; in her college alone there had been more than a dozen deaths ascribed to SDS and it was obvious that at these unheard of levels of mortality rate stats civil stability would become ever more tenuous. She feared for the future, her future and her thoughts were being inexorably channelled towards the SDS situation and a crazy idea began to take root in her mind that perhaps she should delay working on her thesis and instead devote her time to looking at the SDS problem. The newscast had even stated that Oxford University was involved in trying to find a solution; perhaps she could use that knowledge to her advantage.

The bitterly cold easterly wind knifed through her and she gave an involuntary shiver, she sunk her hands deeper into her heavy top coat and strode out with a renewed purpose; Madge felt truly focused for the first time in a long time, at last she was going to do something about her mother's death and not just speculate and keep asking unanswerable questions. She thought she was more than a little crazy to be doing this but what the hell; she didn't have a clue how she would go about injecting herself into the project but she also knew instinctively that time was not on her side, nor anyone else's for that matter.

Her first stop was the university's Admin Office where she enquired about the whereabouts of the SDS project location. The clerk replied that she had no knowledge about it and asked Madge if she would like to speak to Mrs Kay her supervisor. Mrs Kay turned out to be a grotesquely thin woman of about fifty; she looked like a character out of a Bronte novel.

'Yes, can I help you?' Not even a hint of a smile creased her face.

'Yes please,' said Madge, 'I'm enquiring about the whereabouts of the SDS project lab.'

'Why do you want to know?' demanded the severe looking Mrs Kay.

Madge quickly realised that she and Mrs Kay had already reached a critical stage in their new relationship and that a wrong move now would be fatal. She decided that it would be best for her to adopt an authoritative approach so she replaced her usual genial expression with one that she hoped looked at least a little fierce.

' My name is Dr Madge Grant and I'm a research geneticist in Magdelene College, I have been undertaking systematic genetic profiling of specimens from several extinct species and I need to discuss the results with the SDS team as my research work is closely related to theirs and...'

'Alright doctor, I get the message, no need to go on, I need some ID though.'

'No problem Mrs Kay,' having got this far I didn't think a little flattery would go amiss, 'I realise the importance of your position and that you can't let just any Tom, Dick or Harry to wander in here and go wherever they please, here.' I handed her my Oxford University Research ID, it contained my name, designation and photograph but didn't refer to me as 'doctor', which was my little lie when I first introduced myself. I hoped the ever-alert Mrs Kay wouldn't notice, and she didn't.

The lab was in the Science Building a good fifteen minutes walk away, I thanked Mrs Kay, who gave a barely perceptible nod of her head and set off for the lab.

The Science Building was a large three-story block with a collection of labs on each of the floors; the SDS lab was housed on the top floor. Madge opened one of the double entry doors and stepped through. There was an elevator directly in front of her and stairs to the side leading up; she decided to take the stairs.

At the top of the stairs was a solid-looking door with a security punch pad to the side, there was nothing to identify that the SDS project was housed there, underneath the pad was a bell, since Madge didn't know the code she decided to press the bell. No one answered the shrill ringing sound she heard from somewhere within, she pushed the button a second time and she was rewarded by the sound of footsteps approaching the door. A speaker above the door announced the presence of the person with the footsteps.

'Hello, can I help you?' It was a females' voice.

'Hi, said Madge trying to sound friendly and relaxed, 'I'm Madge Grant and I'm a research geneticist, I've come to…' It was as far as she got.

'Oh great,' said the speaker, 'that was quick, wait right there.'

An electronic click told her the door lock had been released and when the door swung open it revealed a woman of about thirty stood in front of her wearing the traditional white lab coat.

'Madge, oh you don't mind if I call you Madge do you? My name's Ada, Ada Morris and I'm a geneticist like you. Oh look at me having you standing there while I prattle on, do forgive me, please, come in.

Madge found herself in a large laboratory but not just any laboratory, it was the best equipped she could ever have hoped to see. There was an array of computers and specialist equipment arranged in workstations almost from floor to ceiling; in fact the room more closely resembled NASA Mission Control than a science lab. Madge stared in open-mouthed wonder.

'Don't worry you'll soon get used to it, it affects everyone the same way when they see it for the first time.'

'It's incredible, in fact it's indescribable, and I've never seen anything like it. The project must have no funding limits.'

'We didn't expect to see you so quick, the last time a replacement was drafted in it took the best part of a week but Carol only died yesterday and here you are already. We had been told not to expect anyone for at least ten days, if ever; I guess our new Head of Project pulled a few strings to get you in. Not that the previous chief wasn't a heavyweight he was but when he died Professor Davis that is, we thought we would get someone less influential but Prof Lofthouse is no slouch.'

Madge heard all these things and soon realised that Ada thought she had been sent in to replace a dead colleague, she didn't want to be morbid but it certainly was an enormous stroke of good fortune. She decided to ride her luck and not disabuse her of the notion.

'Have there been many deaths on the team?' She asked.

'Eight including Carol.' She said

'Were they all victims of SDS?'

'I'm afraid so. There are forty-one of us, I mean forty two of us now you're here but the death rate is starting to affect continuity of effort because some key players were included in the eight. Not that the mortality rate in here is different from that out there,' she gestured to the windows, ' but unless we get a handle on this thing soon the work is going to become so fragmented with the people dying in such quick order that it will start to lose its usefulness. What's your area of specialism?'

Madge decide to stay with the game, she'd done well so far. 'My speciality is the genetic study of extinct species.'

'With a view to what?' asked Ada.

'To determine why species become extinct in the first place. I'm not talking about those species that disappeared because they were hunted into extinction, or died out because of a change in their environment or habitat; my research is with those species that died out for no apparent reason. They simply became extinct.'

'Do you mean like the dinosaurs?'

'Yes, just like the dinosaurs, in fact they're a good example; they ruled the earth for millions of years, far longer than we have and having been so successful they died out and caught the fast train to oblivion, we have yet to figure out why.'

I thought they died out because the earth was in a major collision with a meteor that threw up so much dust it blotted out the sun and as a result the earth underwent a major upheaval; their food chain was seriously disrupted, there were far reaching climatic changes etc, etc.'

'That's a very popular theory but that's all it is, a theory, we don't actually know why they became extinct. It's a case of a story being made to fit a circumstance. It might be accurate but then again it might not.'

'I can see why you were chosen to replace Carol; your research can follow paths as yet untrodden. Let me show you were you'll work and introduce you to some of the team.'

Madge didn't know what would happen when they found her out and anyway she didn't lie her way in, in fact she had only told the truth, it wasn't her fault that wrong presumptions had been made about why she had rung the bell, she just hadn't corrected them. She did have a slight pang of guilt because Ada seemed such a nice person and she wouldn't have wanted to get her into trouble but she quickly suppressed it and followed Ada into the lab.

She was introduced to about twenty people who were her new colleagues and was shown the work station she would be using, it made the one at her designated lab seem like a child's chemistry set. The great thing was that the research work she would be doing with the SDS team was pretty much the same stuff she would have been doing for her PhD.

She told Ada she had brought some specimens with her but she hadn't known where the SDS labs were so she had left them in another part of the university and that she would have to go and get them. Ada gave her the security code so she could let herself into the lab when she returned.

Madge marvelled at her deception, as she hurried back to what she already thought of as her old lab, she saw Mrs Kay and favoured her with her brightest and sunniest smile; Mrs Kay was apparently not impressed because she quickly looked the other way as if Madge didn't exist.

CHAPTER 43

THE WASHINGTON POST – Weekly Edition, Friday 30 March

TIME IS RUNNING OUT

By Laurie Smart

The situation throughout the world continues to deteriorate as governments fall and countries collapse into chaos. It is now a race against time as to whether a cure or even a treatment can be found for 'The Blight'. All civilian flights have been halted and military flights have been cut to the barest minimum. The country is experiencing frequent disruptions to its power grid and six nuclear power stations have been shut down for safety reasons.

The population of the US is now estimated at one hundred and fifty million; about half of what it was before the onset of the SDS epidemic. The story is the same globally. People are dying at an ever-increasing rate and although the WHO continues to make optimistic noises, there is little sign that even the slightest progress has been made.

The civilised world appears to be disintegrating with many of the less stable countries having collapsed already. The US has closed its border with Mexico with border guards having been told to shoot to kill anyone who seeks to gain illegal entry. The border with Canada remains open, in reality the border no longer exists, as Homeland Security doesn't have the manpower to patrol it and Canada is not considered a threat to national security.

Food is increasingly in short supply as the transportation of goods is proving to be a major headache and in too many instances the food producers are finding it impossible to maintain production. Similar difficulties are being experienced in the pharmaceutical industry with drugs and medications becoming increasingly scarce.

In the print media world many of the world's newspapers are barely able to survive, the supply of raw materials like newsprint and ink are unreliable at best, meaning most publications were restricted to only one publication a week.

Radio and television broadcasting is a ghost of the pre-SDS levels, with many stations operating only a dawn to dusk schedule.

Crime is rampant everywhere as undermanned police forces are unable to maintain law and order. There are no records available on the current levels of serious crime but analysts agree they are at an all time high.

The recent ban on the use of private automobiles has placed the responsibility for moving people around on the public transport system; the subway is operating at about sixty percent of its pre-plague service thanks to the high level of computerised automation but the number of travellers is diminishing daily as there are fewer persons using or needing to use the system.

The pre-programmed electric buses are still operating but those buses that rely on drivers have been withdrawn. The Greyhound Bus Company, often referred to as an American icon, has closed its doors and no longer provides a service. Greyhound buses were as much a part of American culture as Mom's apple pie.

The government is fighting a loosing battle in trying to impose its authority on the life of ordinary Americans, it can no longer guarantee power supplies, food supplies, law and order or even the right of individuals to live their lives in peace and liberty.

The Washington Times joins with all other well-thinking Americans in seeking God's deliverance from this dreadful disease that will wipe out the human race if no cure or treatment can be found. God bless America.

Laurie died before this publication went to print.
Editor.

CHAPTER 44

We toiled day and night in our quest to find something, anything that would halt the march of SDS but to no avail. Our colleagues in Oxford and Paris had no better luck and the so-called satellite labs whilst enthusiastic were little more than a cosmetic exercise assigned to the project by the WHO in what was really a public relations exercise.

I can't say that our failure was in any way tied to the deaths of the president and vice president because their replacements were just as dedicated as their predecessors as was their replacements and we were given everything we asked for. The truth was that after several months of dedicated effort we were no nearer to finding a solution and whatever was causing the deaths just marched inexorably on unchallenged.

We kept losing many of our team members to Lord Cyclops; we had the best brains anywhere in the world working on the project and in a short space of time we learned more about the Human Genome condition than we could have thought possible. It seems ironic that in our pursuit of a cure for SDS we had discovered what would be effective treatments and potential cures for Parkinson's, Alzheimer's, MS and many other diseases. We identified genes that caused the onset of many cancers and here also, given time we would have turned our work into effective treatments for these killers of millions of human beings and probably defeated the disease once and for all but none of this was the mission, ours was to find an effective treatment for SDS and in that regard we had failed. The fact is we were no nearer to identifying the cause of SDS than we were at the beginning, we had been unable to establish a single lead and the entire nation looked on hopefully, it was a terrible feeling to think that we had let them down. The testament to our failure was all to visible, mountains of dead bodies in every town and city throughout the world.

Me? I felt fine, friends and colleagues fell around me like ninepins but I never wavered, the funny thing was that I never even developed a sniffle; I don't think I had ever felt healthier in my life.

All the original members of the vice-president's monitoring group had succumbed to the plague, I was the only one left standing, even their replacements had fallen and then theirs as well but we the team was still here, still refusing to give up, as long as we are able to breath we won't give in. If there's a way of beating this thing we'll find it, if not then....

We haven't heard from The Pasteur Institute for a week now but communications with the rest of the world have become fractured and extremely difficult. The last we heard France was having a hard time of things, their government was hardly functioning and they had given up trying to bury the dead, bodies were being burned wherever they fell; if they were indoors when they died they were dragged outside, doused in gasoline and burned. In spite of this action, disease was rampant and the rat population had gotten bigger and fatter as the corpses provided food in abundance. I wouldn't like to have been in France. Not that France was alone in its plight; most of the rest of the world was as bad or even worse, I mean the African countries no longer functioned and few pockets of civilisation remained in the Americas, only Canada and the US had a semblance of what we used to call civilisation.

Asia was in ruins, there had been no news out of many of the countries on that continent for the past two weeks and Japan and China were barely surviving. Russia is a vast country and whatever central government still existed there had long since lost contact with most of the regions. I knew all this and more from the news that occasionally filtered through from the satellite labs. Unfortunately most of those, if not all are no longer functioning and life is becoming increasingly lonely.

The only other outpost of civilisation seems to be Great Britain, there is still a functioning central government of sorts and from what we hear, the Bobbies are still managing to maintain a semblance of control over a population that does its best to co-operate. Most members of the Royal Family have died and Buckingham Palace is lies empty, arsonists torched The Tower of London and Westminster Abby last week and vandals have wrecked Shakespeare's home at Stratford-Upon-Avon but we do receive sporadic contact from the Oxford lab, like us they are somehow surviving and like us they possess a single minded determination not to give in. Their typical dogged spirit comforts us.

Since Bill and the twins died I've spent most of my time at Duke, my home holds far too many painful memories, everywhere I look I see them, not as they were in life, happy and content but how they were in death. First Bill, cold and stiff next to me in bed, he'd died in the night; then Wendy a week later, still stunned by her father not being there anymore and Suzanne two days after that, I'd rather not describe the circumstances of my little girls' deaths it's far, far too painful.

CHAPTER 45

Madge had fitted into the Oxford Project like a hand fits into a glove and her presence had never once been questioned, her colleagues had just assumed that she was Carol's replacement and they immediately welcomed her involvement, her background and training seemed to have readied her for the project.

In other circumstances Madge would have been in awe and felt privileged to be working in such exalted company, her knowledge and abilities had taken quantum leaps forward in a very short time but she was depressed and frustrated that in spite of enormous dedication and application by the team, there had been no progress whatsoever in identifying the cause of SDS.

She had expected that with the quality of minds available and seemingly limitless resources, it would only be a matter of time before the puzzle was solved but whatever it was that was behind the plague it continued to deny them the truth and refused to reveal itself.

Madge had certainly pulled her weight since becoming a member of the team and had earned the respect of her colleagues, so much so that she had been given the responsibility of acting as liaison with the lab at Duke University in North Carolina. She had established an excellent rapport with the head of their team Dr Eve James; regrettably Dr James' team had fared no better than her own. They kept each other fully advised on the lines of investigation each team were pursuing but the lack of progress was frustrating Duke as much as Oxford and she had felt that elements of desperation had started to creep into both sets of reports.

Madge was aware that if the present mortality rates continued to escalate, the human race was staring directly into the face of extinction. She thought of the specimens that now lay in a cupboard gathering dust and remembered how important they had seemed only a few months ago, she couldn't help but wonder if some future race of beings, millions of years in the future, would one day stumble upon the fossilised remains of a human being and marvel at the creatures that had once inhabited the planet.

She looked out of the window, nothing moved, the use of private motor vehicles had been banned some months ago but it seemed only like yesterday that the campus had been a hive of activity but now it resembled a remote part of the earth where humans rarely trod. Someone called her name and it forced her concentration back to the present. The team had lost more than half of its numbers but all that had done was reduce by half the number of failures, the number of dead ends and the number of negative reports to share with Duke. She felt dejected and frightened.

'Madge, would you be kind and pass the papers to me from the top drawer in the Amino Acid file, there's a variation on a previous test I ran that I want to try?'

Madge walked lethargically to what they referred to as the 'Cabinet Room'. She opened the drawer and fished out the papers, her thoughts were elsewhere and as she was handing the papers to her colleague they slipped from her grasp scattering all over the floor.

'Oh hell, I'm sorry,' she said, stooping to retrieve them.

'No sweat, just give me the ones in the blue folder.'

Madge handed over the blue folder and scooped up the fallen files intending to put them in some semblance of order and return them to the file drawer when her eye caught the words 'telomeres erosion' and something in her long term memory teetered on the edge of recognition. Something she had read a couple of years ago on the subject of telomeres was ringing alarm bells at the back of her mind. She put the rest of the papers down after extracting a small manila folder, typed in red letters at the top of the file cover was 'REINHARDT STINDL, INSTITUTE OF MEDICAL BIOLOGY, VIENNA', she picked it up and removed a single sheet of note paper from inside, she began to read the hand-written file notes which were written in staccato fashion:

a. Protective caps on the end of chromosomes are called 'telomeres', like plastic tips on the end of shoelaces – all eukaryotic have telomeres to prevent chromosomal instability.

b. Evolutionary clock that ticks thru generations counting down to eventual extinction date.

c. Cells struggle to copy telomeres properly when they divide and very gradually the telomeres become shorter.

d. Once telomeres become shorter causes disease related to chromosomal instability resulting in a population crash, eg Neanderthals.

e. Shortest telomeres in humans occur on the short arm of chromosome suppressor gene 17.

f. Telomeres can be accurately measured with new DNA sequencing techniques.

g. Telomeres shorten a tiny amount between each generation.

h. Human telomeres already short.

Madge hadn't realised she'd been holding her breath and she let it out with a controlled gasp when she got to the end of the notes. She read them over again, more slowly this time, trying to digest the extraordinary implications of what she was reading. Protective caps, shortening telomeres, population crash, ticking evolutionary clock down to extinction, measure telomeres by DNA sequencing, human telomeres already short. Her thoughts were racing at a million miles an hour. Had she stumbled onto something? What should she do, go tell her supervisor of her suspicions? What suspicions, did she have any and if so what were they? She felt slightly nauseous and dizzy. She felt she was on to something but what was it? She was suddenly frightened, close to panic. She was about to experience a life-altering experience, it was rushing towards her at the speed of light and she desperately wanted to avoid it but knew she couldn't. What to do? What to do?

She sat down and took deep breaths; breathe in and slowly exhale, in and out, in and out; she was back in control, now she could think more clearly and decide on an appropriate plan of action.

She was relaxed now and she knew what she must do. She would conduct the experiments herself using the specimens she had obtained from the British Museum for her PhD project and tissue samples from SDS victims. She would carry out the DNA sequencing and measure the telomeres on all the samples and see what the results were, if her experiments yielded anything she would report it to her supervisor.

Madge closeted herself in that part of the lab designated as her domain, she knew she wouldn't be questioned by the others as they were fully committed to their own workload and assumed that everyone else was looking for answers as diligently as they were.

She assembled the equipment needed to undertake the DNA sequencing; this presented no problem given the enormous amount of equipment and supplies that had been allocated to the project. She then went back to her old lab and collected her five specimens; she decided she would carry out the DNA sequencing on her specimens first and then on the tissue samples from the

SDS victims, which she would get from the lab's freezer unit.

Finally, she would compare the results and learn whether her worst nightmare was about to come true. She wished she had a sample of dinosaur DNA that was capable of sequencing but for the present it remained impossible, DNA can't be extracted from one hundred million year old fossils. She briefly wondered whether there would still be a future in which dinosaur DNA would finally be persuaded to give up its secrets.

Madge chose the Mastodon sample for the first test; there was no evidence of telomeres on the end of the chromosomes. They had obviously become shorter and shorter until they had disappeared altogether and the Mastodon had slipped quietly out of existence.

Next was the Smilodon, more commonly known as the Sabre-toothed tiger, this fabulous creature had roamed the lush jungles of what is now California, many fossils had been found in the Californian Tar Pits. As with the Mastodon, the telomeres were no longer in evidence and for all its fierceness this mega-cat had gone meekly, silently and obediently into oblivion.

The sequencing experiment showed the Woolly Mammoth had fared in much the same way as its cousin the Mastodon; stood eating its food one second and dead the next, no warning, no argument, no fight and no telomeres. There was nothing on the ends of the chromosomes.

The long-horned Auroch had walked the grassy plains of Europe and the Great Auk had skimmed the skies of centuries past but once their telomeres had grown shorter as each successive generation had come and gone, their place in the history of the world had been sealed. They followed the other ninety odd percent of all species that had ever existed since time began, into extinction. That left only the tissue samples from the SDS victims to sequence and to identify what, if any, of human telomeres had still remained on the tips of the chromosomes of those from whom the samples had been taken.

Madge was suddenly terrified; she didn't want to undertake the sequencing because she didn't want to know the answer. It was like when she was a child and something on television frightened her, if she closed her eyes and made it go away, in her child's logic, whatever it was that was the cause of her fear was shut out and no longer existed and by definition couldn't frighten her anymore. She wanted to close her eyes now and make this Blight thing go away but she wasn't a child anymore and that kind of logic could no longer be applied.

CHAPTER 46

The project team now stood at seven down from a high of forty-three, there would be no further replacements for those who had died, we hadn't seen any new faces for two weeks now and anyway we all knew that things were pretty much approaching the grand finale, the final curtain. Oh we would keep going, what was the saying, 'where there's life there's hope' but nothing less than a miracle would make a difference to what we all accepted as the inevitable outcome. The truth was we had failed, we couldn't even point to one success, one breakthrough; that was also true of Paris and Oxford but those thoughts were nothing but cold comfort.

Communication with the other labs was now virtually non-existent and contact with the WHO had been lost altogether following the collapse of the United Nations. The human race was on the brink of annihilation. I had long given up wondering what was happening in other parts of the world, it didn't take a genius to know that civilised society had long since disintegrated, I really didn't need a photograph to see the detail.

Every time I looked out of the window I could see dead bodies littering the campus, they weren't there for long, it's funny how quickly human beings adapt to the worst possible situations, an informal arrangement had arisen whereby those people using the university as a refuge took it upon themselves to drag the bodies away and burn them behind the nearest building. It might have been crude but it was efficient and it did ensure that there were no rotting corpses left to create disease. There was no such thing as looking to inform families or loved ones but bodies were searched prior to disposal and any ID found was removed and left on a table in the main entrance for people to look through if they were trying to locate someone.

The fact that basic services still functioned was thanks to electronic automation and the programmers who had instructed the nation's emergency power supplies to remain operational and maintain an electrical feed to priority locations, of which the university was one. We also had our own standby generator that tripped in automatically if a break occurred in the normal supply. The water remained connected, which meant that full hygiene facilities were still functional and the university had enough food stocks to last for some time to come; what luxury, we could stuff ourselves with food, use the toilet and take a shower, hopefully not all at the same time. Hey, I made a joke, trouble is, nothing is funny anymore and I've forgotten how to laugh anyway.

CHAPTER 47

The 'Bat Phone' started flashing, that was the name I'd given to the telephone that connected us to the Paris and Oxford labs, green flashing light for Paris and red for Oxford. It was the red light that was flashing.

'Hi,' I said, 'is this a malfunction or is there really someone out there?'

'Eve, it's me Madge it's good to hear your voice, I've been trying to get through to you for the past four hours.'

'Hi Madge, who else would be ringing me on the Bat Phone from Merry Old England?'

'Nothing much here is merry right now, in fact things are falling apart, sorry, have already fallen apart and there's nothing anyone can do about it. The government if you can call it that has given up after putting up a good fight; we're flying on autopilot. We long since passed the point of no return.'

'My view is that the worst has already gone, what we have now is a terminally ill patient who has suffered a great deal but has slipped into a coma and is now mercifully about to expire. Sorry to sound so depressing, but it's good to hear your voice as well Madge, are you going to tell me you've found the answer?'

'Yes I am. I have the answer.'

'You're joking right?'

'No I'm not joking, I really do have the answer and I do know why everyone has been dying.'

At first I couldn't believe what I was hearing, for a nano-second I thought Madge was playing games, off her rocker, gone completely mad but then I realised Madge didn't play games, not on matters of 'The Blight' she didn't, Madge was a very serious person when it came to 'The Blight', if she said she had the answer then I could be sure she did have the answer, or at least genuinely thought she had the answer, I gathered myself together and dared to hope.

'Can the situation be reversed, can it be stopped. Have you identified a cure or at least a treatment?' I felt myself starting to hyperventilate; my heart was racing and thumping like a metronome gone mad.

'There is no cure Eve and no we can't stop it, it's going to wipe us all out, every last one of us.'

'Wipe us all out?' I lamely repeated, 'what do you mean wipe us all out?' My voice had taken on a wheedling and petulant tone and I didn't like the sound of it one little bit.

Madge told me of her dropping the file and recognising Reinhardt Stindl's name on a manila folder, she told me how she had first come across his paper on telomeres when she was an undergraduate at Oxford, it hadn't been part of her reading list but she had read it anyway because she had found it particularly interesting.

She told me of the DNA sequencing she had carried out on of her original samples and that in all cases the telomeres were no longer present on the tips of the chromosomes and that according to Stindl, this was evidence that the evolutionary clock had run down taking the species into extinction.

Madge said that she had waited two days before summoning up the courage to subject the tissue samples from the SDS victims to the same DNA sequencing and that as with her original specimens, the telomeres were no longer in evidence on the tips of the human chromosomes.

'We're finished Eve, it's our time to go and make way for something else; it's just like the dinosaurs made way for the mammals and Neanderthals made way for us, it's now our turn to make way for something else. Don't you see, humans are no different from any other species, it's only that our extinction is all the more painful because we are the most intelligent and knowing of all the species that have ever existed and consequently we are being dragged screaming into oblivion, all those that went before us slid quietly away without fuss or as much as a whimper. Think about it Eve it fits, it has been observed for some time that there have been significant ongoing changes taking place in the human condition, for example people have been getting taller, living longer and displaying higher levels of intelligence. On the negative side we've become increasingly violent and intolerant and exhibit ever more extreme patterns of behaviour. Certain illnesses and diseases have also been increasing in spite of our best efforts, cancers are a good example, and the same is true of neurological disorders and many that used to be considered quite rare have become more commonplace in recent times. I believe that these changes are as a direct result of the shortening of the telomeres, which has caused deterioration in our immune systems. It's as if homosapiens, since we left our first footprints on the planet have been treading a pre-ordained path but the cumulative changes that have been going on, both positive and negative have largely gone unnoticed until now and now we are carefully examining our situation we find ourselves fast approaching the end of our journey, the speed of descent has been getting faster and faster and the slope steeper and steeper until we have reached the point where all that is left is for us to crash into oblivion. Eve, are you still there?'

'Yea Madge, I'm still here, speechless but still here. I don't want to believe you, I don't want you to be right but in my heart I think I know you are. None of us has been looking down the road you have. Congratulations Madge, you've just read out the death warrant to the condemned man waiting for his execution.'

The phone suddenly without warning went dead, no sound of static, no disconnected tone, no voice announcing a dropped line just absolute silence, I stared at it for several minutes wondering if it would ring again and I hoped it would be Madge telling me it was all a joke but it didn't ring, it was quite dead and I mused whether the phone's telomeres had disappeared off its chromosomes as well.

I wondered if Madge had died straight after delivering her knockout punch, I hoped not but I had a feeling I wouldn't be hearing from her again.

CHAPTER 48

I turned and faced what was left of the team; no one was looking in my direction so I assumed they hadn't heard anything of my conversation with Madge, just six of them, seven with me, I wondered who would be next and then I wondered who would be last. I sort of hoped it wouldn't be me.

I didn't have to wait too long for the answers, the first to die was Bryn; he was eating a snack when he just keeled over. I'd seen it happen many times but I still found it unnerving. The rest of us quietly and respectfully put down what we were doing and manhandled the body over to the window, we didn't utter a word, George opened it wide and we pushed it through. No one looked to see where it landed, we knew it would be collected and burned. It wasn't a callous act on our part; there was nothing else we could do.

The next to go was Sybil, and then George, when would it be my turn? Greg lasted less than another day and was followed quickly by May. Five down two to go.

CHAPTER 49

Adam South was younger than me by about three years, he had been married with one child, a boy but he lost them both before I lost Bill and the girls. He was a quiet guy, not unfriendly more a private sort of person.

In the days that followed May's death we hardly spoke, we would just sit there for hours staring into space and occasionally looking at each other whilst trying to avoid direct eye contact. I was contemplating whether I would be capable of dragging him to the window and heaving him out if he were to go first.

I continually re-ran the conversation with Madge through my mind and I came to the conclusion that there was nothing to be gained by keeping it to myself so I decided to share her discovery with him, the way things were it seemed quite improper for me to keep the knowledge of his ultimate fate to myself. I raised the subject in a fairly matter of fact manner, as if I might be telling someone where a mutual friend was thinking of spending their next summer vacation. When I had finished telling him he continued to just look at me like he was waiting for me to deliver the punch line to a funny joke, when he realised that nothing more would be forthcoming he just shrugged as if it were no big deal and in an equally matter of fact manner said it seemed to be a reasonable explanation to him. I confess it wasn't the reaction I had expected; I mean it isn't every day that the human race faces extinction and that that included you; I hadn't thought of him as the type who would have a screaming fit of the hebbie gebbies or anything like that but the calmness with which he took the news was surprising to say the least. I was lost for words, I had just read him his death warrant, the only thing missing was when, we already knew where.

Over the next several days I began to realise that Adam and I were bound together in an almost strange and mystical way, not least of which was that we both faced certain death and that one of us would have to dispose of the other, there was no way we could avoid it. In a strange sort of way this knowledge brought us closer together and we started to talk more, not about 'The Blight' and our predicament, that topic had been pretty well exhausted anyway and eventually in spite of ourselves, we started to share stories of what our lives had been like before 'The Blight' had struck. Adam surprised me, when he started to open up and drop his guard I found him to be a very sensitive man, he told me his wife's name had been Lara and that they had dated through high school and married whilst he was still at college. He said he'd loved her very much and still thought of her almost every day. His son, Adam Jnr had been eight, he laughed when he told me of the things he and Adam Jnr used to get up to. The pain that these revelations caused him was palpable, his eyes looked haunted, still, I couldn't ever remember hearing him laugh before and it was good in fact it was very good. I found myself smiling for the first time in ages and was happy to make my own contribution to the conversation. Once I got started I couldn't stop, I spent hours telling him details of what my life had been like with Bill and the twins, I found myself sharing personal anecdotes I'd never shared with anyone else and it didn't seem strange or unnatural.

Over the next weeks we grew even closer, it was inevitable I suppose, in fact I'd never felt this close to any man other than Bill. He told me I reminded him of Lara in many ways and I took it as a compliment. We were both afraid of getting too attached because we knew our days were numbered. It was only a matter of time before we would be included in the big round up.

The weeks became a month and then two months, we couldn't hear any noises in the building and our forays to the other labs and lecture rooms turned up nothing. At first I had expected to find each room littered with corpses in various states of decomposition but apart from signs of food and drink consumption they were quite empty and surprisingly clean. We could only assume that the last one standing had gone downstairs and out of the building after they had heaved their dead colleague through the window. Also, we no longer saw people moving around outside, and within our field of vision not a single corpse littered the university campus, we dared to think that 'The Blight' had claimed every victim but two, Adam and me. It was the fact that we were still very much alive when all around us were apparently not, that made it possible for us to hang onto that one single hope.

We walked up and down the corridors shouting to see if someone, anyone was able to make their presence known but the only answer was the echo of our footsteps on the tiled floor.

We continued to wonder, even dared to hope that we were going to be overlooked; I figured my one-eyed Cyclops friend had given up trying to find me and had climbed down from his perch atop Mount Olympus and gone off in search of another planet to terrorize.

Half way through the fourth month as our feelings for each other had grown stronger and into something more than mere friendship, Adam came slowly towards me and took me in his arms, he put his lips to my ear and whispered that he couldn't help himself, that he was falling in love with me, it wasn't entirely unexpected but it was still wonderful and I told him I felt the same, it just seemed so very natural. We held each other tightly, not wanting the moment to pass and at the same time terrified at thought that we could draw our last breath at any time.

We decided to wait for another three months before venturing outside, we still had electricity, water and plenty of food, we hoped any corpses that had not been burned would have rotted away by then and if things were not as we hoped they would be, we would return to the sanctuary of the Science Block for a while longer. I couldn't help thinking that 'The Blight' was only for humans, Earth's other inhabitants were as far as I knew, unaffected, that meant that every day would be a feast day for the rodent population. I shuddered at the thought.

'Why do you think we are still alive?' Adam asked me.

'I've been thinking about that,' I said, 'at first I thought Darwin had got it wrong, remember his evolution theory was that the survival of the species depended on natural selection, like the giraffe with its long neck equipping it to reach the leaves on the tallest trees, survival of the fittest and all that. When Madge told me of her discovery, I figured that with the entire human race passing into extinction natural selection was seen to have failed, and Darwin's theory was shot to pieces; after all the theory guaranteed the survival of the species not condemn it to oblivion but from what Madge had said it seemed that natural selection was responsible for the erosion and eventual disappearance of the telomeres in the entire human species but the fact that you and I are still here talking about it when it appears that everyone else has died suggests that we might be the exception that proves the rule; for reasons I can't even begin to comprehend it appears at least possible that you and I might be standing hand in hand at the very pinnacle of Darwin's theory, in that our apparent survival in and of itself represents the survival of the species, if that is true then we owe our survival to natural selection, we are the very embodiment of the theory, the living proof that Darwin got it absolutely right.' Adam sat there, staring at the floor, not moving, I waited with bated breath for him to say something. Slowly he raised his head and turned his eyes to mine.

'Does that mean that the survival of the human race is down to the two of us?' he said with a wicked glint in his eye.

I laughed, a real laugh, a hearty laugh. 'Well we do have the right names don't we? Adam and Eve; it seems too perfect doesn't it, it's almost biblical, almost prophetical?'

Adam's demeanour had changed, he looked thoughtful and serious. 'Perhaps you're right, when you look at it that way everything does seem to have an appearance of pre-ordination the final piece in the jigsaw that guarantees the ultimate survival of the species. I know it seems far fetched but in the absence of a better explanation I'll go with it. The fact that you and I are here together as maybe the only survivors of the human race should not be seen as a coincidence You said it all seemed too perfect well here's something else, you will remember the Genesis story of where Adam and Eve lived?'

'Sure, it was the Garden of Eden.'

'Right, but what you probably don't know is that there's a pretty little town not a million miles from here, and can you guess what it's called?'

'Don't tell me, Eden, its Eden isn't it?'

Adam's broad smile said it all, it was, and there and then we made a vow that if we did survive 'The Blight', when we felt it was safe we would leave our sanctuary and strike out for Eden. I couldn't predict what it would be like out there or what we would find, I was still petrified when I allowed myself to think of the kind of life that waited out there for us but I believed that our survival had to have been for a reason, perhaps Darwin's theory of Natural Selection had more to do with God than he thought and less to do with evolution. There might be others out there like us who had lived through the nightmare and are still able to tell the tale. Perhaps Madge is still in her lab in Oxford vainly trying to re-connect with me to tell me she is still alive. Who knows, I don't and for now there's no point in dwelling upon it. The only thing I know for sure is that there is Adam and me, we are real and we are human and like all humans we are imbued with the instinct to survive and I have to confess, Adam and Eve in Eden has a distinctive ring of truth to it and that is what I'll hang on to for now.

THE END?